The Medici Guns

Other books by Martin Woodhouse

TREE FROG

BUSH BABY

PHIL & ME

MAMA DOLL

BLUE BONE

THE MEDICI GUNS

by

Martin Woodhouse

and

Robert Ross

E. P. Dutton & Co., Inc. · New York · 1975

The Medici Guns was first published in 1974
by J. M. Dent & Sons Ltd of London, England,
in somewhat different form.

First Edition
10 9 8 7 6 5 4 3 2 1

ISBN: 0-525-15460-4

Library of Congress Cataloging in Publication Data

Woodhouse, Martin, 1932–
The Medici guns.

1. Leonardo da Vinci, 1452–1519—Fiction.
I. Ross, Robert, joint author. II. Title.
PZ4.W8873Me4 [PR6073.0616] 823'.9'14 74-22075

To Penny again
and Ranette always

CAST OF CHARACTERS

The Principals

LEONARDO DA VINCI	The Inventor of the Medici Guns
Guido Toscanelli	Condottiero who commands the mercenary army employed by Florence
Andrea del Verrocchio	Artist and master of the studio where Leonardo da Vinci works
Dr. Cino di Lapo Mazzone	Scholar and court advisor to Lorenzo de'Medici
Fra Sigismondo Carregi	Cleric and tutor to Bianca Maria Visconti
Matteo Barletta	Archer and boyhood friend of Leonardo da Vinci
Federigo da Montefeltro	Condottiero employed by Rome. He commands the mercenaries defending Castelmonte

The Medici Gunners

Roderigo Leone	Captain-Gunner, the Army of Florence
Scudo	Lieutenant-Gunner
Agnolo Fulvio	Lieutenant-Gunner
Cipriano di Ser Giacomo	Gunner
Giachetti di Lucca	Gunner
Tesoro di Veluti	Gunner
Andrea di Veluti	Gunner
Marco di Carona	Gunner
Piccio Berignalli	Gunner
Balestraccio	Gunner
Guccio Berotti	Gunner
Tomasello Cennini	Gunner
Giunta di Lenzo	Gunner

The Florentine Court

Lorenzo de'Medici	Ruler of the Republic of Florence
Giuliano de'Medici	Brother to Lorenzo de'Medici
Guido Toscanelli	Condottiero in the employ of Florence
Bianca Maria Visconti	Ward of Lorenzo de'Medici; Cousin to Ludovico Sforza, Regent of the Duchy of Milan

Constanza d'Avalos	Ward of Lorenzo de'Medici, betrothed to Giuliano de'Medici
Carla d'Avalos	Sister to Constanza d'Avalos
Silvio	Prince of Savoy
Andrea Verrocchio	Artisan
Dr. Cino di Lapo Mazzone	Scholar and advisor to Lorenzo de'Medici
Fra Sigismondo Carregi	Cleric and tutor to Bianca Visconti
Matteo Barletta	Archer and boyhood friend

The Papal Court

Sixtus IV, Francesco della Rovere	Pope
Rodrigo Borgia	Cardinal
Domenico della Palla	Cardinal, Apostolic Chancellor
Girolamo Riario	Captain-General to the Armies of the Holy Roman Church
Rafaello Sansoni-Riario	Cardinal
Manfredo Romolo-Paro	Bishop

The Conspirators

Jacopo Pazzi	Banker of Florence
Francesco Pazzi	His son
Paolo Pazzi	His son
Ippolito Pazzi	His son
Benno Foscari	Assassin
Bernardo Bandini	Assassin
Mario Bandini	Assassin
Francesco Salviati	Archbishop-Designate to Pisa

The Defenders of Castelmonte

Giovio della Rovere	Governor of Castelmonte
Bona della Rovere	His wife
Federigo da Montefeltro	Condottiero, Duke of Urbino
Guido Falcone di Riccomano	Captain
Ridolfo Peruzzi	Watch Commander
Guaspare di Piombino	His second-in-command
Nofri	Soldier
Alessandro Gambacorte	Soldier
Mariano di Gaddo	Soldier
Noldo Pellegrini	Shoemaker

Science is the study of things possible.
—Leonardo da Vinci.

The Medici Guns

One

All day long, under a yellow and smoking Tuscan sky, the two huge guns vomited fire. For seven weeks they had done so, weeks lost in futility, their monstrous strength pitted against the endurance of a granite wall ten feet thick. The distant stone cracked an inch, releasing a soft fall of dust, but stood against the onslaught of the hundred-pound shot.

Each gun fired three rounds in every hour. Thus, from one side or the other of Roderigo Leone, Captain-Gunner to the army of Florence and the Medici, the deep roar surged at intervals of ten minutes, pounding upon his cotton-stuffed ears. His lieutenants laid their slow matches to the cannons' bellies. The powder trains hissed and sparked, died into a half-second of silence while fire crept like a serpent through the touch holes. Power gathered, growling inside the eight-inch thickness of Milanese bronze. Then it flamed and erupted, rocking the immense guns to the height of a man, before driving them back into the piled earth of their redoubts. Woe to the powder boy who allowed a careless foot to linger in the trenched groove as nine tons of cannon lunged back in recoil.

In that long moment of stillness before explosion, Rigo Leone's head would turn away from his men to face the massive wall he sought to breach half a mile away, across the valley. Sometimes his gunner's eye would pick out the nine-inch ball in flight; occasionally, he imagined it. More often, he would miss the hurtling shot until its impact against the gray, implacable breastwork of the citadel of Castelmonte.

High upon its rocky peak, Castelmonte controlled the road between the Republic of Florence and its principal enemy, Rome. So long as Castelmonte was in Roman hands, as now it was, Florence was in danger. Indeed, Lorenzo de' Medici expected the army of the Holy Roman Church to march up that road the following spring and invade his republic. And so he had hired Rigo Leone and his professional artillerymen to break the Castelmonte defenses with their colossal cannonry, so that the citadel could be taken by Lorenzo's troops.

Castelmonte was no ordinary fortress. On nearly three sides it was surrounded by sheer cliffs, and from these three sides it was absolutely invulnerable to attack. It was the fourth side at which Rigo now gazed. At his extreme left, at the northwest corner of the fort, was the main gate. But the gateway, with its gigantic oaken doors, was in such a position that Rigo's guns could not be brought to bear upon it. Far around to Rigo's right was another entrance, the postern gate. But it offered even less opportunity. It too was poorly placed for Rigo's guns. It was also tiny, much too narrow to mount a large attack through. And Rigo suspected that behind the postern gate were still heavier fortifications. Worst of all, the land between the river and the postern rose so sharply that attackers would be at a great disadvantage.

Only the three-quarter mile western and northwestern aspect gave any hope to attackers coming from the river valley below; and for the full length of this—the citadel's only natural weakness—ran the vast and forbidding wall which had defied the bombardment of Rigo Leone's siege cannon.

Watching the spurt of shattered rock fragments, he would know, before the ball fell to the sloping earth at the wall's foot to roll into the muddy river, what damage it had made. He longed for the spreading fissure, the tumble of stone which would announce that this blow—*this*—had brought about the beginning of the end. Meanwhile Rigo measured his success in ounces, in handspans of flaking surface or gouged crater, like a sculptor carving his will into a block of marble, chip by slow chip. Now attacking with a chisel blow. Now standing back to assess its worth. Patience, he would tell his guns, reaching out to them with his mind. And, from right and left, the blackened muzzles replied in turn: Patience. What can withstand us? Given time, all must fall. Only wait.

It had been, thus far, a long and idle war, fought through a sunlit autumn. Only the gunners sweated, their skins tattooed with ingrained powder at finger and wrist and neck. Forty strong, they slaved, ate and slept on the ridgetop overlooking that small tributary of the Arno River which formed the perimeter defense of Castelmonte. That the wall of Castelmonte had survived for seven weeks they took as a personal affront, few among them having developed the tolerance of their Captain-Gunner. Yet survived it had, and seemed likely to last longer. If his guns spoke to Rigo of patience, nonetheless patience was not all. For in a week or two would arrive Castelmonte's strongest ally—winter.

On this late afternoon in October 1477, two men on horseback watched the siege of Castelmonte from a rise above the Roman road. Below them, in the basin between guns and city, the foot soldiers of the *condottiero* Guido Toscanelli, mercenary in the employ of Florence, milled aimlessly between rows of tents and along the willow-lined banks of a stream which fed the small river beneath the citadel wall. Few approached the river itself. It ran a bare ten paces from the battlements and was within easy bowshot of the besieged.

The man on the big roan patted his fretting mount and pointed to where, a hundred paces away, the flap of a scarlet pavilion had opened and a figure in dulled campaign mail was emerging.

"Ha," the man on the roan said. "Our good Toscanelli takes the sun. An idle man." He laughed, waving a white-gloved hand. The man in the distant tent mouth returned the greeting. "An idle man," Giuliano de' Medici repeated, "yet a good soldier for all that."

"Why idle?" asked the rider on the piebald horse beside him. He was holding his reins in his right hand. With his left, he drew upon the top page of a notebook resting on his thigh, tied into place by a narrow thong and chained to the waist of his tunic for security.

Both men were in their twenties. The harness of the piebald was of simple, serviceable leather, while that of Giuliano's mount glittered with gold and silver chasing. Otherwise, both were well attired, equally handsome, and equally flamboyant in appearance and temper. They might have passed, at a distance, for brothers.

The man on the piebald dropped his stub of charcoal deliberately to the ground beside him, let go of his reins and dusted his fingertips together.

"Why call Toscanelli idle?" he asked again. "He has little to do. Until your Captain-Gunner rips that wall apart, a circumstance for which we may all wait yet awhile, how should he occupy himself? In knocking upon the main gate for admittance?"

"There speaks the artist," Giuliano said mockingly. "Stick to your easel, my perceptive friend. Here we are soldiers, Toscanelli and I. Where you see flowing wreaths of smoke, I smell brimstone. Where you see figures in a landscape—"

"How do you know what I see?"

"I imagine it, Leonardo. I imagine it. When I was ten, perhaps twelve, I recall my tutors encouraged me to dabble paint on canvas, play the lute and indulge in other sorts of foolery. I told them that my fingers would not answer my soul, which was nonetheless that of an artist, and made the canvas into a kite."

"Which never left Mother Earth," said Leonardo with good humor.

"I allow that. I insist, however, upon my artistic soul."

"Continue, then, Giuliano. Where I see figures in a landscape with the eye of a ten-year-old lad, what do you perceive?"

"Idle soldiers. Look for yourself. Being too idle to carry their pitchers more than ten steps, they have set their tents on low ground in order to be near the water. Therefore, they are choked by Rigo's brimstone. Whereas, Leonardo, had they but the industry to hoist their water a mere thirty paces uphill, they could breathe easily. Do not ask me why guns should smell of brimstone. They do. I—"

His words were drowned in the boom of one of the siege guns from the ridge to their left. By the time the echoes of its roll had died away, Giuliano had lost his advantage; the man on the piebald was speaking.

"I have no need to ask you," said Leonardo da Vinci. "Guns smell of brimstone for the excellent reason that gunpowder contains brimstone, along with saltpeter and charcoal. Therefore, ride with me and learn. All friendship brings profit, the more so to the thickheaded. Tomorrow, if fortune smiles, I may teach you to fly kites."

Upon their ridge, the gunners of Florence still tended their massive charges, levering them forward from the recoil banks with balks of timber and with shoulders that strained against wheel rim and carriage. While the staveman thrust his fifteen-foot ash pole, tipped with bound and oil-soaked rags, down the muzzle to scour the bore, Rigo Leone stood fingering a smooth pebble and estimated what daylight he had left.

The retreating sun announced the close of the day's bombardment; it remained for Rigo to announce it too. He cast away the pebble.

"Enough," he said. He turned away from the cannon to witness the arrival of the two horsemen who had just ridden up the reverse slope of the ridge.

Leonardo da Vinci and Giuliano de' Medici dismounted, looping the reins of their mounts around one of the upright posts of the rudely thatched hut which served as field magazine to the siege guns. Leaving Leonardo at the hut, sketchbook once more in hand, Giuliano strode forward.

"How goes the day?" he asked.

"Badly," said Rigo. "Yet there is always tomorrow."

"And the day after," said Giuliano. "Well . . ." He looked across the valley at the citadel of Castelmonte. "A strong wall, then," he went on. "I begin to think this a fruitless exercise—by which I intend no reproof whatever to yourself, Captain-Gunner. What is your opinion?"

"A gunner's opinion, as always," Rigo said. "It is a strong wall, but I shall bring it down."

Giuliano de' Medici looked at the Captain-Gunner closely.

"Come, Rigo," he said coaxingly. "You speak to me alone, not to my brother Lorenzo. Nor are you some half-witted knight who must give me phrases and flourishes. Therefore, tell me. Five days? Or ten? Twenty?"

"Ten," Rigo said. "Ten, but the ground softens. I have heard it said that horses catch the scent of bad weather before men do. What does your horse say? Give me rain, as in September, and I am in difficulty. Give me snow, and I am lost. Do you see?"

"I do indeed. Bones of God, but Federigo da Montefeltro must be laughing at us, over there," Giuliano said. "He sacked Volterra for us, and Forli. Now he holds Castelmonte against us, and with more success than ever."

"He is a fox," said Rigo, "a professional. Still, God willing, I will dig him out for you." He broke off. "Look there," he said. "Is that Montefeltro himself, do you think?"

From the wall of Castelmonte, a trumpet sounded a single, drawn-out note. There was a moment's silence and then, softly, the slow beat of a drum arose, deliberate and menacing. All the men on the ridge turned their faces toward the city. The last rim of the setting sun at their backs picked out the battlements in glowing red. To the left of the wall's summit where Rigo Leone's flying shot had reduced its granite teeth to intermittent and ragged stumps, figures were gathering.

"Not Montefeltro," said Agnolo Fulvio, one of Rigo's lieutenants. "I count eleven, but the Duke is not among them."

"I trust your eyesight," Rigo said. "Who are they, then?"

"Give me time," murmured Agnolo. "The light is poor, but Montefeltro I would know by his gait, were he there. I have studied him often enough."

"One is Giovio della Rovere," said a quiet voice from behind them. They turned. Leonardo da Vinci had come forward from his vantage point beside the thatched powder magazine, his right hand inside the breastfold of his tunic. "Also his wife, I judge," the artist continued. "A woman large with child? Am I right?"

"Aye," growled Rigo. "That would be Della Rovere's sweet Contessa. A bitch from the hound pack of hell itself. It seems you have sharp eyes too, sir. Who else?"

"Six soldiers, and a prisoner," Leonardo replied. "A tall man, fair-haired and with no beard. He wears a hacketon . . . a cavalryman. Giuliano, what do you say?"

"Tedesco Giasone," said Giuliano. "They took him in a sortie four nights ago."

"Pray for his soul," said Leonardo grimly. "They have their executioner with them. The eleventh man . . . you see him there, in the shadow of the turret? Also—I do not recognize him—a man of medium height, and armored."

"Armored?" Giuliano frowned.

"In light mail, fluted, after the fashion of some Saxon knights I have seen. The breastplate is flexible, its seams picked out in black. Toward his left shoulder he wears a golden cross."

"You can see all this, Leonardo? I cannot, and I have a keen eye for hawking, so they tell me."

"He is as I describe him," Leonardo da Vinci said. "Shall I draw him for you?"

"No need for that," replied Giuliano. "I know well enough who he is. Riario, Count of Imola."

Beside him, several among the gunners crossed themselves. Rigo Leone thumped the cannon's oaken carriage with his fist.

"Yes," said Giuliano. "Pray, indeed, for the soul of Tedesco Giasone." He turned toward his friend. "You are sure, Leonardo? A black-haired man with gold insignia?" Leonardo nodded. Giuliano pulled off a glove, slapping it against the palm of his other hand. "Riario, then. Riario. Yet how did he come there? He has not shown himself before now. No matter. Blood of the saints! A man with such a treaty with Satan, as Riario must long since have signed, could doubtless ride through our lines invisible, or in the guise of some wild beast. Or so my knights would tell me."

Upon the ramparts of Castelmonte, Girolamo Riario, Count and Protector of Bosco and Imola, and Captain-General to the Armies of the Church of Rome, watched impassively the preparations for the death of Tedesco Giasone. Had he been able to hear the words being spoken by Giuliano de' Medici upon the distant ridge, he would have approved of them as showing an attitude in his enemies that he wished to foster. Indeed, it was the purpose of the scene being enacted, since he bore no particular animosity toward the man who was now being trussed in an embrasure, his head downward and half hanging outside the wall, his legs spread wide apart and strapped to the short pillars of stone at either side of him.

Girolamo Riario's face, then, was neutral. Not so the faces

of his natural half-brother, Count Giovio della Rovere, and of Bona della Rovere, the woman who gripped her husband's arm. Under the green and fur-trimmed cloak she wore, her belly was swollen with the seventh month of her pregnancy. Her eyes, like those of Count Giovio, glinted with anticipation.

Within the turret, in whose doorway Riario stood fingering the neck of his mail jacket, the unseen drummer ceased his slow tattoo. The hooded axeman stepped forward, testing his blade with broad thumb as della Rovere raised a hand. Tedesco Giasone uttered a single, cut off, weasel's scream, his head falling back limply in the instant that the swinging, razor-sharp edge clove him from groin to breastbone, spilling blood and entrails in a slaughterhouse gush that fouled the stone notch of the embrasure and dripped crimson fingers down the wall's outer surface.

The executioner stepped away, looking toward his lord for approval. Bona della Rovere, her fingernails clutching at the skin of her cheek, buried her face in her husband's sleeve. Riario turned his back on the ruined and stinking puppet that still jerked a dozen feet from him, passed through the turret doorway, and disappeared from the sight of those assembled on the wall and of the far watchers upon the ridge beyond the river.

The midnight moon hung in a clear, cold sky, spilling its light on the sides of the tents below. Giuliano, with Leonardo da Vinci to keep him company, had completed his round of the guardposts, answering their quiet challenges with his own password and some small talk. Then the two men sat astride their horses and rode to a low ridge, to the side of the gunners' summit, which directly overlooked the postern gate of Castelmonte.

"The Count of Imola, then, is a monster," Leonardo was saying. "But what of it? More to the point, what will happen tomorrow? Rigo Leone will hurl some sixty more shot at

Castelmonte, and another sixty the next day, and the day after that. And then it will snow and Riario will split or skewer another captive or so. Christmas will come, and your guns will lie idle."

"As you would not," Giuliano said irritably.

"Not I. I would consider a tunnel."

Giuliano turned to him. "A mine?" he asked. "Castelmonte's walls are bedded in rock. How would you drive your shaft, and how long would it take you?"

"Not eight weeks and more. That is certain."

"We should have consulted you earlier, I can see," said Giuliano. "We had need of your suggestions in August. You talk with hindsight, which all men can do."

"Did you consider a mine, then?"

"No."

"Then that is all my argument," Leonardo said. "I do not insist upon a mine. There are other methods. But had you spent three of the last seven weeks in thought, you might, by now, be inside Castelmonte."

Giuliano patted his horse. "Well," he said. "No doubt there is some truth in what you say, but show me the soldier who will spend three weeks in thought when he might be setting up his guns, and I will account you a wizard. For myself, I would sooner hawk than think, believing that thought is better left to monks, who have no time to spend upon war. Or women. In which connection . . ."

"Aha." Leonardo smiled.

"Tell me, Leonardo, what you think of Constanza d'Avalos."

"You seek my opinion as a painter?"

"As what you wish."

"A most gracious and fair lady, then."

"Well said indeed. Also virtuous."

"Aha."

"I pray you to spare me your 'ahas,' Leonardo, or we shall fall out with one another before the night is much older." He sighed. "All Medici campaigns are unsuccessful this autumn, it seems. My brother has his fortress to besiege, and I have mine—Constanza d'Avalos. Now here, Leonardo, is a campaign in which I might even welcome your instruction."

"I perceive no campaign," said Leonardo. "You are betrothed to her."

"Not yet."

"But you will be. Do you love her?"

"As to that . . ." Giuliano began cautiously but his companion was already pressing on.

"In two years' time, when she is eighteen, you will marry her. Where, then, is your campaign? If there is one, it is certain of success."

"By God," Giuliano broke out, "and what conquest is that? To bed by political convenience? Do I need a parade of bloodless nuncios and chamberlains to sound me a victory by contract? A plague on that! I want her now, not when she is told to come to me."

"So speaks the child when the toy is taken," said Leonardo. "Constanza is wise here. Consider this—"

"I am not interested in her wisdom," Giuliano interrupted. "Shall her mind give me pleasure? No."

"Possibly she thinks it might, were you to notice its existence inside her body."

"And doubtless, therefore, you would have me lay out matters like a geometrician. Is that your advice? By all the saints, Leonardo, where is your romance? What of her breasts?"

"They are charming, and will serve admirably to feed her children."

"More romance. I thank God I am a simple cavalryman."

"Or so you delude yourself," said Leonardo calmly.

"Meaning that you know me better than I do myself? I doubt it. However, friend artist, let me reward you for your advice, poor though it may be. I shall introduce you to a girl who is bound to take your fancy—Sforza's cousin, Bianca Maria Visconti. Have you seen her?"

"No."

"A little narrow in the bosom for my taste, though this may cure itself, she being but fourteen," said Giuliano. "Brother Sigismondo insists that she is too clever for her own good; so, she should suit you very well. Also she has a sharp tongue and might eventually distract you from your admiration of thought—or wisdom—in women. What say you?"

"I thank you for your courtesy," said Leonardo gravely. "Burdened as you are with two campaigns of your own, it is indeed noble of you to find another and press it upon myself. However . . ."

He stopped.

"What is it?" Giuliano demanded. The artist was staring intently toward the battlements at the far side of the river.

"Who is that?" he asked. "There . . . at this side of the turret to our left. You see him?"

Giuliano looked where he was pointing.

"Andrea di Veluti," he said. "The pickets knew he was passing through our lines. It seems that he had some notion of examining the effect of Rigo's gunnery upon the wall. I am bound to say . . ."

He broke off. The man they were both straining to watch was all but hidden in the deep shadow beneath the wall. But now, immediately above Veluti's position, gleamed the light of a torch.

"Trouble," Giuliano said. "I—" But Leonardo had already set spurs to his horse. The cavalryman at once did likewise, and both began the descent of the ridge face, sliding in a welter of loose pebbles. At their right, and some three hundred paces south of the unlucky gunner's figure, the postern gate had swung inward, and a detachment of foot soldiers was emerging from it. At almost the same instant, the gunner collapsed, and his body began to roll downward toward the far bank of the river.

"Stones," said Giuliano as they reached the level expanse of meadow at the bottom of the ridge. "They have dropped stones on him from above!" They reined in their horses. Leonardo, already turning to ride along the riverbank, found himself blocked by his friend. "No," Giuliano said. "You are not thinking as a soldier. We cannot reach him before they do. We must cut off their retreat."

Leonardo hesitated but was urged to his right by Giuliano's insistent maneuvers. Together they rode for the ford immediately below and opposite the postern gate, and plunged into the water. It foamed around the bellies of their horses as they breasted the current. The soldiers on the far bank were now strung out in a line. Their vanguard had almost reached the motionless gunner. At the party's rear, five or six pikemen were forming up where the slope of the ford rose up from the river.

The disadvantage was clear to both before they were halfway across. The climb from the far bank to the postern was steep. The halberdiers who opposed them could easily prevent their leaving the river at all, let alone forcing a passage to any higher ground. Setting horse against pikes was futile. Leonardo stood in his stirrups for a brief moment, and dived from his mount. The water was cold. Surfacing ten yards away, he saw Giuliano had done the same.

They reached the shore at almost the same moment—Leonardo upstream from the confused pikemen, Giuliano below them. Pulling himself out of the water, Leonardo gained a purchase on the turf with one knee, stood upright, and headed for the defenders' rear. The pikemen, in some disarray, abandoned their bristling outward formation and made a loose semicircle to protect their flanks.

With drawn sword, Giuliano suddenly fell upon the nearest man, slipping under his point and hacking at his ribs. The halberdier fell, shouting curses and hampering his neighbor's parry. Leonardo, his weapon unsheathed, gripped the shaft of the pike swinging toward him and wrenched it away. Using it as a quarterstaff, he charged the remaining group. Off balance and badly placed to counter this surprising assault, they tried to set their pikes in two directions at once, staggered, and toppled backwards into the river under the combined onslaught of their two assailants.

Suddenly finding themselves in command of the bank, Giuliano and Leonardo grinned at each other. Behind Giuliano and downstream from the ford, indistinct shapes could be seen around the prostrate Andrea; while more were beginning to return along the sloping grass in order to combat the counterattack they had seen developing to their rear.

"Good," said Giuliano. He looked across the river. In Toscanelli's camp, shouts and the clanging of weapons being buckled on told of imminent reinforcement for their hard-won but precarious position.

"Nothing of the kind," said Leonardo shortly. "Look behind you again."

The gunner's captors, wisely, had never intended to retrace their path back to the postern gate, across poor terrain and burdened with an unconscious man. A rope had already snaked downward from the wall top, and they were fastening it about Andrea's body. Even as Giuliano watched, the tightening cord dragged the captive to the foot of the battlements. His feet left the ground, and he began a jerking ascent, hauled upward by invisible hands overhead.

"God rot their entrails," said Giuliano. "I had not thought of that."

Leonardo pointed toward the postern at their right. From beneath the arch of the doorway, more pikemen were appearing.

"Let us not stand here and consider it now," he panted, "since there is nothing we can do."

The defenders they had knocked into the river were also retrieving their weapons and preparing furiously to regain the shore, while from the guardhouse above the gate a crossbow bolt hissed unseen and buried itself at Giuliano's feet.

Giuliano sheathed his sword.

"I agree," he said. "And since we are already wet . . ."

They turned as one, ran the few necessary steps, and launched themselves once more into the dark waters of the river.

Two

Piled high with a load of rough-hewn barrel staves, a little cart trundled slowly across the Ponte Carraia, along the Via dei Fossi and into the piazza that spread like a tiled lawn around the steps of the Church of Santa Maria Novella. The bells of Florence chimed eleven times to mark the morning hour as the cart negotiated the entry to the street which passed the front of the studios and workshops of Andrea del Verrocchio. It pulled to a sudden halt at the emergence from a nearby alley of two dogs, growling and snapping in a furor of combat. The noise of their quarrel was too much for the horse. It reared in panic and tumbled the overladen vehicle onto its side, spilling staves in a hundred directions.

The snarling of the dogs, the crash of the falling wagon and the hoarse imprecations of its owner all filtered through the casements of the upper-story studio, lifting heads and hands from wood and canvas. Work stopped and the two north-facing front windows were crowded in an instant with the artisans and students who called Andrea del Verrocchio their master.

Two men paid no attention to the commotion.

Leonardo worked on, skimming quick lines of charcoal across the whitewashed surface of a wooden board. Behind his shoulder stood Verrocchio himself, watching intently as the lines flowed together to form the delicate shape of a young man's head. Scarcely pausing, the artist brushed his thumb confidently over the soft carbon outlines, maturing the features and adding years with a few more rapid strokes. A crease here and there, a furrowed brow, aged the young man to thirty, forty, and then, magically, the head seemed to wither and a grasping, tired old man's face took form, with cheeks sunken and lips pulled and puckered over toothless gums. Da Vinci paused, changing his charcoal for the final thrusts, and the ancient face itself dissolved to reappear as a skull, with polished planes and eye sockets dark as death.

Verrocchio had been so absorbed in these transformations that when he expelled his long-held breath Leonardo turned, grinning cheerfully.

"Look well, Master Andrea," he said. "Consider the power you have given us, to create a lifetime in a moment." He returned to the drawing, now holding two charcoal pieces, one in his left hand, one in his right. Both moved over the death's head, working together, and from the skull emerged again the face of a young man, laughing with the joy of life.

Verrocchio shook his head.

"A conjuror's trick, Master Leonardo," he said. "Better to do the work I set you with one hand, and well, and save your conjuring for the fêtes and fairs."

In mock chagrin, Leonardo spun on his stool and rose, dusting his darkened fingers on the sides of his smock. "And does my work displease you, then, Master Andrea? No matter. It was, as you say, a jester's trick. I will come back this evening and work on the head of my little angel there," he pointed to a panel at the other side of the room, "and it shall be exactly as you wish it done, I promise you." He turned again, and began to gather a random array of papers and sketches, dropping them swiftly into a large portfolio.

"This evening?" inquired Verrocchio, looking stern.

"God sparing me, yes," said Leonardo.

"You come in late this morning, and leave before noon? No, Leonardo, I fear not. I need you here, to work on your angel while there remains some light to see by." The master craftsman's body assumed a stance much like a barrier. "No more holidays, I pray you, Leonardo. Not today!"

"No holiday at all, good Master Verrocchio," said Leonardo, continuing his preparations unperturbed. "I'll return after sundown and work until midnight if need be. The candlelight serves me well. Do I cheat you, sir? You know I do not. Have you not crept in here of nights, many times, to assure yourself of the fact?"

"And what is it you wish to do with the daylight?" Verrocchio demanded acidly. "More riding through the countryside—for the purpose of sketching, no doubt—with our young Medici prince?"

"Not this time," Leonardo said. "Though I am sure you would not grudge me such pleasures, seeing that each time I ride with Giuliano, there is another commission for you. Even the Medici hounds must by now be eating from platters of your engraving, Master Andrea. I have been considering charging you a fee for my services as agent."

Unwillingly, his employer broke into a smile.

"True," he admitted. "Yet I cannot allow even the best of my artists to overthrow what little discipline I manage to achieve here." He broke off and called the watchers at the windows back to work with a few choice oaths, then turned back to da Vinci. "Another experiment, then?" he asked. "The third time this week, Leonardo, which is three times the license I would extend to any of my other workers." Curiosity now tempting him, he added, "And what are these experiments that drag you from my studio so often? What do you seek from them?"

Leonardo lifted his head and stared briefly at a gable beyond one of the now vacated windows.

"What is it I seek?" he asked thoughtfully. He shook his

head slightly. "Why, it is but a light matter, Master Andrea. I seek to know everything there is to know."

"Indeed," said Verrocchio, his voice mildly sarcastic. "I see. You wish merely to achieve the sum of all knowledge. Well, well. There being a full seven hours of daylight remaining today for your search, let us devoutly pray that it will prove time enough to make some headway. And you will work tonight, though how any man can lay down a true tint by candlelight is another thing I have yet to argue with you."

"Why, as to that," Leonardo said, "there is no argument. Your own teaching suffices. When I came to you as a green journeyman, did you not tell me always to seek out the manner in which light varied, and both form and color with it?"

"I was speaking of the daylight," replied Verrocchio testily, "and not of peering about in the gloom like an owl."

"Then, as a good student should, I have advanced upon your wisdom," said Leonardo. "For the light of a candle, or a fire, brings its own tones and shadows, which belong to the technique we call *sfumato*—a technique I have not yet studied deeply enough. This is what I hope to capture, and therefore, must work at night. So, with your permission, may I use the sunlight for other purposes, good Master Andrea?"

"Aye, go," the craftsman grumbled. "I would sooner have you gone than contest matters with you."

"I thank you, again and always, for your kind consent."

Verrocchio watched as Leonardo's tall figure moved easily down the narrow center aisle that separated the work tables upon either side. He scratched his head.

From the whitewashed board, the face of the young man looked out at him serenely, smiling, he imagined, with the same faint mockery as its creator. Verrocchio caught the drawing by its edges and carried it away, past the hastily lowered heads of his work force.

His boots, hose and doublet spattered with mire, Captain-Gunner Rigo Leone stood beneath the marble colonnade of the Medici Palace courtyard and argued briefly with the tall and gorgeously arrayed page who sought to detain him. Around the central fountain, courtiers drifted like peacocks, posturing in trivial discussion and casting occasional and mildly disdainful glances at the gunner's drab hawk like figure before returning to their daily business of seeing and being seen. The page was querulous.

"Sir," he said. "Your dress—"

"Is muddy. I am aware of it. I thank you," snapped Rigo.

"If you would care to change your attire, sir—"

"I would not."

"Il Magnifico, sir, may feel . . ."

"Lorenzo de' Medici will know, as you do not, that I come from work and return to work. His work. Stand aside, boy!"

The page sighed in infinite weariness. "I will conduct you then, sir, to the library."

"I did not ask you to," said Rigo. "I requested you to stand aside and permit me to find the library for myself. Now move—and do not try my patience." He pushed the blue and silver clad chest in front of him gently—as a battering ram nudges a gate before trying its strength in earnest—and proceeded on his way in the shadow of the cloister, the page fluttering in his wake.

The library was on the upper floor connected by a wooden stairway to the gardens in the rear of the palace. Rigo reached its twin doors twenty steps ahead of his insistent guide and went in.

Two women stood in the arch of a window to his right, their gowns bright against the oak wainscoting between the shelves of leather-bound volumes. The younger, Bianca Maria Visconti, slender and fair, waved to him in silent gaiety and then turned back to her companion. Acknowledging the greeting with a bow (and with a frown), Rigo crossed the room to the three men who sat at a table in gilt-lined chairs beneath the gaze of two statues. Guido Toscanelli and Giuliano de' Medici made room for him, while at the head of the table Lorenzo de' Medici, Ruler of the Republic of Florence, looked up from a parchment map.

"You come late, Rigo," he said, "though doubtless with good reason. We excuse you."

"Of your kindness, sir," said Rigo. "I had already mounted my horse when there arrived a cartload of powder from Ser Nencio, and I was forced to see to its stowage."

"And hence—as ever—you must return tonight," Lorenzo said.

"I fear so, sir."

"And have you eaten?"

"No."

"Then do so, before you leave. For now, if you please, state us your case."

Lorenzo de' Medici—The Magnificent—was a man of twenty-eight, though few would have guessed him to be younger than either his Captain-Gunner or the condottiero he employed. Dressed always in sober brown, his only concession to personal adornment was a rough piece of amber hung about his neck on a silver chain. He gave those who surrounded him an impression of rock like strength. His somewhat squat and ugly face was impassive but for his eyes, which roved slowly yet continuously as though in restless search or in assessment of other men's worth. He had appeared the same at twenty-one, when the people had come to him upon his father's death and begged him to assume responsibility for the Republic of Florence. Changeless, formidable, untiring—friends imagined he would appear the same in middle age.

Beside him, his brother Giuliano seemed a light and dashing jewel of a man. Though differing extremely in appearance and temper, Lorenzo and his brother had reached an accord which few in their position achieved. They loved each other, respected each other and went their own ways. Imprudent factions arose from time to time, proposing that Giuliano supplant his elder brother. Giuliano laughed, and took hawk to fist. Similar but opposite factions had proposed to Lorenzo that the presence of his popular younger brother at court might lead to danger and unrest. Lorenzo did not laugh, but banished one such proposer and hanged another. Thereafter, no more such suggestions were voiced. Giuliano managed horses and women; Lorenzo handled money and men: a division under which Florence prospered mightily in both pleasure and commerce.

"My case," Rigo Leone said. "My case, sir, is swiftly put. My guns sink in mud. Two weeks ago, they placed nine shots in every ten within an area of Castelmonte's wall no bigger than the doorway of your library here. Last week, the rain came, though mercifully at night only. Yesterday I had to shore my wheels with timber, and my spread at impact is twenty paces from side to side. My chance of breaching the wall is small, and lessens each day. When the snows come, I must stop. Also one of my gunners is captive as a result of a foolish escapade by moonlight which I blame myself for permitting."

"His name?" Lorenzo asked.

"Andrea di Veluti, sir. An impatient youth, but competent."

"And valued?"

"Yes. As are all my men in your service."

"By which you imply that I should value him too. I do. What price must I pay Montefeltro for an impetuous but competent gunner? A thousand florins, I dare say. It shall be paid."

"I thank you."

Lorenzo de' Medici gestured impatiently. "Would that I might purchase time so easily," he said. "Your opinion is that I shall be forced to raise my siege, then?"

"Save by God's grace, sir, that is so."

"Very well. Toscanelli?"

"Long sieges are always unsatisfactory, my lord," said Guido Toscanelli, a swarthy man, angular of face, with graying hair. Booted, as was the Captain-Gunner opposite him, he wore a cloak of dull blue, thrown back from the shoulders of an azure tunic. "I have some two hundred hard soldiers, Magnifico," he went on, "these being men who understand the need to wait out a bombardment. For the rest of my *condotta,* I collect such as are willing to serve me for the duration of any campaign upon which I may be engaged. I collected them, in this instance, after harvest. Your Lordship will therefore rightly comprehend them to be peasants."

"There are no lordships in this room, Guido," Lorenzo said brusquely. "What of your peasants, then?"

"They are, on the whole, stupid," Toscanelli replied. "Good men in a fight they may be, but while your guns batter Castelmonte, they swill, fornicate and grow fat. Were it possible so to arrange matters, I would have gathered the bulk of my force after the wall had been breached, not before. Yet such a course would be impossible. Therefore, I dislike sieges."

"And if we make no breach, then I have wasted your hire, and theirs," Lorenzo said.

"It is not entirely wasted," Toscanelli pointed out. "We have enforced your blockade. Someone must do so, else your siege cannot exist. Nonetheless, it is unsatisfactory."

Lorenzo grunted.

"Giuliano," he said. "Your cavalry?"

"In like case to Guido's infantry and pikemen," Giuliano replied. "What have I done these past months? I ride bravely from Florence to the upper Arno. I wave greetings upon every hand. Where I can do so, I encourage my horsemen. Some few arrows and bolts, it may happen, are fired on me from the city's walls. I take wine with your Captain-Gunner here and return gloriously to Florence. A healthful way to spend the fall. But, as Guido says, unsatisfactory." He paused in recollection. "So also says Leonardo da Vinci, when he rides with me," he added. "I am forced to tell you, Rigo, that nobody loves your cannon."

"Leonardo da Vinci?" said Lorenzo. "The artist who painted the frescoes in my belvedere?"

"The same," said Giuliano. "An artist, and a notable singer of bawdy songs, though no drinker. He proposed a mine, in preference to your cannon. I disagreed. Yet he is a man of surprising mind, for all that."

"Evidently," said Lorenzo. "And what of the Count of Imola?"

"Riario? As to him," Giuliano said, "he has done nothing but to kill Giasone in a foul and cowardly fashion. As a demonstration of scorn, I take it, since he gained nothing by it."

"Yet he is Captain-General of Rome," remarked Lorenzo. "Why is he at Castelmonte?"

Giuliano shrugged. "Who knows? He is a vulture, as all men know. Which reminds me . . . by your leave, brother?"

He rose from the table at Lorenzo's nod, and strode across the room to where the two women now sat, sewing and murmuring quietly.

"A pretty picture you make, my ladies." Giuliano smiled confidently, bowing minutely and taking a grape from a rose crystal dish that lay on the sill between them.

"Or is it the thought of the grapes that drew you here, I wonder?" Bianca Maria Visconti tipped her head at him pertly. "Men think first and most often of food, so I have been told." Her dark-haired companion raised eyes briefly toward Giuliano and returned to her embroidery.

"You do me wrong," Giuliano said. "I came here to feast upon your grace and beauty, my ladies. From across the room—could you but see it—the sun strikes glints from the hair of my lady Constanza here, as from the wing of a raven. Did I say a pretty picture? A glorious one, rather, that dazzles me as I draw closer!" He bowed again.

"My lord," said Constanza d'Avalos dryly, "I pray you take several more of these grapes." She laid her sewing aside and, detaching a generous cluster, offered it to him.

"I thank you. Since they come from your hand, each shall

taste the sweeter," Giuliano said. "Yet so many at once? I had rather eat them one by one and slowly, thereby remaining with you the longer."

"And we," interrupted Bianca, "had rather you devoured them all at once, Giuliano, since the more you eat the less will you talk, and thus we shall finish our work the faster. Besides, for the making of such long and courtly speeches you need sustenance, surely."

"Cousin, you overwhelm me," Giuliano said. "I am abashed." He spoke blandly, but with a faint edge to his voice. This disconcerted Bianca not in the slightest, though it brought a blush to Constanza's cheek as she bent her head swiftly to her sewing. "Directly to my purpose, then," Giuliano continued. "Constanza, does not your sister, Carla d'Avalos, journey to our court from Arezzo?"

"She does," Constanza replied.

"And when does she arrive, Madonna?"

'Tomorrow, Giuliano. Why?"

"It is no great matter. With your permission, I propose to ride out and escort her party. The Republic is no longer as safe as it once was."

"You alarm me, sir," said Constanza.

"There is no need for alarm," Giuliano replied. "Merely for sensible precaution. Ladies, I thank you for your courtesy."

"It is I who should thank you for your concern, Giuliano," said Constanza d'Avalos. "And I do so."

"Then, by your leave," Giuliano said, and bowing, left them. He sauntered easily back toward the table at the far end of the room.

Bianca laughed. "He takes the last word, after all," she said. "It is an uphill task to teach him to speak plainly, but I shall succeed."

"Have a care that he takes no offense at your sharp tongue," Constanza said crossly.

"Have a care?" Bianca demanded. "What do I care? I am a

Visconti. Nor do I gaze at him with your round and adoring eyes, cousin. Is this the fashion in which you speak at night in the gardens? Somehow I cannot believe it. Will this mountain of 'by your leaves' and 'of your sweet permissions' persuade you to his bed, Constanza? It would not persuade me."

"Since you are barely fourteen and therefore a child," Constanza said, "I am glad to hear it. Have you been spying on us?" Anger flickered in her eyes. "You go too far, Bianca."

Bianca laughed gaily. "We Viscontis learn early the lessons that others learn too late," she said. "Of course, I have watched you. In Milan, cousin, we survey the field before we fight upon it, and how else should I learn the tactics of love save from those who—being sixteen—are older and wiser than I am?"

"You have too much wisdom, child," said Constanza, glancing at Guiliano's back. "And insufficient sense. Get on with your work."

Guiliano stepped up beside his brother.

Lorenzo de' Medici passed his hand across the map before him, smoothing its edges.

"Assume that I am forced to lift my siege," he said. "What then, Toscanelli? Would you have us conclude a formal truce for the winter?"

The condottiero brooded, stroking the side of his face. "That is hardly my decision to make, sir," he said finally. "It lies between yourself and the Count of Castelmonte, Giovio della Rovere, as principals in the matter. As between myself and Montefeltro—who represent you and the Count as professionals—such would be my choice. And his, I believe. Truce or no, the result will be the same. Your war will stop until next spring. Nature, God and snow will stop it. There remains the question of Count Girolamo, Rome's Captain-General. What his attitude may be, and what power over Della Rovere he may have to enforce it, I know not."

"But you would recommend a truce?"

"I would, sir."

"A truce during which they will repair Castelmonte's wall."

"That would be unavoidable," Toscanelli admitted.

Lorenzo leaned back in his chair and closed his eyes in concentration.

"Let me lay out the facts of this campaign," he said. "I must take Castelmonte. Not for itself but because it controls—by reason of its commanding position—the road from Rome." He opened his eyes again, resting his glance upon the mercenary. "You agree?"

"Most surely," Toscanelli said.

"The road along which, sometime next year, the Pope will march against Florence with an army twenty thousand strong. More, it may be."

"With respect," Toscanelli said, "that is a question of military and political strategy. I am merely a tactician, and accepted the case to be as you stated it when you came to me in July. Failure now stares us in the face, and I must ask you again what I asked you then. Do you not here deal in guesses? Can you be sure what His Holiness intends?"

Lorenzo considered.

"Not guesses," he said. "Calculation." Then, appearing to digress for the moment, he went on. "Tell me, Guido. Girolamo Riario, Count of Bosco and Imola—of what family is he?"

Toscanelli smiled, almost invisibly. "The Captain-General is the son of His Holiness's sister."

"Is he so? Is it not whispered, discreetly, that His Holiness bears a closer relationship, shall we say, to the Count?"

"Riario is a della Rovere bastard," said Rigo forthrightly, "and the Count of Castelmonte another, so let us spare ourselves discretion."

"Spoken like a gunner," laughed Giuliano de' Medici.

"I thank you, Rigo," Lorenzo said. "Papal bastards both. Well then? Pietro Riario was made Cardinal, and died of his excesses in that holy office. Francesco della Rovere is now our Holy Father and Giovio della Rovere holds Castelmonte for Rome. Girolamo Riario is greater, both in ability and in evil, than either, and is Captain-General of the Armies of the Church. And he is in Castelmonte too."

"And where does this lead us?" the condottiero asked.

"It leads us, good Toscanelli, to this question again—why is he there? If the Captain-General of Rome's army thinks it worth his while to join a beleaguered garrison, then it follows that he places the same value upon that garrison as I do. If I must take Castelmonte because it guards the upper Arno, he must hold it for the same reason. Therefore, Rome intends to march. But my case does not rest on this alone." Lorenzo raised a finger as he went on. "One. Sixtus has denied us Imola by purchasing it four years ago from Milan; thereby, he intends to deny us the Adriatic Sea. Two. He has removed Rome's banking affairs from our uncle, Giovanni Tornabuoni, and transferred them to the Pazzi family in Rome; thereby, he denies us profit. Three. He has appointed Francesco Salviati to be Archbishop of Pisa in our domain, against our wishes and against formal agreement; thereby, he deliberately seeks to provoke us."

"And has succeeded," Giuliano said.

"Admirably," said Lorenzo. "Four. He holds Castelmonte against us, and has armed and provisioned it from his own purse. Five. He has sent Girolamo Riario there. Therefore, the question I ask myself is not whether he intends to proceed to open warfare with us, but when? Riario's presence tells me the answer: early next year. Do you find fault with my reasoning?"

"Not I," said Rigo. "You state the case adequately enough."

"Guido?"

"You persuade me, sir," Toscanelli said. "I agree."

"Guiliano?"

"I agree also."

"And therefore," Lorenzo drove the point home, "Castelmonte *must* be in our hands no later than two weeks after the start of campaigning weather next spring. Does this follow?"

"It does," said Rigo.

"And if you begin your bombardment again as soon as the ground will hold your guns—in April, let us say—how long will it take you to reduce the wall, Rigo?"

"You know the answer to that as well as I, sir. It must take me the eight weeks I have already spent this year, since they will by then have repaired what damage I have achieved. Unless Toscanelli here is prepared to sit out the winter surrounding the stronghold and prevent them from doing so."

"Impossible," Toscanelli said. "Spend four months in tents, brush-fighting with repair parties? It cannot be done. In any case, they have only to build themselves a second redoubt behind the damaged portion. In four months, they can do so with ease, and keep warm in the bargain. I cannot stop them."

"Eight weeks and more, then," Rigo said. "Moreover . . ."

"Yes?" Lorenzo prompted.

"Sir, I have no wish to add to your troubles."

"You do not do so, Roderigo, by pointing them out to me. Speak."

"Then," said Rigo, "as soon as I have made my breach next spring—say summer, rather—and Toscanelli has taken the city through it, you will at once become the defender rather than the attacker. Rome will be on the march. Thus the wall, which I shall have knocked down for you at great pains, will have to be repaired yet again, by yourself. And will His Holiness grant you the time in which to do so?"

Lorenzo de' Medici drummed his fingers upon the map, then turned to Toscanelli.

"Guido," he said, "what chance of taking the wall of Castelmonte without breaching it?"

"Small," Toscanelli answered. "It can be done, but not with the troops I have. They are good enough for a blockade, but not for storm attack. The Swiss, perhaps, could do it for you."

"At enormous expense."

"Most certainly. And, again, not until next spring. Furthermore, for such an enterprise you will need siege engines—towers, bridges, rolling ladders, ballistae, rams. These are mechanical matters, and I have little skill in them."

"But there exist men who have such skills."

"Assuredly. Your best military engineer is Francesco di Giorgio Martini, the Sienese. His fee would be some twelve thousand florins per month, which is a full third of what you now pay myself and my condotta—and still does not include the engines themselves. Your good siege engineer is a rare man, and an expensive one."

Three

"Gold," the Supreme Pontiff said. "This, then, is what it comes to, as always. Gold, Borgia."

"An excellent and necessary tool," the Cardinal agreed.

"You speak truly," said Sixtus. "A tool. And yet I perceive it also as a rock, Borgia—a rock upon which our work, our love, our grand design *in excelsis* may founder, my old friend."

Francesco della Rovere, Pope Sixtus IV by Almighty Grace and the expressed will of the College of Cardinals at Rome, former General of the Franciscan Order, past professor in Padua, Bologna, Pavia, Siena, Florence, Perugia, Venice, and now Vicar of God's Kingdom upon earth, raised jeweled hand to chin and shifted impatiently in his ornate chair.

About him the walls of his chamber rose thirty feet and more into shadowed magnificence above silken hangings and carved architraves above paneling in cedar and olive, pilasters in ebony and bronze. All around were the portraits of his predecessors since the Great Schism: Nicholas V, Callistus

III, Pius II, Paul II. Looking down, they seemed to radiate their spiritual blessing upon his driven purpose.

Gross, dissolute, shrewd and hypocritical, Sixtus drew strength both from his surroundings and from the webs of policy woven at his accession. He advanced his family, repaid his supporters and bought time from his opponents. The world, it had been revealed to him by the light of reason, was the Mediterranean. The Mediterranean—despite the Turks—was Italy, and Italy was Rome. And Rome was himself. Hence, reason and revelation both demanding it, the grand design was there, and the purpose. It was purpose that twisted the Pontiff's face into a mobile and wrenching grimace as he talked and forced his pace when he strode the corridors of the Papal Palace; purpose that led him into smoothly concealed impatience with legate and nuncio.

It was something of this purpose, perhaps, which those who supported his election had seen in him, and for which they had lent him the weight of their favor. His grand scheme they had not perceived so readily or they might have had second thoughts. His predecessor, Paul II, an ascetic, had left Rome with few friends, being as parsimonious with others as he had been with himself. Sixtus, his supporters hoped, would retrieve the situation with purpose but also with moderation, restoring to Rome her power through the judicious distribution of money, the golden pollen of power.

Francesco della Rovere, upon his election, overrode their hopes of moderation like a pious and flabby juggernaut. He had, it was apparent, larger aims for Rome and for himself.

"Florence," said Pope Sixtus IV. "Florence, Siena, Ferrara, Mantua, Venice, Milan. You see it, Borgia? Rome cannot be squeezed like a nut between south and north. She must extend, Borgia, extend and consolidate."

"I see it, indeed, Your Holiness," Cardinal Borgia replied, "and approve. Yet this is a large meal for Rome to digest."

"Your metaphor," said Sixtus, fluttering pudgy fingers, "is inept. Digestion implies a crudity of which we are incapable. Let us rather think of Rome as a swan spreading her wings in protection over the City-States of our torn and misguided Italy."

"By all means," said the Cardinal equably. "I accept the correction happily, since Milan and Venice would, as morsels, strain the mouth of Gargantua. Adopting your more delicate phrase, then, it remains my feeling that Rome's wingspread may be too short to accommodate them."

"It must do so."

"Eventually, perhaps," Borgia said, "since Rome must control the Adriatic no less than the west. Moreover, through Venice—if I understand the thoughts of Your Holiness correctly—pours incalculable wealth."

"You understand me, Borgia, as always."

"Then let Rome proceed slowly."

"Slowly?" Sixtus shifted in his chair again, his mouth working. "Slowly?"

"With circumspection."

"Better. We are not, I hope, to be thought of as rash."

"Certainly not," Cardinal Borgia replied. "And what of Naples?"

"Barbarians! Let Ferrante brew his own soup, and his dung-stained brats with him. We have given the Abbey of Monte Casino to one of those same brats, thus diverting to Naples revenues which should be ours. Beyond such gestures, nothing to the south is worthy of our consideration."

"Very well. Let us fix our eyes upon Venice and her river of gold—but circumspectly."

"Her river of gold," Sixtus fluted. He clasped his hands across his ample stomach and looked toward the ceiling. "Admirable. A trifle worldly, but admirable nonetheless. Bringing our gaze nearer home, however . . . Ferrara we may leave, since if we achieve Venice, Ferrara is surrounded and must fall to us by treaty. The same applies in the case of Siena, to my mind."

"If Florence is overcome," Cardinal Borgia agreed, "Siena cannot stand. Now Milan—"

"—is powerful," Sixtus interrupted. "There is no doubt of

that. Were the Duke Galeazzo still alive, our problems with Milan would not exist. But they murdered him, Borgia, murdered him most foully." He sighed. "And the Duke Ludovico Sforza has not the same love for Rome that Galeazzo bore us. Ingratitude, my friend; it is sharper than a serpent's tooth. Sforza and Medici now walk hand in hand. Of our great love, Borgia, we must have them both."

Cardinal Borgia stood up, a handsome and striking figure. Well-knit and robust, he was attired more sumptuously even than the Pontiff. His pleasant and yet noble bearing had been widely extolled in popular writings, and his attraction for women was the subject of a highly indelicate tale by Masuccio Salernitano. This fable had not incurred Rodrigo Borgia's displeasure. His Spanish ancestry encouraged him to take a certain pride in such stories and in the tales of his youth, when he had fought bravely for his uncle, the Borgia Pope, Callistus III. Now, in his prime, he was a politician of both charm and presence.

"We return, it seems, to Florence," he said.

"Florence," agreed Pope Sixtus IV, sighing. "Ah, Borgia! If Rome is a swan, must she not yearn to enfold rebellious Florence as a swan does her cygnet? A city of such beauty, so near to God and yet so far! If we lend them not our care and guidance, may not her people slip into heresy? And is it not our holy duty, then, to care for the Republic of Florence? It must be, Borgia."

"Your Holiness is too kind, as befits your Office," said the Cardinal. "Florence is a city of freethinkers, and damned thereby."

"My dear friend, be not too harsh. She could be the flower of Italy, and a jewel in our crown."

"Not while a Medici rules her," said Borgia.

"The Medici," Sixtus said irritably. "What are the Medici but usurers who have hoodwinked Florence these many years into accepting their rule? Our first kindness to that city, Borgia, should be to open her eyes to the stiff-necked greed of the Medici. But enough of that. Next year, Borgia

. . . next year, we shall address ourselves, in love and good will, to Florence."

Cardinal Borgia pinched the bridge of his nose in thought.

"If Castelmonte holds," he said.

"It will. Our most excellent son Girolamo Riario will assist Count Giovio in this."

"I had rather trust in Montefeltro," Cardinal Borgia said, "if Your Holiness wishes my frank views on the subject. The Counts of Imola and of Castelmonte are sometimes overgiven to excesses."

"To our sorrow," said the Pontiff gently. "It grieves us continually. Yet they *are* effective."

"I admit that. Girolamo Riario strikes terror into the hearts of your enemies wherever he goes."

"Terror, Borgia?" The Pontiff's voice was filled with tender reproach. "How can that be, since he strives only to extend our benevolence to the lost and blind? Say rather, awe."

"As Your Holiness pleases. As for the matter of the Medici themselves, I gather that certain notions have been put forward concerning them, for the greater comfort of Rome and of yourself."

"They have not," said Sixtus quickly. "Understand this, Borgia. They have not. Rumors—wild rumors—have reached our ears. Infamous suggestions, to put it bluntly. Our ears are closed to them."

"I understand perfectly, Your Holiness," Cardinal Borgia said. "Perfectly."

Four

"Again?" protested Matteo Barletta, the archer. "I am a wounded man, Leonardo."

"So you have been at pains to tell me, some fifty times or more. Again, if you please, since your wound is a trifle, and of no concern whatever to me. Science is merciless, Matteo. We must all suffer in her cause."

"So I see. Your own suffering moves me to tears," said the archer caustically. "And furthermore, there is no science in bowmanship. It is an art, and it will take more than your continual foolery with sticks to persuade me otherwise." He took his stance once more, feet apart, his left shoulder toward the target seventy paces away at the far end of the field. The nock of the arrow rode back between his fingers as he drew the ash wood bow. The string thrummed, and a moment later, the shaft thudded into the mark alongside four others, their heads buried deeply in the coiled straw behind the canvas.

Leonardo lowered the two pieces of wood he had been holding in front of his eyes. They were hinged together at one end to form a rough protractor with which he was measuring the angle made by the arrow's shaft with the level ground in the instant before Matteo Barletta loosed it. He entered the result in the notebook which, as ever, swung at his hip, using for the purpose a small quill recharged from a stoppered inkhorn that dangled alongside the notebook's spine.

Matteo glanced at the sun. "It is four already." They had repeated this procedure one hundred and forty times since noon of this, the first biting day of winter. Each time, in the brief pause before Matteo released the bowstring, Leonardo would rapidly set the arms of his measuring device and then take notes.

Between groups of a dozen shots, Leonardo walked the length of the field to collect the arrows while Matteo rested.

They had spent nine days upon this exercise in the small water meadow behind the Medici Palace. A shallow stream divided it, beyond which the ground rose upward to the base of the high stone wall that surrounded the lawns and formal terraces of the *palazzo* itself. Occasionally, the figure of one watcher or another had appeared at the wicket gate in the palace wall, surveying the two experimenters; but no one had approached, either in curiosity or to protest their obvious trespass. From noon until sunset, therefore, they had followed their routine without interruption, and Matteo Barletta was beginning to tire of it. He was also becoming impatient with the continual stream of questions directed at him by Leonardo da Vinci.

"I have told you," he said, resting the foot of his weapon against his instep. "I do not know how it is done. It is a question of skill, and of practice by those who have the skill to start with."

Leonardo eyed him. "Do not unstring your bow, Matteo, if that is what you intend. We are not finished yet."

The archer groaned and replaced the loop of the bowstring in its notch.

"No?" he asked. "I had hoped that by now you might be

as weary of writing figures as I am of this child's work. Enough, Leonardo."

"Rest awhile. However, we still have . . ." The artist scanned his notebook, rapidly counting, ". . . some sixty shots to complete the day's tale. Now, as to this question of skill: Tell me, at what point do you aim the tip of your arrow when shooting thus?"

"At this distance?" the archer asked. "A man's height above the target's center."

"And how do you know that this is the true point of aim?"

"I know it," Matteo Barletta said tartly, "because I have shot in some hundreds of tournaments since you and I were lads in Anchiano and have even taken a few modest prizes for this skill of mine. That is how."

"And if we move the target to a hundred paces distant?"

"Then my point of aim is so much the higher. Every fool knows this. I have called this child's work, Leonardo, and I find your questions more childish still."

"Because I approach these matters as a child does," Leonardo said imperturbably. "To get a direct answer from you is like trying to squeeze juice from a dried fig. At a hundred paces by how much higher is your aim?"

Matteo Barletta scratched his neck vigorously, frowning.

"It is beyond me," he said. "I àm no mathematician. I perform no calculations, as you put it. I am an archer. Do you think I have time to reckon this and compute that when I stand in front of a charging knight at arms and must bring him down before he rides me beneath his hooves? A wondrous sight I should make, sharpening the end of my quill and scratching away at some tablet, begging my enemy to hold off while I worked out how far away from me he sat! I take aim and loose, and there's an end of it, Leonardo. If I miss with my first shaft, Providence may grant me a second. If I miss with that also, then I am a dead man. Yet not so surely dead as if I were to stand like a stockfish and count upon my fingers."

"All this is well argued," said Leonardo. "And yet . . . you are weary of shooting, did you say?"

"Exceedingly weary."

"And your wound is troubling you?"

"My wound, as you call it, is a scratch, as you well know, and therefore I suspect your sudden concern for it. Are we done here or are we not?"

"We are not. But you may sit on the ground awhile and rest, prince of archers, while I walk to the house of Piero Novara and beg some timber from him," said Leonardo.

"Timber? In God's name, what now?"

"Timber and nails. Wait for my return. There remains a full hour of daylight," said Leonardo, "so take your ease, and wait."

The archer sat down, resting his bow across his knees.

"Then bring some wine too."

In the studio of Andrea del Verrocchio, heads were bent over work tables and benches in silent industry, real or simulated. Now and again, however, one apprentice or another stole a glance from his appointed task toward the small group of persons in a far corner of the room, clustered around a whitewashed board.

The light was failing. Had this been a normal evening, subtle moves would have been taking place here and there, suggesting with the ease of practice that the day's labor was all but finished. Tidy pyramids of wood shavings or of gold and silver swarf would have been brushed together, workpieces covered with protective cloth, briefly muttered conversations begun to the accompaniment of smiles betokening imminent release.

In the presence of Lorenzo de' Medici, the artisans' lord and chief patron, such gestures were considered injudicious. Cleaning up could be done, if need be, by candlelight when he had gone.

Lorenzo de' Medici put down the drawing he had been examining. The portrayed face smiled out at him from the board's surface, as it had done at Verrocchio on the day of its execution.

"And where is Master Leonardo himself?" inquired the ruler of Florence mildly.

"He is not here, sir," Verrocchio replied.

"So much I observe. Were he present, I doubt that he would have escaped our notice. Nonetheless, since it was chiefly to speak with him that I came here, it would be convenient to know his whereabouts. Has he gone upon some errand?"

The master craftsman hesitated.

"Why, not exactly, sir," he answered. "That is . . . I am not certain. But I believe him to be in the field which adjoins your palazzo; though to be truthful, I have never asked him where it is that he goes."

"Have you not, Andrea? But he is absent with your consent, I take it?" Lorenzo smiled, and Verrocchio permitted himself to do likewise.

"Unwillingly given, perhaps, sir," he said. "But he has it."

"Playing truant, I'll wager," put in the young man who stood beside Lorenzo. "Is it not always thus with artists, good Verrocchio?"

The speaker was tall and supercilious of manner, with a handsomely flared nose down which he gave the constant appearance of looking at the world. It was an appearance amply confirmed by all that he did, said and implied. He was Silvio Grimiani di Torino, Prince of Savoy. Colorfully dressed in a slashed doublet of purple with gold embroidery, he sniffed delicately at a scented handkerchief, the better to keep at bay the smells of paint, turpentine and heated chasing irons. This delicacy of breeding had earned him the admiration of many ladies at court and the amused tolerance of a few more, including Bianca Maria Visconti, who now stood at Lorenzo's other side.

"I imagine, Lorenzo," the prince continued, "that he will

be found riding with your brother. Upon a borrowed horse, I have no doubt."

"Then in this you are mistaken, my lord," said Lorenzo, "or so I believe." He turned back to Verrocchio. "There have been two men in my meadow these last nine days, practicing archery, as I am informed. Do you mean that one of them is Master Leonardo? Curious. Why is he doing it?"

"You must ask him that yourself, sir. I have no idea, nor, indeed, do I swear that he is there at all."

"He is." Bianca Visconti spoke up, gently pulling the sleeve of Lorenzo's cloak. "I saw him there not two hours ago, from the roof of the belvedere."

"Did you, child? Then you could have saved me my journey."

"If you had told me why you were making it, sir, perhaps I might have. Since you did not—"

"In any case," interrupted Lorenzo, "it is no longer dignified for you to go scrambling about the walls and roof of my gallery, as I have repeatedly asked Brother Sigismondo to impress upon you. Without effect, it seems. How do you know it was Leonardo da Vinci you saw from this unsuitable position of yours?"

"By the book at his waist," replied Bianca promptly. "Is this not so, Master Andrea? On a chain, thus?"

"Indeed," said Verrocchio. "Leonardo, beyond a doubt."

"There you are, you see," said Bianca triumphantly.

Her guardian surveyed her with a certain grim fondness.

"Very perceptive of you," he said. Then to the master craftsman, "Whether you grant your employees freedom from their labors to practice archery or not is your affair, Master Andrea, though I am bound to say I find it somewhat odd." He tapped the drawing. "May I see some further examples of his work? The decorations he undertook for me in the belvedere, of which the Lady Bianca speaks, pleased me well. As does this trifle here."

"With pleasure, sir. His portfolio lies on that table."

Verrocchio led the way to the spot he had indicated. There, Lorenzo de' Medici turned over a wide leather cover and began to thumb through the collection of sheets and tattered paper scraps that lay beneath it, turning them this way and that.

"A study for the 'Incredulity of St. Thomas,' sir," Verrocchio commented. "And what you hold in your hand now is a cherub in the style of Desiderio da Settignano, I believe; a poor thing, in my judgment. As you see, I cannot prevent him from borrowing my competitors' techniques when it suits him, many of which are unsound. But he has a good eye. One cannot deny it. He is, of course, too free in his sense of composition, far too free. I have often told him so, but he is impatient of instruction. He insists that he paints things as he sees them; in which case, as I have often been at pains to point out to him, his perception must be vastly different from my own. He is, sir, a hard man to dispute, and needs discipline, badly. When he is ready to accept it, his eye for movement may be turned to good account."

Lorenzo nodded, abstracted.

"And then again," Verrocchio continued, "he has no appreciation of allegory."

"Has he not, indeed?" said Lorenzo. "How reprehensible of him. How old was Master Leonardo when he first came to you?"

"Twenty-one, I believe, sir. Before that, he was under Ser Antonio Pollajuolo."

"Well, well, Master Andrea," Lorenzo said, "when I was twenty-one, I too was somewhat impatient of instruction, as I recall. As for our good Leonardo, my guess is that he will shortly be thinking of setting up on his own account. Which, I imagine, is one of the reasons for your permitting him . . . certain liberties. Do I guess aright?"

"You do, sir. When all is said and done, he remains my best workman."

Lorenzo grunted and took up a torn, triangular paper from the portfolio in front of him. After scanning it closely in the fading light, he passed it without comment to the Prince of Savoy, who accepted it with an air of surprise. Lines creased his noble forehead. He turned it end for end once or twice, and handed it back.

"I can make neither head nor tail of it," he confessed loftily, "one thing being drawn on top of another. What is the writing scrawled there? 'Tis Greek, I fancy."

"I had not thought Your Lordship capable of Greek," said Lorenzo, "though I am sure you are right in your analysis. What do you think, Bianca?"

Bianca Visconti took the proffered scrap.

"No," she said at once. "Here is no Greek."

"Do you say so? You hear that, Silvio? Not Greek. Tell us further, little one. What is it?"

"I think it is written backward," Bianca announced. "As in a mirror. Yes, I am sure of it. See, here is an *s*, and here an *e*."

Verrocchio spoke up. "Your ladyship is quite correct," he said. "He often writes thus, though for what reason, I do not know."

"For the mystification of others, perhaps?" Lorenzo suggested.

"I hardly think so," said the craftsman. "It has, after all, failed to mystify the Lady Bianca for very long."

"But then her perception is very acute," Lorenzo said, "as must be evident to all of us. Master Leonardo begins to intrigue me. Have you a mirror anywhere?"

"Not here, sir. I could send next door for one, if you wish me to."

"No matter. I see a piece of polished metalwork there." Lorenzo pointed. "Bring it to me, if you please, and a candle, perhaps. It grows dark."

Verrocchio removed the silver dish which his patron had indicated from under the nose of one of his apprentices, and fetched it to the table on which the portfolio lay. He lit a candle stub from a spirit lamp and carried it, with flaring wick, to set beside the platter.

"Bianca," said Lorenzo de' Medici. "Decipher it for us, if you can. Here, let me hold our makeshift looking-glass for you—so."

After several false attempts, his ward succeeded in placing the torn leaf so that she could read its reflected script. "It makes little sense," she said in a disappointed voice. "For all our trouble, it is but half a sentence upon . . . upon gunpowder, it seems. Do you wish to hear it?"

"By all means."

"It says . . ." Bianca squinted at the distorted image in the silver surface, ". . . *that force contained within gunpowder being like to the force of a man's arm.*" She stopped.

"That is all?"

"Yes."

The Prince of Savoy lowered his kerchief. "Very enlightening," he said sarcastically. "My lord Lorenzo, these nursery excursions are fascinating, but if you have finished here, might I suggest we return home? Night draws in, and besides . . ." He flourished the silken square. ". . . It is somewhat airless in here, I find."

Lorenzo straightened up, laying the plate down upon the tabletop. "Then we must have you under the open sky before you are quite overcome, Silvio," he responded briskly. "Which being so, Master Verrocchio, I thank you for your courtesy in indulging our childish curiosity, and we shall now leave you in peace."

"You are always welcome, sir," Verrocchio said. "And what of Master Leonardo? Shall I instruct him to attend you tomorrow?"

"No need for that. If he is indeed in our meadow then we shall meet with him shortly, since I propose to return that way now."

The Prince of Savoy opened his eyes wide in protest. "No," he said. "This is an overlong walk for my liking, and damp besides. I do not care to plod through mud and wet grass."

"And perhaps step on a toad, my lord," laughed Bianca.

"Our meadow is full of toads at night. Great ugly ones, that squash underfoot." She studied the expression on his face closely. "Some say, I believe," she continued innocently, "that they are venomous."

"And your manners, Bianca," interrupted Lorenzo coldly, "leave much to be desired, as always. Be not so pert, or I shall have you confined all tomorrow with your tutors. Come, Silvio. The walk will clear your head."

Leonardo da Vinci spat the remaining nail from between his teeth into his hand and took a purposeful grip on his hammer.

"Hold firm, Matteo," he commanded. "Have you got it?"

"I have, blast and plague it. And strike your own fingers if you must, not mine," said the archer.

"I am somewhat unhandy at this work, I concede. I should have given more study to the framing of my canvases when I was an apprentice. But it will serve, I dare say."

Leonardo drove the last nail into the structure of planks he had built with his friend's unwilling aid.

"There," he said. "A most excellent machine. Does it not appear devilish like a ballista to you?"

"Somewhat," Matteo Barletta admitted grudgingly. "Somewhat. Is that what it is intended to be? Where is your string?"

"That will be provided, tomorrow, by your bow."

"Will it? Having missed my supper tonight, I had hoped to spend tomorrow in resting." The archer hacked at the frame moodily with his foot. Two lanterns rested on the ground beside it, casting a flickering but necessary light. There being neither moon nor stars visible, the darkness a mere ten paces away seemed impenetrable. A thin and cutting night breeze had arisen, and Matteo Barletta hunched his shoulders against it inside his leather jerkin.

"Then lend me your bow, and stay at home," said Leonardo.

"By no means. Where my bow travels, there do I travel

also. Without it, I feel like a tortoise without its shell. I shall bring bread and cheese, and watch you at your labors. It will be a new sensation for both of us."

"As an alternative," Leonardo suggested after a minute's thought, "you could borrow a crossbow for me. It would serve as well, and might be more convenient to handle."

"A crossbow!" snorted Matteo in derision. "The crossbow is a contrivance of the Father of Lies himself, ungainly and ineffective. I can loose ten shafts in the time it will take your crossbowman to handle his winch or goat's-foot lever alone. I do not understand what it is you intend to do tomorrow, but I can promise you that with a crossbow, it will take you from dawn to sunset to fire ten shots."

"This smacks of prejudice, Matteo," said Leonardo. "But I will be advised by you, and use your bow. The effect is the same with either weapon."

"Not so," said Barletta stoutly. "The arch of your crossbow is of steel, and therefore, unnatural."

"But the principle, my friend, is the same. It is similar for all missiles, however launched. By crossbow, catapult, ballista, mangonel, cannon."

The archer sat down heavily on one side of the sloping wooden framework they had completed. It creaked, but held his weight.

"What nonsense is this?" he said. "I will allow, if you like, that both bow and crossbow use—in some sort—the same force, which is that of the string. But there is no such force in your cannon."

"Yet force there must be," argued Leonardo, "else the ball would not fly."

"It is the noise of the powder which propels the ball," said Matteo confidently, "as all men know. And it does so but feebly, at that. Which is why the cannon is an invention still more useless than the crossbow, and fit only to frighten horses. I would not give you a *soldo* for all the cannon in the world. Rigo Leone's guns have been roaring at the wall of Castelmonte all autumn, and to what effect? None whatever.

Whereas I, Matteo Barletta, have killed six men there, and been wounded in the leg by a man who—though doubtless a black, thieving and misbegotten son of a Roman whore—was, nonetheless, a bowman like myself."

"Well spoken, archer," said a dry voice behind them.

They turned. Lorenzo de' Medici stood just inside the circle of light thrown by the two lanterns, a wing of his cloak around Bianca Maria Visconti. Beside him was the Prince of Savoy. Matteo Barletta jumped up from his sitting posture in confusion.

"My lord," he said, "I did not see you."

"Be easy," said Lorenzo. "There is nothing wrong with a man's expressing his opinions upon his own trade. Master Leonardo da Vinci, I believe?"

"At your service."

"And what deep undertaking is this, Master Leonardo, that you must drag a wounded bowman of mine from his sickbed in the middle of the night? To say nothing of using my meadow in its pursuit without seeking permission to do so."

"I had not thought, sir," Leonardo said easily, "that you would object."

"I have not said that I do object. It is an explanation I seek, not an apology."

"I am conducting experiments."

"Of what kind?"

"Upon the flight of missiles."

"And for what purpose?"

"For the gathering, sir, of knowledge."

"Very praiseworthy," said Lorenzo. "Let me reshape my question: to what immediate and practical end?"

"To no immediate end. The gathering of knowledge is sufficient end in itself."

"Is it? I am far from certain that I agree with you, Master Leonardo, though it may rest upon opinion. What harvest of knowledge do you wish to garner by the use of this contrivance I see?"

"I hope to determine at what upward angle an arrow must be discharged to achieve a certain length of flight. And whether, as I suspect, this angle remains constant for any such given length. Also, to what height the arrow may rise in its path between bow and target; and whether there is any simple mathematical relationship between either the angle at which it is discharged, or the height to which it rises and the distance it flies. And a few other such matters."

"What other matters?" asked Lorenzo.

Observing the two men with their eyes fixed upon each other, Matteo Barletta began to feel uncomfortable. "If your lordship would permit me," he said, "it is late, and my supper—"

"We will not keep you from it, Barletta," said Lorenzo. "Eat well, and a swift recovery to you, bowman."

"Thank you, sir." The archer melted inconspicuously into the night.

"What other matters?" persisted Lorenzo de' Medici.

"There is the further question," Leonardo said, "of whether any such mathematical relationship as I may discover between the angle of discharge and the distance flown by the arrow also holds good for other types of missiles, or whether the size, weight or shape of the missile affects the relationship. And also, whether the amount of force used to propel the missile can be deduced from the curve and distance of its travel—an important matter, since it would lead to speculations upon the nature of gunpowder."

"I see. A brave harvest, Master Leonardo," said Lorenzo. "Is that the sum of it?"

"By no means. Gleaning knowledge—to use your metaphor—is like gleaning barley. In the act of picking up one straw, the eye strays farther and perceives others to be garnered; and in reaching for these, still more appear within reach. The harvest is endless."

Lorenzo de' Medici lifted his hand and rested it idly upon the golden head of his ward.

"Yet the mind," he said, "is finite."

"Save for the mind of God, that is true."

"Hum. Well, Master Leonardo, I suppose that a start to such a harvest may be made as well in my meadow as elsewhere. I hope your contrivance here may withstand the onslaughts of the urchins of Florence, who avail themselves as freely of my streams and pastures as you seem to do."

"I confess, sir, that the same thought had occurred to me. Nor can I spend all day here, as I would wish."

"No, indeed. Master Andrea has some small need of your services." Lorenzo surveyed the machine thoughtfully. "What work are you engaged upon at his studio?"

"For the present," Leonardo replied, "I am painting an angel or two for an altarpiece."

"And is this important?"

"That depends, sir, upon one's point of view. Di Credi could paint them as well as I, it is true. But a man must earn his wage, else he is a poor thing indeed."

"So he is," Lorenzo agreed. 'Nevertheless, I will make you an offer, if you care to hear it. You may move your contrivance into my archery range and work with it for as many days as it may take you to gather—shall we say—the first two or three straws of your harvest. I will approach Master Andrea on your behalf, and perhaps free you from the painting of angels for awhile. How does that strike you?"

"As being exceedingly generous," Leonardo replied. "I offer you my thanks for it, since a few undisturbed days at this time would be more precious to me than gold. But a bargain has two sides. What might I give you in exchange?"

Lorenzo smiled fleetingly.

"Allow my doctors and mathematicians to pester you with such questions as their learned minds may produce upon the subject of the flight of missiles," he said. "I cannot guarantee that you will not be similarly plagued by my courtiers, I regret to say, though they will not damage your contrivances as others might were you to continue working in this field. Well?"

"I accept with pleasure," Leonardo said.

"Then present yourself to me early tomorrow, Master Leonardo. And now good night."

Lorenzo nodded affably and made as if to move on.

"Will you not take one of my lanterns?" Leonardo asked. "The night is dark."

"A kindly thought. Bianca, will you carry it for us? Come, Silvio." Lorenzo turned back to the artist, still with a faint smile on his lips. "We are," he said, "somewhat afraid of toads."

"There are none here," said Leonardo. "Toads, sir, croak, and thereby make their presence known."

"So they do," said Lorenzo de' Medici. "So they do."

Five

By midmorning, the scattering of frost on the lawn had melted though the sun had not yet drawn the remaining beads of moisture from the short turf. Water still gathered, trickling on the beaten copper roof of the belvedere, and dripped unevenly to the cobbles beneath its eaves. Around the long, narrow enclosure, the high, stone walls, glowing with patches of golden lichen, threw back reflected glints of an icy fire where the night's coldness still lingered in dark crevices.

It was three days since Leonardo's first meeting with Lorenzo in the field beyond the wicket gate, and his first experiments with the framed bow, that now stood at one end of the archery range, were almost completed. He sat on a wooden bench in the sunlight and surveyed his untidy columns of figures, his breath steaming in the crisp air.

Matteo Barletta, whose initial caution at working within the Medici precincts had by now left him, was as skeptical of their joint labors as ever. However, he regarded their apparatus with the proprietary air of a watchdog, barring the approach of those who showed any signs of wanting to lay hands on it.

Leonardo himself had spent only eight hours of the past seventy-two in sleeping, yet showed no sign of it. From dusk until midnight, he performed calculations on the previous day's results, and rose before three to prepare the next day's trials.

After some discussion, he had reached a compromise with the archer upon the nature of their equipment. Their missiles were still arrows—chosen with care from among Barletta's finest—rather than crossbow bolts. But the device he had rebuilt and refined. Still a crossbow in essence, its drawn string was held taut by a filed and polished metal sear and was released by a trigger. The bow itself lay horizontal, clamped to an independent wooden mounting whose angle of elevation could be altered by raising or lowering it within the main body of the framework itself.

Thus far their onlookers had been only the more curious among the ladies and gentlemen of the court. Lorenzo de' Medici had not been seen. Such arrangements as Leonardo deemed necessary had been delegated to a chamberlain who, in his turn, had referred them disdainfully to the head gardener. Nor, up till now, had any of the mathematicians of the Medici court appeared.

This suited Leonardo very well, since he preferred the company of courtiers to that of savants. The questions of the strolling noblemen and their companions, while often delivered in a somewhat condescending fashion, obliged him only to give the barest outline of what he was attempting to do. Since they knew him by sight as Giuliano de' Medici's constant riding companion, they were, in their turn, prepared to accord him a certain acceptance as one of themselves, their condescension springing more from defensive ignorance than from snobbery. A painter, they reasoned, was a tradesman. But a painter who rode at hawk with the brother of Il Magnifico and thus showed an amiable disregard for his trade, might be socially admissible—pen, inkhorn and notebook notwithstanding. Besides, life at court was often tedious, and to be able to take a turn through the gardens and comment upon the strange contraption which had been set up in the practice butts—for what purpose, Providence alone knew—gave a conversational edge to the day which it formerly lacked. Leonardo answered them cheerfully and in words they could understand, and they chattered and passed on.

A shadow fell across the page Leonardo was studying, and he looked up.

"How goes it, artist?" asked Giuliano de' Medici.

"Well indeed, I thank you."

"What have you discovered?"

"Poetry."

"Have you? I am uncertain what you may mean by that."

"A certain symmetry in nature, then," said Leonardo, "which has a poetical air, and pleases me thereby. Giuliano, you have a face like a thundercloud. Sit down."

"Not for long," said Giuliano, seating himself on the bench beside the artist. "I had hoped that you might have discovered some means of taking Castelmonte tomorrow, not the poetical aspect of nature."

"Not tomorrow, or the day after. Why?"

"For good reason, indeed, my friend," said Giuliano. "Constanza's sister, Carla d'Avalos, lies prisoner within its walls."

Leonardo closed his notebook with a snap and turned to face the man beside him.

"How?"

"Through the stupidity of that damnable popinjay, the Prince of Savoy," Giuliano said bitterly. "Had I not restrained myself, I could have killed him on the spot. They took her in a *camisado* two nights ago, and I was too late to do anything save clatter about in the dark, shouting curses."

"Tell me precisely what happened, Giuliano. A camisado? I would have thought the defenders of Castelmonte had better things to do than ride about the countryside at night with shirts over their armor."

"It was but a chance piece of blockade running, I think," said Giuliano, "though it turned out more profitable than they had intended. Very well, then. As you know, I had arranged to ride out and escort Carla d'Avalos and her party from Pistrola to Florence, since they had been ill-advised enough to travel close to Castelmonte rather than taking a harder path through the hills to the north. I sent word to the inn there, telling them to await my arrival. They did not do so. And why? Because our Prince of Savoy, if you please, took it upon himself to ride to Pistrola before me, with the foolish suggestion that the easiest way to pass Castelmonte would be under cover of darkness. And that very night. He found one Corsario de Soto, a cousin to Carla and as stupid as himself, in agreement. Whereupon what must they do but ride out under a good half moon with but five men as escort—and one of these a friar. Toscanelli heard them coming a league away. He let them by, thinking that they were accompanied by myself and therefore secure. I told Toscanelli that if he supposed I would have less than a quarter squadron of cavalry with me upon such an errand he must be nearly as dull-witted as Silvio, but no matter for that. As for me, I arrived at Pistrola shortly after midnight to find them gone, and straightaway rode after. A mile beyond Castelmonte, they were attacked in a defile by some thirty fellows from the citadel wearing tabards over their mail. I found de Soto wounded, the friar picking at his beads in prayer, one man dead and Silvio engaging their rearguard, which fled at my approach. I wished him in like case to de Soto, and said so, at which he took great offense. Blundering fool! There was nothing I could do except ride in pursuit, which proved futile. I came back, damned his princely soul again heartily, and that was the end of it. A bad business."

"Doubtless, however, he meant well."

"I am sure he did. Who in the devil's name asked him to interfere? He is no soldier; he is a blowfly who prances about thrusting with a rapier after the fashion his French fencing masters teach up there in the north. Having killed a few men at *duello* with his effeminate mincing and prodding, he probably thought himself excellently suited as a ladies' escort. Well, it is done now, and we shall pay the price of his conceit. If della Rovere is prepared to release us Carla d'Avalos for a lesser sum than fifty thousand florins I shall be greatly surprised. They may also try to use her capture to advantage in arguing a truce. And unless matters move faster than I dare hope, I shall have to break the news to Constanza."

"You will have to do that in any case," said Leonardo.

"But not necessarily now. There is a chance, though a small one, of sparing her some anxiety."

Leonardo shook his head. "I do not see how."

"Some, I said. Not all. But I would rather leave it until a ransom has been demanded and agreed upon by my brother, which may be today or tomorrow for all I know. They are not likely to let the chance slip while they have it, and both Rigo and Toscanelli agree that a winter truce must be declared within the next few days. It will now cost us more than if the Prince of Savoy had not decided to give us a show of his addleheaded gallantry, that is all. You look thoughtful, Leonardo."

"Unpleasantly so," Leonardo rejoined, "though perhaps for no good reason. Tell me, when did you arrive here in Florence?"

"An hour ago."

"Then take my advice, Giuliano, and seek out Constanza. She has as much right to know of her sister's plight as I have."

"You do not think it would be better to wait?"

"No. Your reasoning is good-hearted, but wrong. Have I not already pointed out to you that she has a mind, even as you and I have minds? Therefore, tell her—now."

"Well," said Giuliano, rising, "I will consider it. And I have kept you from your work long enough, and your archer there. Though I see someone coming who will keep you from it still longer." He pointed to the pillared archway which led from the range to its neighboring inner courtyard.

Framed in the arch stood an imposing man with a forked, gray beard, wearing a flowing robe of brown and velvet cap to match.

"Who is he?"

"That, my dear Leonardo, is Dr. Mazzone, scholar extraordinary to my brother, The Magnificent. I wish you joy of him. As for myself, I shall bid you farewell before I am forced to share your conversation."

Giuliano crossed the stretch of level grass between the bench and archway, bowed to the doctor, and hastened out of sight. Dr. Mazzone, having inclined his head gravely in answer to this greeting, thrust out his chin and strode toward Leonardo, pausing briefly in the center of the range to examine the framed bow and to receive a paralyzing glare of discouragement from Matteo Barletta, who was testing its string for wear. Leonardo got up as he approached.

"Your servant, sir," Dr. Mazzone announced insincerely.

"As I am yours, sir."

"They tell me," Dr. Mazzone said, "that you are presently engaged here in mechanical pursuits. I had meant to come and offer you mathematical advice and assistance long before now, but it is hard, sir, very hard—as you may appreciate—to leave one's own labors and one's books. I seldom stray far from my suite these days, being engaged upon three separate proofs of a theorem by Anaximenes, my third especially being one of considerable refinement. You are familiar with the tenets of Anaximenes, I daresay?"

"To a degree," Leonardo said.

"How, sir, to a degree? One is surely either familiar with Anaximenes or one is not. His reason shines upon us like a beacon; his philosophy is limpid; his mathematics superb; and his theory of the universe far superior, as I believe, to those of either Xenophanes or Anaxagoras. He is, sir, the greatest of the ancients."

"It may be as you say," Leonardo replied. "Yet I find he has a singular disregard for facts."

Dr. Cino di Lapo Mazzone was taken aback, though not for long.

"Facts?" he said. "We do not know the facts. Until we do, we must rely upon hypotheses and systems, accepting or rejecting them as our intellects dictate. When, as in the case of Anaximenes, we come across a system of thought which is both harmonious and consistent, then you may depend upon it, sir, that the facts will eventually be found to agree with it. Such is the nature of philosophy. May I hazard a guess that you are a Pythagorean?"

"Sir, I am nothing of the kind."

"What school, then, do you follow, may one ask?"

"I follow no school. Nor any man. If there is one among the Greeks whom I admire, it would be Eupalinos the Samian."

"Eupalinos," said Dr. Mazzone slowly. "I believe, sir, that I am unfamiliar with his work. Remind me of it, if you will."

"He bored a double tunnel one hundred and fifty fathoms long beneath a mountain, so Herodotus tells us, for the supply of water to the city of Samos."

"Ah," said Dr. Mazzone, relieved. "Then, sir, he was no philosopher, but a mere engineer?"

"Even as I am," replied Leonardo in amusement. "Naturally, I am aware that the intellect of an engineer must, in all respects, be inferior to that of a philosopher. Does not Plato tell us so? In *Georgias*, does he not point out that a man of sensibility will use the very title as a taunt, and that he will refuse to allow his daughter to marry an engineer's son? An ignoble calling indeed, then, we may be sure. But we must all follow that road in life along which God beckons us."

"I perceive, young sir, that you are at least well read."

"Thank you."

In choosing to ignore any possible irony in Leonardo's argument, Dr. Mazzone had reassured himself that his position of superiority was no longer under attack. He was, therefore, prepared to be gracious. "This device of yours," he went on, "what is it, pray tell me?"

"It is a snare," Leonardo said.

"Indeed? I do not quite understand you, I fear. What is it designed to catch?"

"Why, facts," said Leonardo.

Dr. Mazzone grew frosty again. "I think that you attempt to reprove me," he said.

"By no means. I speak but the truth. Facts are elusive, as Anaximenes might tell you were he alive. Yet by means of my machine, I entrap them, caging them upon this paper." Leonardo held out his notebook. "When I have caught a sufficient number, I may then proceed to theories. Or again, I may not. Such, sir, is the nature of engineering."

"Is it? It sounds, if I may say so, a rather molelike approach to knowledge."

"Excellently put. Would it interest you to see a demonstration?"

"It was for that express purpose that I came here," said Dr. Mazzone, "upon the instructions of Lorenzo de' Medici himself, I may say, who has requested me to . . . ahem . . . evaluate the work you are doing under his protection. I have been but awaiting the arrival of a colleague."

Hurrying toward them was a tall and thin-lipped man in Franciscan robes, who peered about him with birdlike darts of suspicion as he walked. Leonardo went with Dr. Mazzone to meet him.

"May I present Brother Sigismondo Carregi," Dr. Mazzone announced. Leonardo bowed, and introduced his learned guests to the bowman, who uncrossed his arms and nodded to them silently.

"Proceed," said Dr. Mazzone.

While Matteo Barletta drew back the string of the bow and hitched it over the protruding brass sear at the back of the framework, Leonardo consulted his notebook.

"If you would care to select any particular distance from where we stand to the target," he said, "please do so. At the moment, it lies seventy paces distant."

"Is this a matter of importance?" inquired the mathematician.

"None whatever, save as part of our demonstration."

"Ninety paces, then."

"Very well," Leonardo said. He walked the length of the range, picked up the little straw target and its tripod, and moved them twenty paces farther. Returning, he fitted an arrow into the groove on the top of the frame and adjusted the angle of the contraption. Then he nodded at Matteo, who stepped forward and knelt behind the framework, reaching for the trigger. The sear slid downward a fraction and released the string. The bent arms of the bow straightened with a whirr and a click, and the arrow flashed briefly in the pale sunlight before burying itself in the target's center. Matteo, his grin of relief hidden from the three men who stood behind him, got to his feet again.

"And is that all?" asked the friar.

"I am afraid so," Leonardo rejoined. "We can, of course, repeat the procedure as many times as you wish. The result will be the same, within an inch or two."

Brother Sigismondo circled the contrivance warily and with evident disdain, stooping once or twice to touch one part of it or another.

"It does not seem to me," he said, "that there is much of a mystery here. The bow being once fixed—as you have it here—one would expect the arrow to strike in the same place, would one not?"

Dr. Mazzone, pursing his lips and parting his beard with his fingers, agreed.

Leonardo bowed once more, his face open and cheerful.

"Gentlemen," he said, "this also is the nature of engineering. That a thing being once achieved, all men readily perceive it as obvious. I wish you good morning."

Six

The day dawned peacock blue, and bitter.

Matteo Barletta, returning thankfully to the arms of his long-suffering wife, had taken his bow with him upon the dismantling of their experimental arbalest the previous evening, and Leonardo had been forced to borrow another for the casual practice he had been engaged upon since daybreak. Being an unskilled archer, he had already skinned two of his knuckles and burned his wrist with the string. Nonetheless, he whistled blithely, there being no one about at this early hour to observe him making a fool of himself.

In theory, he was still working with angles, distances and scholarly matters, though less rigorously than before. In fact, he was merely enjoying the air, the morning and his own high spirits.

He raised the bow above his head and loosed an arrow vertically into the sky. Watching the shaft climb against the glare of the sun, Leonardo shaded his eyes, counting. The time of its trajectory was an aspect of flight which he had not, until now, considered; and he wondered if its fall would take exactly as long as its ascent—as seemed logical. If so, then it would follow . . . what would follow? That its speed upon striking the ground at the end of its descent must be the same as the speed with which it left the bow? Would this, of necessity, be true? He lost his count, and laughed. The wind caught the arrow at its zenith, drifting it sideways as it turned end on end and began to tumble. Plunging down beyond the stone wall of the archery range to his right, it vanished.

Laying the bow on the bench beside the dismantled sections of his framework, Leonardo walked to the wicket gate that led to the meadow beyond the palace confines and pushed it open. The lay of the land outside was discouraging. The sloping bank from the gateway to the edge of the brook below was tangled with briar and myrtle, and he was now at a level with the tops of the stunted willows that canted over the glinting water a bare score of paces away. It was unpromising terrain in which to search for a lost arrow unless it had been carried over the stream and into the long grass of the field beyond it.

He made his way down the slope, his feet sliding on the loose and granular soil. Arriving with a rush at the crumbling margin of the stream and clutching at a branch to halt his momentum, he at once saw the striped feathers and varnished shaft protruding above the water's surface in midstream.

Removing his boots, he slipped cautiously into the icy flood, wincing, and waded out. The brook was no more than twelve feet wide and, though fast running, was shallow everywhere. Searching for footholds on its gravel bed, he reached the arrow and bent to pluck it out, but then stopped. A precise and narrow pattern of ripples streamed out from around its shaft and tiny, perfect vortices coiled against it where it broke the water's swirling surface. He reached for the quill and notebook at his waist and began to draw these designs of nature, oblivious to the growing numbness of his feet, and whistling softly once more.

He had been thus engaged for five minutes when he was startled by a girl's voice behind him.

"And is the water, then, warm?"

Leonardo straightened up, turning his head. Standing on the bank by his discarded boots was the slight and fair-haired figure of Bianca Visconti, wearing a flowing dress of apple-green silk, stained at the hem and bodice with mud. A stray twig had grazed her face, leaving a smudged line across one cheek. Neither these small accidents of her descent to the river's edge nor the unsuitability of her clothing seemed to trouble her. She was laughing merrily.

Leonardo closed his notebook, but remained where he was in midstream.

"My lady," he said.

"You know me?" she asked, brushing a strand of hair away from her forehead. "I know who you are, of course. You are Master Leonardo da Vinci, a painter of summerhouses and an indifferent archer, from what I have seen. But who am I?"

"The Countess Bianca Maria Visconti of Abbiategrasso, cousin to Duke Ludovico Sforza, Regent of Milan," said Leonardo.

"So you do know me. How is that?"

Leonardo grinned at her in turn. "I am not such a poor archer in matters of the mind as elsewhere. Guiliano de' Medici pictured you to me, both in temper and in appearance. And it was, I thought, impossible for there to exist two women to answer his description. For the rest, have I not seen you peeping like a mouse from beneath the cloak of Lorenzo de' Medici? Your guardian, I believe. Very simple, you see."

"Good. Though I like not your phrase," said the Countess. "I am no mouse."

"It was dark at the time. I acknowledge my error, and repent of it."

"Better. And how, may I ask, did Giuliano describe me?"

Leonardo, having drawn the arrow from the bed of the stream, began to wade toward the bank.

"Why," he said, "as impudent, my lady, and small-breasted, as I recall." He stopped in front of her, knee-deep in the water. "At least, I think he said 'impudent.' He may have used the term 'sharp-tongued.' I am not sure."

"Let us forget my temperament for the moment, if you please," said Bianca sternly, looking down at him. "I am more enraged by these loose comments of Giuliano's upon my . . . my personal appearance. How dare he? And I am still further enraged that you should dare to repeat them to me."

"I am afraid that men, when riding together, have the vulgar habit of making comments of that kind," said Leonardo. "But since you asked me a plain question, it would have been unworthy of me to withhold the truth, however vulgar."

"I could have you beaten. Do not think that I cannot arrange it."

"I am sure you can. If you wish to terrify me, however, you must learn to control your laughter better than I see from your eyes. And if you will meanwhile grasp that willow branch beside you with one hand and extend me the other, I shall be grateful."

The Countess obeyed him, with some loss of dignity. Leonardo sat down on the grass beside her and began pulling on his boots.

"Now," she said. "Tell me why you were standing in the middle of the river, making pictures of . . . I know not what. Let me see."

He obligingly unfastened the notebook from its chain and held it out to her. She examined its top sheet critically.

"What are these?"

"What do they look like?"

"Like lines in the water, and curls."

"Admirable."

"But what for?"

"That," said Leonardo, "is hard to explain."

"I do not see why. It is as plain a question as any, and we

know—do we not—that you are capable of giving plain replies."

"Well, then," said Leonardo, standing up, "you should understand that I have been studying the flight of arrows—"

"I know that," Bianca said impatiently. "I have been watching you do so."

"Is that so? I did not see you."

"I doubt that you are capable of observing anything more than a span from the end of your nose when you are working, if one may call it work," said Bianca crisply. "You did not even hear me approaching just now."

"True."

"Continue, then. What has the flight of arrows to do with ripples in water?"

"Perhaps nothing. The connection in my mind was made by the arrow itself. The ripples you see, and which I have set down there, prove that water resists motion, and is resisted by it. It occurred to me a few minutes ago that the air may resist the arrow's flight in the same way. If it does, then I must take this into account when I study the motion of an arrow through the air. Do you understand?"

Bianca frowned.

"Hold up the arrow, then," she commanded. Leonardo picked up the shaft and held it out to her. "Where are the ripples in the air?" she asked. "I see none."

"They are invisible."

"Or they do not exist. If they are invisible, how do you know they are there at all?"

"Because," Leonardo replied, "I can see them elsewhere."

"And where?"

"Had you a mirror, my lady, and could you therefore see your own hair blowing in this selfsame air, you would perceive them too," said Leonardo. "Also, you would see that your face is smudged with grime, by the way."

"There was no need to spoil your compliment."

"That is the difficulty with the eye of an artist," said Leonardo in apology. "Blowing hair and grime are all one to him."

"I see. To return to this matter of the air," Bianca said, eying him with some humor, "it seems to me that you are mistaken. Water is heavy. Air is not. Air is . . . nothing."

"Not so. Look over there." He pointed to where some few remaining leaves drifted in the breeze, to rest lightly upon the surface of the brook and be swept downstream. "The air sustains the gliding leaf," he said. "If this were not so, then the leaf would fall directly down, like a stone. Hence the air has substance, even as the water."

"But the leaves fall," she objected. "Slowly or swiftly, they still fall. This proves nothing."

"You are hard to convince."

"I am not. Ships do not fall through water. They float upon it."

"As the clouds float in the sky, and fall not."

"Clouds have no weight. Can a cloud bear a cargo? No. You will have to do better than this."

"Say, then, as a kite floats," argued Leonardo. "You will agree with me that a kite has weight? Or a bird?"

She rubbed her cheek, still watching him.

"Yes," she said slowly. "I will admit that. Perhaps you are right after all, though it seems a peculiar notion. I must think upon it." Then, swiftly, she changed. "Do you know what my Aunt Francesca would say of you, sir? That you are a dreamer."

Leonardo threw back his head, laughing. "I cry mercy," he said. "I cannot withstand both your aunt and yourself, and survive. Yet I am no dreamer, Lady Bianca, I promise you. Quite otherwise. I do but deal with what I perceive, and cannot prevent myself from doing so; but this is not dreaming. Painters, perhaps, see things more clearly than other men. And some, having seen clearly, draw lessons from what they see."

"Lessons," said the Countess. "I have no liking for lessons.

Indeed, I came down here to escape them. So keep your lessons to yourself, I pray you."

"I wondered why you were dressed as you are. Silk and thorns hardly go well together. Who gives you your lessons?"

"A friar with the air of a Pisan hound," said Bianca. "He bores me. His name is Brother Sigismondo Carregi. Doubtless he is storming about the palace courtyards even now, looking for me, and will lock me in my room this afternoon. Much I care! I would sooner read books than listen to his droning. That is why I said that I have no liking for lessons."

"You have not objected to this one," Leonardo pointed out to her.

"Nay, sir," she protested. "This has been no lesson."

"You are once more mistaken, little Contessa. Lessons are not always given by friars, nor even drawn from books. My own tutors are more congenial than either."

"Your tutors? And where, then, are they?"

"All about us," he replied. "For this morning, at least, they have included arrows, leaves, water and . . ." He reached forward gently. ". . . perhaps even blowing hair. Consider this when you are locked in your room this afternoon, my lady. It is a matter of even more importance than the relative weights of clouds and kites."

Chin in hand, Lorenzo de' Medici sat behind a table of pinewood in a small room which much resembled a monastic cell, being bare of all decoration save for a map by the cartographer Petrus Vesconte upon one of its whitewashed walls. Its window, though large, was barred. From it could be seen a pleasant and commanding view of the palazzo gardens and the distant Florentine countryside.

It was a room used often by the ruler of the republic. To it he retreated for private consideration of state problems or to escape the conversation of the idle. Apart from himself, few entered it, and none without express invitation.

"Your experiments are satisfactorily concluded?" he asked.

"They are, sir."

"Good. I must tell you that neither Dr. Mazzone nor the worthy Brother Sigismondo Carregi have given me encouraging reports about them. But this you may have already surmised."

Leonardo, seated on a low, wooden stool at the other side of the table, crossed one leg over his other knee and held his ankle comfortably.

"I confess to no surprise," he said. "They seemed to believe that I was concerned with accuracy, and of course I was not." He would have continued, but Lorenzo raised a discouraging hand.

"Spare me your science," he said. "I deal in men, a subject of which I have some little knowledge. What the good doctor and Brother Sigismondo may have said to me is of little importance. I offer you a position with me as military engineer. I propose to pay you but little until you have proved your worth to me. On the other hand, you may have such freedom to continue with your experiments as your duties allow. What do you say?"

"Your terms are fair. I accept them as before. With gratitude. When do you wish me to start?"

"Now."

"Now?" said Leonardo equably. "Very well."

"I will procure your release from contract with Andrea del Verrocchio at no expense to yourself. You will lodge here with us, as a condition of your employment. But not tonight. This evening, you will ride to Castelmonte. You will carry my personal warrant to Captain-Gunner Leone, and assist him in reducing the wall of that city." Seeing Leonardo about to speak, he raised his hand again, his eyes hard. "Do not trouble to point out that you are no miracle worker. I am aware of it. I expect no miracles. However, even at this late hour, it may be that something will occur to you that others have missed. You know that the Lady Carla d'Avalos is prisoner within Castelmonte?"

"So your brother told me, sir."

"We have, as yet, received no demand for her ransom. That we shall receive one, I am sure. I will be frank with you. My aim, at this moment, is to save my exchequer a matter of some fifty or one hundred thousand florins—which sum it will certainly cost Florence to obtain her release if the Count della Rovere can hold his citadel intact until the day after tomorrow. If it must be paid, I do not grudge it, naturally. But those are the facts. Do I make myself clear to you?"

"Yes," Leonardo said. "I shall do my utmost, sir, as I trust always to do in your service."

"Then good fortune go with you," said Lorenzo de' Medici.

"Good Master Matteo," said Bianca Visconti, "I pray you, tell me." They were standing together on the small footbridge that spanned the brook behind the palace.

"It was nothing, my lady," said the archer. "That is to say . . . it was but a dream of his, and we were children at the time."

"So you said. Tell me of it."

"I thought it great nonsense," the archer grunted. "As he recounted it to me, he dreamed that he lay in a hayfield on the farm, and that a hawk fell upon him from the sky, beating him about the lips with its tail. Afterward, he refused for many months to go to school in the village, though his father, Ser Piero, thrashed him soundly many times on account of it."

"Indeed?" said Bianca. "And why did Leonardo refuse?"

"He said that the bird had revealed to him his destiny, which was to speak the truth as he found it. His teachers, so he claimed, did not know truth when they saw it and were feeding him nonsense. He was strange even in his youth, my lady."

"And you were his friend."

"In some sort," agreed Barletta.

"Had he many friends? Or did these notions of his drive them away?"

"My lady, it is hard to say. There were many who sought his friendship, but few that he would himself accept. He could always draw men to him, and women too, whether he tried to or not. But I think that until he came to Florence with his father, he was often lonely, though with no good reason that I could find."

"But he accepted you," persisted Bianca.

The archer laughed. "Perhaps because I never made the mistake of admiring him. Or of seeming to. I loosed arrows at rabbits, and told him not to be a bigger fool than he could help. And he was unhandy with a bow, as I was not, and I too had small love of teachers. So we went hunting together, which is to say that I hunted while he watched the sky and pulled leaves from trees. And since I understood barely a quarter of what he said and could nonetheless fight as well as he could—"

"Did he fight with you?" interrupted Bianca.

"Often. He was stronger than I, but since he seldom gave his mind to it, we were evenly matched. I would lose my temper, my lady, and Leonardo would not, and that's the difference between us."

"Say no more. It is clear that you understand him well enough, Barletta, and I begin to understand him better. He has need of friends like you, I think."

"And perhaps like you, my lady."

Bianca Visconti threw a twig into the water beneath them. "Possibly," she said. "And possibly not. We shall have to see."

Seven

Allowing his sword point to rest briefly upon the packed earth at his feet, his back hard against a side column of Castelmonte's postern gate, Guido Toscanelli took stock of his situation.

For the moment, he was protected from above by the overhang of the archway; his right shoulder was pressed against the studded timber of the door he sought to shatter. But the men, who under his blasphemous urging were swinging a steel shod ram against the planks an arm's length away from him, were not so fortunate. Of an assault force of thirty, five had already fallen and as many had been wounded by enfilading crossbow fire and rocks hurled down from the slotted embrasures of the guardhouse above the gate.

He cursed himself for having allowed impatience to overcome good sense. His hope had been to force an entry within a few minutes at most. He had failed and every blow of the battering ram cost him another man.

From postern to river's edge was a scant fifteen paces, but

every foot of it uphill. It was impossible for his men to put much energy behind the heavy ram. Not able to back off with it and charge, they could only swing it back and forth at arms' stretch. The defenders, now gathered in strength above the postern and along the walls at either side, opposed him with a deadly hail of missiles. Even at forty paces, a crossbow bolt could punch through a chain-mail corselet.

Penned in between river and wall, he was helpless. The door itself might have been built of solid stone for all the damage the ram was doing.

Toscanelli stepped out from beneath the archway and looked back across the river. Sheltered in a tumble of boulders, his own arbalestiers were giving his party what covering fire they could. Their bolts rattled off the parapet above him. As he turned to gauge their effect, a defending bowman, his neck skewered, clutched feebly and fell forward. Dead before it struck the ground, the body rolled down the steep embankment and splashed into the water. This was the only casualty his supporters had to their credit. And, even in the instant it took to make this judgment, the rearmost of the men swinging the battering ram grunted hoarsely and slid on his back, arms outflung, to rest at Toscanelli's feet. The reddening vanes of the short iron quarrel in the man's brain stared up at the commander like a third, and malignant eye.

A useless enterprise, Toscanelli thought, then cursed. It was no part of a condottiero's task to waste lives in fruitless battles. A quarter of his attacking force consisted of his own regulars, the remainder being Florentine volunteers eager for death or glory in the service of their city and of Lorenzo de' Medici. Would-be heroes, in Toscanelli's estimation—fools. But on this occasion they were no more foolish than himself.

The call for retreat was almost on his lips when the postern door swung inward under the impact of the ram. Dropping it, his vanguard swept through the mouth of the archway, urged onward by the cheers of those behind. Surprised, Toscanelli followed them, almost the last man to jostle through the opening.

In times of peace, the narrow postern gateway gave passage to washerwomen and to those who wished to draw water from the river. Under siege, it was impregnable in its own fashion, as were the main gate and walls of the city.

Its defenders called it, in grim jest, the Serpent's Mouth.

Above it stood Federigo da Montefeltro, Duke of Urbino and nominal commander of Castelmonte. Sardonic and competent, he was of military rather than of noble bearing and held his title through knowledge of arms rather than by inheritance. He looked down through a slot between the timbers of the gatehouse floor at the milling Florentine attackers surging through the passage beneath his feet, their weapons scraping against its stone walls. He heard the first faint note of uncertainty creep into their cries of battle, and smiled to himself.

"Wait," he said softly to the men who stood about him. "Not yet."

Expecting to meet hand-to-hand opposition beyond the door they had just forced, Toscanelli's men had found none. Those in the forefront were beginning to suspect the truth—that the gate had not yielded to the blows of their ram, but had been deliberately opened to lure them in.

Certainly Guido Toscanelli had realized it. Among the last to enter the long defile, he took rapid note of the unbroken bolt and socket, and undamaged hinges. He stopped, allowing the remaining hotheads to elbow him aside. The defile itself was readily defensible. It ran for twenty-five paces through the solid outcrop of rock that was the foundation for the gatehouse. From here, he could see little of the terrain at its far end.

Where were the men who could so easily have held such an entry against him?

Ten paces ahead, rough-hewn doorways gaped darkly in the flanks of the passage. These must, he knew, lead upward by stairways to the guardhouse overhead. Three men, descending from either side, could hold the passageway against his twenty. Crossbowmen at the far end of the tunnel could have dropped a dozen of his soldiers before they could fight through into the open. Yet his opponent had not taken this precaution.

He turned and looked behind him once more. On the other side of the river, another hundred of his troops were massed on the ridgetop. They waited only for his signal to charge across.

Six feet above the defile, Federigo da Montefeltro watched the attackers' reinforcements undisturbed. Almost conversationally, he gave his orders to the captain of the gatehouse and to the archers outside on the battlements. At his command, they crossed to the rear of the parapet and aimed their weapons down at the Florentines, swarming like bees from the inner mouth of the tunnel. Four men in the small room with him were heaving a portcullis of wrought-iron gridwork into place, its lower edge fitting into the slot at his feet. The top of the portcullis—the door of the trap he was about to close upon his victims below—was supported by cords and pulleys from the roof beams. Four more men held the cords, awaiting his signal.

"Wait," he said softly.

The stillness was unnatural. A stray bolt from beyond the river clattered through an embrasure and rebounded harmlessly off a wall, a bench and then fell to the floor, its metal shaft ringing. Then Montefeltro's own archers methodically began shooting down the Florentines who had emerged into the small vineyard beyond the Serpent's Mouth.

Making his decision, Toscanelli raced up through the passageway after his men. If his assault force was about to be killed to a man, the loss of thirty lives must at least be justified by closer reconnaissance.

He saw at once that he had been correct. The defile he had been allowed to capture gave onto a sloping, stony field across which he would now have to advance. Any such advance would be useless. The field was planted in regular rows with stunted vines and totally surrounded by the citadel wall. Beyond it was yet another gateway, the twin of the postern he had taken. The builders of Castelmonte had been clever. If the outer postern was the Serpent's Mouth, here lay its entangling belly, ready to digest its prey.

Hemmed in on all sides by steep walls and with no enemy they could reach, his men were stumbling about in all directions, vainly trying to escape the arrows raining down from all around. One or two, quicker to sense defeat than the rest, were already running back down the slope toward Toscanelli. There was nothing he could do to save the situation, except shout. He did so and then ran back through the passage. Panting, he reached its outer end a narrow half second before the portcullis dropped from above, sealing the tunnel with a clang. All those behind were condemned to inescapable death. Plunging down the riverbank, he dove into the water, cursed with what breath he could spare and swam for the far side and inglorious safety.

A light and penetrating rain was driving into the faces of Rigo Leone and his gunners. Leonardo da Vinci, his horse once again tethered by the powder magazine, stood with flapping cloak by the master gunner and tapped his arm, pointing.

"One man only," he said. "It is Toscanelli himself, I think."

Rigo turned a streaming and irritable face to him.

"I have little time for Toscanelli's troubles," he said tersely. "The more so since he brought them upon himself. It was an ill-conceived and foolhardy attack. He knew its impossibility and has paid for it."

"I agree. But he may, at least, have brought back some new information."

"None in which I have any interest. The postern gate is no concern of mine," Rigo said. "What concerns me is the accuracy of my guns, which at present is pitiful. Since that warrant of yours from Lorenzo describes you as an engineer, perhaps you have some advice to offer me upon the question of working siege guns waist-deep in mud. Have you?"

"No," said Leonardo, "except to stop doing so."

"I thank you. In which case, do not distract me with Guido's misfortunes. I have enough of my own. Out of my way, engineer."

He stepped down from his small hillock, thrusting Leonardo aside as the right-hand cannon roared. Leonardo, not yet accustomed to keeping his mouth open so as not to be deafened by the blast, shook his head to clear it. Then he knelt, pushing his fingers into the sodden turf. To his left, Agnolo Fulvio's crew strained feverishly at their enormous weapon, levering its carriage sideways with twenty-foot timbers, five men to each lever. Plastered to the eyes with reddish clay, the men were barely recognizable as human. Rigo might have been exaggerating his difficulties, thought Leonardo with amusement, but not by much. The gun slewed sideways, canted, and settled at an angle. It would take them half an hour to shore the sunken wheels again with wooden balks, which would only sink into the softened and trampled ground with the next recoil. He stood upright again to find Rigo at his side.

"You are right, of course," Rigo announced. "A man with more sense than myself would have quit this task days ago. I cannot. Were I to stop now, I would be telling myself for the rest of the winter that one more shot might have been enough to tumble that damned wall." He coughed and spat, sulphur thick at the back of his tongue. "Well," he continued, "after tomorrow, it will not matter."

Leonardo grunted in acceptance of this, the closest to an apology Rigo would ever achieve.

"Given firm ground," he asked, "how accurate are your guns?"

Rigo grimaced. "It has been so long since I saw firm ground that I can hardly remember," he said. "At this range? Ten feet upon either side of my aiming point—with good powder. Sometimes they will do better. Often they do worse."

Leonardo walked away from him to where three of the great iron shot lay side by side. Crouching, he lifted one with both hands and straightened, hefting it at shoulder level.

"How heavy?" he asked.

"A hundred pounds. Your build is deceptive, engineer. I should employ you as one of my loaders."

Leonardo lowered the ball gently into place again.

"How many more rounds will you fire today?"

"As many as God grants. Perhaps eight before sunset."

"In that case," Leonardo said, "I had better be on my way."

"Where to?"

"Down to the wall over there. I have a fancy for observing the flight of your cannonballs from either end."

"Then you take your life in your hands," said Rigo, "my present accuracy being not ten feet at either side, but forty. This is folly."

"Perhaps. I trust in God, and in your competence. Have you never wished to watch the fall of your own shot?"

"Me? Never. Why should I do that? A gunner's job is to stand behind his guns, not in front of them, and you would do well to follow my example. I had not thought engineering to be a dangerous calling."

The lesson was going badly. Brother Sigismondo Carregi sat primly upon the edge of the one comfortable chair, his pallid and scholarly finger marking a page of his book. He awaited Bianca's reply. The silence lengthened in the room so that, even through closed windows, the cry of a street urchin could be heard. Bianca heaved a sigh.

"I am sorry, Brother Sigismondo. I truly am. But I have forgotten your question."

Her tutor's smug nod suggested that he had been expecting just such an answer. "We were speaking, my child, of St.

Agatha," he said. "Perhaps you now recall her? St. Agatha. Why was she sainted? When was she sainted? Let us grant St. Eusebius to be difficult, and St. Felicitas. But except for St. Francis of Assisi, who is known to every babe in arms, all our blessed saints appear to be a mystery to you."

"St. Agatha," said Bianca. "No, I do not think I have heard of her. I'm sorry."

The friar wet his narrow lips. "Pay attention, then, please. Her intercession stopped an eruption of Mount Etna, madam, in Sicily. She was martyred in the year of Our Lord two hundred and fifty."

Bianca laughed.

"She stopped Mount Etna from erupting? A volcano? Do you truly believe this, or is it a legend?"

Brother Sigismondo arose and drew his habit about him in anger and agitation.

"How much more of this must I listen to?" he demanded. "Let us hope that Il Magnifico, your guardian, never hears you speak thus. That you ignore your lessons is bad enough. That you challenge them is far worse." He stood over her. "Listen carefully to what I tell you, my lady. Whether you choose to listen to me or not may be your affair. But when you mock my teachings, you do not mock me. You mock our Mother, the Church, and that is heresy."

"I do not mock you or the Holy Church," said Bianca with some spirit. "I but asked you a question because Master Leonardo da Vinci has told me that it is only through questions that we learn. Am I not here to learn? I think you fear questions, sir, unless you already know the answers to them. Yet Master Leonardo says that it is such questions—"

"Master Leonardo, Master Leonardo," said Brother Sigismondo angrily. "It seems you now have two tutors, my child—one who would lead you toward grace and one, so it appears, who would do otherwise."

He turned his back on her and looked out of the window. Bianca studied him with distaste.

"I am sorry if my questions offend you," she said with

deceptive meekness, "yet may I ask you another? One more churchly, I think. Do angels have wings?"

Somewhat mollified by her tone, the tutor faced her again.

"Why, yes, child, they do," he replied. "Each of them, as we know, is a messenger from God, and therefore winged. Have we not seen them depicted thus, in paintings?"

Bianca nodded. "I have seen such pictures," she agreed. "But I would ask you why?"

"Why?"

"Why do they have wings?"

"So that they can fly, of course," said the friar indulgently. "A foolish question."

Bianca adopted a tone of intelligent interest. "Are angels, then, heavy?" she went on.

"Heavy? I do not understand you, madam. They are spirits."

"And weigh nothing?"

"Only things material have weight."

"Then why," she asked, "do they have wings? For I have also talked with Master Leonardo about birds, and wings and the air. And he has shown me that wings are needed to lift the weight of the bird so that it may not fall to earth. If, therefore, an angel has no weight to lift, why should it need wings?"

Brother Sigismondo considered her for a long minute. "I will not be angry with you, child," he said piously. "You provoke me. But it is not, I think, entirely your fault. This Master Leonardo has poisoned your mind so that you can no longer distinguish wisdom from mere cleverness. Evening draws in, and perhaps it is time your lesson for today ended. You may go. And I, for one, shall pray devoutly for your guidance."

Leonardo stood precariously beneath the wall of Castelmonte, his heels dug into the steep and treacherous slope of the riverbank his back turned to the ramparts which soared overhead. His footing was the less secure for the many loose fragments of rock which lay about him, together with the occasional deformed cannonball which had not tumbled down into the water to join its fellows.

He was staring alertly in the direction of the far ridge, his view of it uncertain because of the drifting rain and vapor. He had already learned that by the time the sound of one of Rigo's cannon reached him, its shot had passed the halfway mark of its trajectory. The muzzle flash gave earlier warning, allowing him a full count of six in which to pick out the hurtling sphere in flight, though it was still all but impossible to predict whether it would strike to his right or left. He had calculated, however, that his chance of direct annihilation was small. His chief concern was to avoid being knocked from his perch by a rebounding ball as it fell and rolled.

Wet from swimming the river, he was cold. Hunching his shoulders and shivering, he waited.

Scudo's cannon spat flame and smoke, to vanish almost instantly as a rain squall swept across the intervening valley. Leonardo swore softly. Whatever his calculations might have been, it was still unnerving to think of the compact, deadly and now invisible power rushing toward him. In the swirling mist, he heard its murmuring hiss overhead, and ducked in nervous reflex. The wall and ground shook at its impact. Chips of stone spattered about his ears, then the shot thumped to earth short paces away. He scrambled upward at once and stood below the spot where he had seen it strike the breastwork, an arm's-reach high and close to the angle made between the wall and the forward bulge of a turret.

Over an area many yards across, the wall's surface had been gouged into a crater at whose edges several clinging masses of stone seemed ready to fall away. At either side of this were smaller scars. Rigo's shots had fallen close enough together to make—given time—a single breach, but many had flown wide and to little effect. He felt the raw margin of the wall's major wound, and edged across toward the spot where the turret curved outward.

Here, he saw, was the rampart's weakness. A crack, wide

enough to admit his hand, had developed in the recess. Thick and massive as the wall might be, it had been pushed back fractionally under the pounding of successive balls, allowing the stonework to spring apart and shed mortar. He raked lime out of the crevice with his fingertips and tried to crumble it. It was hard, but not impossibly so.

Count Girolamo Riario withdrew his head from a window in the turret and beckoned to a man-at-arms.

"You serve under the Duke of Urbino, do you not?" he asked.

"Sir, I do."

"Were you in his service for Florence, a year or two since?"

"I was, sir."

"And are you, therefore, acquainted with that city?"

"Sir," said the man, growing uneasy, "I am a Florentine by birth, though . . ."

Riario cut him short with a gesture. "Excellent," he said. "I care not if your mother were kitchen maid to Lorenzo's own household. Just tell me what I wish to know. Look down from that window and tell me what you see."

The soldier obeyed. "I see a man, sir, standing at the foot of our wall and looking upward. I fear he caught sight of me."

"I care nothing for that either," said Riario. "Do you know him?"

"I will not swear to it, sir, but I believe him an artist who once worked in the goldsmiths' quarter by the Ponte Carraia. His name is Leonardo da Vinci."

The Count scratched his neck. "Good," he said, after a moment's consideration. "What is your weapon?"

"I am a pikeman, sir."

"A pity, but of little importance. Go and find me a crossbowman from among your fellows, and send him here to me. Quickly, man."

Leonardo had seen the halberdier's face at the turret window and decided upon prudence as his best course.

Of the several bolts that were fired at him as he swam back across the river and into the protective mist, none came close enough to trouble him. He reached the gunners' evening fire some twenty minutes later. Wrapped in a horse blanket, he accepted Rigo's wineskin gratefully.

"Well, Sir Scholar?" said the latter with amusement. "What did you find?"

Leonardo lowered the skin. "That, on the whole, you are wasting your time. In another month or so, perhaps you will have made a worthwhile dent in Castelmonte's wall, but that is the best of it. You would do better to move both your guns over there," he pointed to the southern ridge, "and concentrate your fire upon the side of the turret rather than upon the wall itself. The turret would fall within a week. The wall behind it might remain undamaged, but a determined force of infantry could easily scale the ruins of the tower. Shall I draw it for you?"

"No. And save your breath to warm yourself. Tomorrow I move my guns, but not to your ridge. We go to winter quarters in Pistrola. In the morning Toscanelli will parley with Montefeltro. His herald is at the main gate even now. Since all of us, no matter what side we fight upon, have known the cost of my failure to breach their wall for some time now, I can assure you they will reach agreement by early afternoon. How much ransom the lady Carla d'Avalos, my young gunner and the Count della Rovere's other prisoners will cost Il Magnifico, I cannot tell. That is a matter for tomorrow's haggling. But, until next spring, this war is ended."

Eight

By noon, the weather had worsened, the rain becoming sleet. Nonetheless, among the gunners who sat beneath the shelter of their magazine with backs resting against powderkegs, there was an air of cheerful relief and even of festivity. Leonardo had been admitted to their society after his feat of pure bravado the previous evening, and had won their further approval by now lying at full length atop the rearmost stack of barrels with that disregard for the explosive power of gunpowder which few, except gunners, ever achieved.

Giuliano de' Medici, in maroon riding habit, stood by his horse and stroked it with concealed impatience. He had ridden from Florence overnight in order to negotiate, on his brother's behalf, the financial aspects of their truce with Castelmonte, and would not be needed until Toscanelli and Federigo da Montefeltro, as soldiers, had finished their discussion of military matters.

Of the assembled company, only Rigo seemed dispirited.

"Where is Guido?" he demanded, of no one in particular.

"God's blood, he has been inside their damned citadel long enough, and we have work to do."

"And why should he hurry?" asked Agnolo Fulvio. "Doubtless they still have a skin or two of good wine left, even after so long a siege. We have been at war for three months. Let them take the whole day to bring it to a conclusion if they wish. My gun is not yet cold, and a few hours less of polishing it between now and next year will make little difference to it."

"It would not have taken me this long," Rigo said sourly.

"True," his lieutenant agreed. "That is because, being no politician, you would at once admit that Florence has been the loser and pay the price for it. Toscanelli is somewhat more subtle. Give him time."

"I mistrust politicians," was all that Rigo would say. He stood in the open, looking across the valley and trying to penetrate the day's gloom.

An hour passed.

Then from beyond the river, a trumpet sounded. Giuliano mounted and set off down the face of the ridge. The sleet had now thickened and turned to snow. He checked his horse as its hooves slid, and was hidden from his comrades by the falling flakes before he reached level ground below. Rigo removed his fur-lined cap, slapped it against his knee and silently rejoined his men under the thatched roof of the powder hut.

Giuliano reached the riverbank and reined his mount to the left, intending to follow the line of the river until he reached the unseen bridge that would lead him to the main gate of the fortress. From beyond the blanketing snow and mist, he could hear, as though at a great distance, the sounds of Toscanelli's troops and his own cavalry going about their daily tasks as best they could in the foul weather. Yet, with the sullen water and the gray backdrop of the looming wall upon its farther side, he felt closed in and alone. He shivered.

"Welcome, Prince," a harsh voice said.

He pulled in his reins, startled, and looked across the shallow river to the ramparts above. Dark figures were grouped on the wall's crest. In one of its notches stood Count Girolamo Riario, the gilded cross between breastplate and shoulder of his mailed suit glinting dimly as he leaned his elbow on the parapet and gazed down at the horseman.

"Welcome," he repeated. "And where do you ride, Giuliano?"

"To speak with the Count Giovio della Rovere, as agreed, Captain-General. Where is he?"

"At the gate," said Riario. "But save yourself the journey. He is with the Duke of Urbino, engaged in farewell courtesies with our worthy and stupid friend Guido Toscanelli. Your business, Prince, is not with them, but with me."

"That I doubt," Giuliano said. "I have little to discuss with Rome's vulture for the present, being not yet formally at war with her."

"Spoken with spirit, if discourteously," said Riario. "I shall not detain you long. I have something to show you."

Impatiently, Giuliano loosed his rein to move onward, but then stopped. A horrible suspicion was forming in his mind. He looked up again. Four soldiers were lifting a wide plank with a body bound to it to the top of the parapet. For an instant, Giuliano thought they bore a corpse; but then, the bound man's head moved, and he saw that it was Andrea di Veluti.

"Your gunner," Riario said. "I believe you have come to ransom him, among others. Well?" He moved across from the embrasure to seize the young gunner's jaw, rocking his face back and forth casually as if inspecting a carcass. "He is healthy," Riario continued, "despite some small discomforts he has undergone. A valuable specimen, one might say, though foolish. Come, what do you bid for him? A thousand florins? Two thousand?"

"Do not mock me, Captain-General," said Giuliano, between his teeth. "Set the boy free, and we will talk."

"Indeed? A moment ago you were not so eager for discussion. We must, accordingly, teach you manners."

He signaled to a man behind him, who now stepped forward into view. It was, Giuliano saw, the hooded executioner who had once before committed public murder at the Count's behest. He held in his left hand a pouch of deerskin. Horrified, Giuliano helplessly watched as he raised this object.

"Your gunner has not proven talkative, I regret to say, despite our persuasions," Riario said, in an offhand manner. "Since he has thereby angered us somewhat, we shall now silence him permanently, and in a fashion which befits his calling."

Deliberately, the executioner took a short iron bar in his free hand and forced it between the gunner's teeth, prying his jaws apart. The boy screamed, but his cries were cut off as the hooded man above him trickled a black and grainy powder into his mouth from the pouch, choking him as it filled his throat. It overflowed his lips, spilling down the side of his face, and Giuliano could see the veins bulge in his neck as he tried to fight against leather bonds in animal desperation. The executioner thrust a short length of stiff fuse into his packed mouth and lit its end from a slow match. In the long instant of quiet while the cord sputtered, the young gunner's eyes rolled, half-unconscious, yet staring with the terrible knowledge of what was about to happen. Then there was a monstrous and repellant hiss of smoke and a noise, like the bursting of a rotten melon, as the gunpowder, which packed his mouth and windpipe, flared into a rending, muffled explosion.

Giuliano leaned to one side and retched, his horse pacing nervously. When he was able to sit erect again in his saddle, the gunner's body was falling to earth at the foot of the wall. Still bound to its plank, it rolled down the slope, mercifully hiding in the discolored water the charred ruin of what had once been its head. Giuliano lifted his eyes from it to the wall top and to the man who stood there, wreathed in smoke and mist.

The curse he was about to utter died unspoken. In the embrasure now stood Carla d'Avalos, supported by two men. Her hands were tied in front.

"I see that I still have your attention," Riario said softly, fingering his collar. "Therefore, tell your Captain-Gunner that a similar welcome awaits him or any other of his men, should they be unfortunate enough to fall into my hands. And now to other matters. You know the Lady Carla d'Avalos, I take it?"

Giuliano steadied himself in his stirrups.

"Hear me, Count," he said, with death in his voice. "Spill one drop of her blood, and I will hunt you down and kill you, though I perish in the doing of it."

Riario ignored this as though unsaid. He held out his hand, and the executioner put into it a soft and heavy cloth of black velvet.

"I have a message also for your brother Lorenzo," he said, "and for Florence. Let him not imagine that he can play at war with me. The Medici have laid siege to me here, as they have to others in the past. And, as in the past, they would seem to believe that success or failure in such things is a matter for settlement as one settles for an evening's gaming—with money and a few knowing smiles between winner and loser. You had better know me, Prince, and Florence had better know me also. I am Girolamo Riario, Count of Bosco and Imola and Rome's Captain-General, and I do not play at war."

Taking the velvet cloth, he advanced upon the trembling girl, stunned and silent in her terror. Delicately, he placed the soft cloth over the lower half of her face, and held it there. The men holding her gripped her arms fiercely as her body arched and her forehead grew livid. Pinching her nostrils through the material and pressing it into her mouth, the Count waited until her struggles had ceased with her suffocation, then stood away.

She collapsed in the embrasure. Riario pushed at the body with the toe of his boot, urging it toward the edge of the wall until it tumbled loosely to join the other in the waters at the foot of the bank.

"Take, then, the Lady Carla d'Avalos," he said, tossing the deadly cloth aside. "I give her to you freely and at no expense. And when, in due course, Rome calls upon you to submit, remember this day—and comply."

“Unnecessary,” said Sixtus IV in reproof, his eyes fixed upon the gorgeously illuminated ceiling above him. “Completely unnecessary, Riario, and thus reprehensible. Have I not cautioned you many times before this, my son, to control yourself?”

“A lesson which I have taken to heart, Holy Father,” said the Count of Imola. “I assure you of this with all the sincerity at my command. And it follows, therefore, that I must disagree with you. The example was needed, and I supplied it.”

“Needed?”

“Certainly. Demonstrations of will, however brutal they may appear, are tools of war no less than our Montefeltro's soldiers or the cannon of Florence. I need hardly add, Your Holiness, that my tools are the more effective. If Rome considers war essential, it is not for me to disagree.”

“And do you disagree?” asked Sixtus mildly.

“Not in the least,” Riario replied. “And if I did, I would not say so. I am Captain-General, and Rome's servant. But the means of my service are mine to consider and to select in Rome's cause."

The Supreme Pontiff rubbed the arm of his chair uneasily.

"But a woman, my son? The gunner, perhaps, though even there I cannot condone your . . . severity. The Countess d'Avalos . . ." His voice trailed off.

"Which reminds me," said Riario. He reached into his doublet, beneath the fluted breastplate of his armor, and produced a small piece of jewelry. He held it out to the Pontiff. "Your Holiness will recognize this, I am sure. I removed it from the finger of the Countess before her most regrettable demise."

Resting in his palm was a ring of chased gold, bearing a single emerald. Sixtus recoiled from the sight of it.

"I see that the memory of Your Holiness is as keen as ever," continued Riario. "This is the ring which you gave to the Countess on the occasion of her betrothal to the eldest son of the Duke of Ferrara. Since the alliance, in the nature of things, cannot now take place, I return it to you."

They were alone in the audience chamber from whose gilded walls their muted voices seemed to echo and press inward upon them, locking them into a complicity which neither desired. The Pontiff's shoulders moved uncomfortably beneath his embroidered robes of Barbary silk. Riario smiled.

"Why?" demanded Sixtus. "I have no need for it."

"As you wish. It was merely that I believed seeing it might remind Your Holiness of the further fact that an alliance between Ferrara and Florence is something which, upon reflection, neither of us would consider to be in Rome's interest."

"True. We would have prevented it politically at the time, if we could have done so without provoking offense," Sixtus said. "I think I begin to understand your intentions."

"Quite so. It would have been unbecoming for Rome's Father to offend in a matter of such seeming triviality. Rome's Captain-General, however, has a duty to offend. I take no pleasure in doing so, but if I may say without arrogance, I am Rome's right arm just as surely as you are her head and her heart."

"A mailed arm, my son? Is that what you seek to tell me?"

"Precisely. As for the gunner, I beg you to trouble yourself no further over him. The Medici cannon inconvenienced me. I put it no higher than that. I do not permit things to inconvenience me for long, as Your Holiness knows, and therefore used the man—whose soul, we must pray, is now in heaven when all is said and done—yes, used him to impress upon the Medici the wisdom of submitting next year. A like reasoning applies in the case of the Countess d'Avalos. If I was severe, I regret it. But my conscience remains clear." He stood easily, looking into the eyes of Sixtus IV, his own eyes innocent of any particular challenge.

Repelled and yet fascinated by this man, so closely tied to himself both by blood and by what he saw as Rome's need, the Pontiff found his emotions to be compounded by fear and distaste. He had summoned a monster to his service—as had others in legend—and began to wish he had not done so. He gathered himself.

"A mailed arm," he said softly. "Even so. I notice, my son, that you wear your armor now, as always. It is said that you have been known to sleep in it." Suddenly and surprisingly, he uttered a falsetto laugh. "Well. His Eminence, the Cardinal Borgia, has often pointed out that you feel yourself safe from a stiletto in the back. No doubt your wisdom and your conscience go hand in hand. We are pleased with your defense of Castelmonte, and you may convey our similar approval to the Duke of Urbino and the Count Giovio della Rovere, who are also among our beloved sons. You may leave us."

Rodrigo Cardinal Borgia, handsomely dressed for riding, sat on the balcony of his apartments with a plate of figs and a flask of wine before him. Hospitably, he pushed these in the direction of his guest, his Spanish ancestry and manners concealing the fact that his opinion of the latter bordered on contempt.

The Count of Imola refused them.

"We have received," said Cardinal Borgia, "a somewhat interesting letter. To be precise, His Holiness's secretary has passed it to me *sub rosa.* I am, in turn, to give it into the safekeeping of the Apostolic Chancery, where my good friend Domenico Cardinal della Palla will proceed to copy it, file it, cross-index it and finally bury it irretrievably in one of the many ways he has devised since he took over the office of chancellor. I took the liberty of asking you to visit me before it vanishes forever."

"The Apostolic Chancery—" began Riario.

"Is the bane of our lives, my dear Count," said the Cardinal. "It was far more useful, to those of us who thrive upon information, in the days when it consisted largely of several cellarsfull of bundled documents, gathering soot. At least one could get at what one needed in private, and without fuss. One cannot do so nowadays. However, that is neither here nor there. This letter—my clerk will show it to you if you wish—is from an artist. It requests permission to consult the libraries of the Church upon what its writer calls 'the highest of all arts.' Observe the curious phrase. His Holiness is uncertain what action to take in replying, but that too is by the way. My own interest in it arises from the name of its author."

"Well?" Riario said.

"The letter comes from Florence. It is written by a man called Leonardo da Vinci."

He paused, as though expectant. Riario did not gratify him.

"And so?" he suggested.

Cardinal Borgia raised the wine flask and held it to the light.

"I find that the cold weather makes our northern vintages cloudy," he remarked. "Perhaps you are wise to decline it.

Well, now. Master Leonardo describes himself as an artist, and indeed, we have heard of him even here in Rome. I am informed that he is a brilliant young man. I am also told that he has recently added a new dimension to his career, since he is now military engineer to our cousin Lorenzo de' Medici." The Cardinal paused. "My dear Count, if you do not remove that expression of feigned ignorance from your face I shall begin to fear for your sanity. You have your informant at the Medici court, as I have mine. I can hardly be amazing you with these revelations."

"Occasional news does reach me from Florence," Riario admitted. The Cardinal smiled in delight.

"But, of course, it does. I would scarcely be enjoying your company now if it did not; therefore, let us be candid with one another. Your informant there, by the way," he added casually, "is seriously annoyed with you at present. I have not found out why, but there it is. Money, I dare say. However. One wonders exactly what Master Leonardo means by 'the highest of all arts.' To those of us with a classical bent, sculpture would spring to mind as, no doubt, it is intended to. But then again . . . you don't by chance know this young man, I suppose?"

The Count of Imola, changing his mind suddenly, thrust a crystal goblet across the surface of the table. Borgia filled it for him.

"Yes," Riario said. "I have, as it happens, seen him."

"Ah."

"I confess I had not heard that he was Florence's engineer."

"Perhaps my informant has been in Florence longer than yours," said the Cardinal graciously. "It takes time to build these . . ." he dabbled his fingers in the air, "these networks. I am delighted to have been able to assist you. What, then, do you know of Leonardo da Vinci?"

"That he was undertaking a study of this high art of his, beneath my wall at Castelmonte," said Riario.

"The art of war? Yes. Excellent. We may infer a sense of

subtlety in him, then. Rome's enemy wishes to tap Rome's springs of knowledge. I like that. I really am most pleased that you could join me this morning. We make progress, dear Count. Would you imagine him dangerous, all things considered?"

"Possibly."

"Then I am sure I can prevail upon His Holiness to welcome him to Rome. It is always better to know what one is dealing with in cases like this, is it not?"

Riario lifted his goblet and drank.

"By all means," he said. "Invite him here, and I will have him killed."

"But you would, perhaps, like to talk with him first?" asked the Cardinal. "We all admire your sense of priorities, of course, but let us not crush the grape untasted. He will be conferring, for the most part, with His Eminence Cardinal della Palla, as librarian. However, I see no reason why you should not assess the lad before having him disposed of. Though I am sure your instincts are sound, as always."

"As you wish," said the Count indifferently. "My assessment of him at this moment—putting your information together with mine—is that he is likely to prove a nuisance. Which is sufficient cause for removing him. Should I find no reason to change my mind, I will at least defer to Your Eminence to the extent of killing him on his way *out* of Rome rather than the moment he arrives. Unless, that is, you have some reason of your own for wishing him to remain alive?"

"I have none," said Cardinal Borgia, "except for a mistrust in overhastiness. No matter. In the meanwhile, do prod that fellow of yours in Florence. It is always annoying to receive one's news thirdhand. A lazy informant is worse than useless. I speak from long experience and trust you will not resent my advice."

Ten

In Florence, the Advent bells pealed. The season of good will was at hand. Under the ringing bells, friends, neutrals and undeclared enemies gathered together in harmony amid the appetizing scents of roasting meats. Christmas hymns were sung in cathedral and church, wine barrels were broached, and rich and poor alike rejoiced.

In the courtyards and the Great Chamber of the Medici palace, a swallow throng of visitors assembled to wheel, eddy and settle or disperse as fancy took them. Earnest discourse and idle conversation flourished among legates, ambassadors, nuncios, archbishops, guildsmen, minor nobles, poor scholars, wise men, virtuous women, whores, wits, jesters, priests, learned counselors and fools. In costumes plain and colorful, in linens, silks, furs and fustian, adorned with pewter and gold, with trinkets of Venetian glass and clustered diamonds, with emeralds from Nubia and the Indus, Circassian tin, ivory, opal, lapis lazuli, pebbles, bezoars, pyrites and pearls, they came. Old alliances were warmly confirmed or quietly severed, as prudence might demand;

new ones were forged with money and power and arrangements for marriage. The common business of the City-States of Italy was carried on, publicly and in private corners, and Lorenzo de' Medici moved among his guests like a courteous shadow, listening to its hum.

Lodovico Sforza, Regent of Milan, *Il Moro*, surveyed his young cousin with fondness, looming over her as she sat demurely beneath the pergola that formed the eastern wall of the archery range. It was evening, and brief flurries of snow winked in the light of bracketed torches set at intervals along the covered walks. A pavilion of green and orange silk had been erected in the corner by the belvedere, which itself served as stage for a group of Flemish lutenists; beside them, a miniature fountain bubbled a gentle stream of Calabrian wine into an alabaster bowl decorated with floating peaches and artificial water lilies.

"They tell me you are becoming quite a Florentine, madam," said the regent.

"Indeed, sir? I do not know what they may mean by that. Is it intended as a compliment?"

"What others may mean by it, I am not sure. My impression is that it implies your having become both disputatious and unruly, as the ladies of Florence have been for as long as I can remember."

"Then you disapprove, my lord," said Bianca.

"I did not say so. I am not sure of that either. I admire independence of thought, even in womankind. But I must tell you that it will not do in Milan, little cousin, however admirable it may be here. We are less given to affairs of the mind and prefer a decent reticence in the fair sex. Nor," he added, "will it be welcome in Savoy."

Bianca colored with anger.

"In Savoy?" she said. "I had hoped that by now you might have dismissed Savoy from among your plans for my future. Must I defy you again?"

"It would be unwise."

"Nonetheless, I do so. My grandfather would not have wished me bartered with Savoy like a prize heifer, for the political benefit of the house of Sforza. I am a Visconti, as your mother was, my lord. And you are my guardian, not my owner."

Lodovico Sforza laughed in admiration, his teeth luminous in his darkly handsome face.

"Child, child," he said, "I shall do with you as I see fit. Your grandfather is dead, and the Viscontis scattered through France and Lorraine. Your father gave you into my charge before he was murdered, relying upon me to seek the advantage neither of the Viscontis nor of the Sforzas, but of Milan. Besides, what are your objections to the Prince of Savoy? Your grandmother was of their house. I do not understand you."

"He is stupid, boorish, and vain. I detest him, as you well know. If you have any love for me—"

"And do you doubt it?"

"Sir, I . . . I do not know. Perhaps I presume too much. There is no reason why I should expect you to feel affection toward me. We are cousins, but God knows that means little enough in these times. Yet I trust you as a man of honor. Moreover . . ."

"Yes?" prompted her guardian.

"My lord, it seems to me that your purpose in wishing me to marry the Prince of Savoy cannot be altogether firm, else you would have us betrothed by now. I shall be fifteen next year."

"And old enough for any man's bed? Is that your meaning?"

"Old enough," said Bianca, looking at him, "though, as yet, unwilling. And is Milan so feeble that you must bed me with a fool against my will?"

The regent laughed again, this time so loudly that several passing couples stopped to look curiously in their direction.

"Little cousin, you delight me," he said. "Rightly despairing of my good nature, you appeal to my honor, my presumed subtlety and Milan's pride. By the saints, they have taught you, these Medici! I shall begin to regret sending you here. Well, I make you no promises, and I insist on your obedience; but it may be that my plans for you will change. If they do, be sure that I will so inform you. If they do not, may I remind you that many women have gone to the marriage beds of men they detested."

"Many women, no doubt," rejoined Bianca. "But not I."

"You will be no exception," Lodovico said, "and do not overreach yourself, cousin."

Sitting at a laden trestle table in the Great Chamber of the Medici palace, Paolo and Ippolito Pazzi chewed on capons' legs while their brother Francesco drank from a silver cup. Beside him, old Jacopo Pazzi, their family head, stood with folded arms. Though they were surrounded by a swirling throng of festive people, the noise was such that they were effectively in private.

"Nothing passes my lips here," announced Jacopo Pazzi. "I do not eat in the house of my enemy."

"Then I wonder, Father," said Paolo, "that you came here at all."

"Do not think I take any pleasure in it. Our absence would be remarked upon, that is all. But the food you are devouring so shamelessly would choke me. I marvel that you can touch it."

"If I allowed hatred to interfere with my appetite," replied Paolo, "I should have starved long since. This fowl is excellent. Though expensive when set against the loss to our bank of Cardinal Borromeo's lands. That I grant you."

"You speak as though it were a matter for jest," said Jacopo, "although it is but a tithe of the wrongs these Medici upstarts have done us."

"I agree, Father. Do not mistake me. I am not here as a gesture, but in order to speak with certain people whom I might otherwise be forced to meet in some inconvenient alley." He pointed across the room with the bone he held. "Grimiani, for instance."

"A clown," said his father.

"Again, I agree. Let us think of him, for the moment, as a liaison, which is a function admirably performed by clowns. We cannot move without Rome's agreement, and Rome's *imprimatur* may be hard to come by."

"Rome will support us," said Francesco Pazzi with confidence. "His Holiness loves the Medici no more than we do. Did he not remove the assets of the Church from the Medici bank in Rome and transfer them to us?"

"It does not follow that he will wink at violence," said Paolo. "But we may hope that you are right." He turned back to his father. "If so," he continued, "then you will admit that a mere seven or eight hundred thousand florins, stolen from us by an infamous piece of Medici legislation, can safely be forgotten. We may regard it as . . . how shall I put it? An enforced loan, to be called at our leisure, and at a high rate of interest."

At the far end of the room, Leonardo was arguing with Florence's Captain-Gunner.

"In the name of St. Barbara—who is, so I believe, your patroness—can you not forget your cannon for the space of a day and enjoy yourself?" asked Leonardo. "Here we have music, wine, food, lovely ladies, well-dressed gentlemen. All are wasted upon you, since you do nothing but stand there scowling."

Rigo Leone rested a foot on the edge of the vast open hearth and looked around him.

"There is nothing the matter with the food, or the wine, for that matter," he said, "but I find your costumed gentlemen effeminate. I invite you to inhale their scent, my friend. This place reminds me of nothing so much as a whorehouse in Rabat. As for your music, we have better in the taverns of Pistrola, and with less of this pestilent twanging. Moreover, a man may break wind there without some damned overbred jackanape looking as though the sky had fallen in. I shall return to my cannon as soon as I may, and I would suggest you join me."

"No," laughed the artist, "that I cannot do. I am commanded to build fountains here, devise tableaux, and in general, make myself useful. You see me now in the role of kitchen knave."

"I wondered why you were standing in the midst of the ashes. What are you doing?"

"Designing a turn spit. I can see no reason why one should not turn a roast mechanically, by means of the rising draft in the chimney above a fire such as this. There are several advantages in doing so. First, since the strength of the draft depends upon the fire's heat, it follows that the brisker the fire, the faster the spit would rotate. Second—"

"I wish you the joy of it," said Rigo hastily. "And after Christmas?"

"After Christmas, I travel to Rome."

"To Rome?" said the gunner, startled. "In God's name, why?"

"To read books."

"We have plenty of books here in Florence. Why stick your head in the lion's mouth?"

Leonardo, trying to look up the chimney stack without getting singed by the heat of the embers, extricated himself and shot a look of innocence at his companion.

"What is this talk of lions?" he demanded. "*I* am not yet at war with Rome. Or, if I am, then Rome does not know it yet. I am a poor artist with a head full of curiosity. That is all."

"A head full of misplaced optimism would be nearer the mark," said Rigo.

Having left his unruly young cousin to her own devices, Lodovico Sforza sat opposite the half-Moorish Ferrante of Naples in an alcove decorated with cherubim. Their conversation, though seemingly casual and interrupted by waves of passers' greetings, was to the point.

"I am untroubled," Lodovico pointed out. "Have I not Genoa, Modesta and Lucca between myself and Florence? And is not Rome's hold on the Apennines tenuous, at best? No, Rome does not frighten me. Her arm must grow long before it reaches out to Milan. All the same, I am by no means against alliance."

"Nor I," King Ferrante said, "though our good Sixtus is unlikely to look covetously southward toward me. Tell me, does Lorenzo press you?"

If the regent noticed this familiar reference to His Holiness, he let it pass. Naples, Milan, Venice and Florence dealt with the Papal States as equals, as all men knew, and the easy flattery of smaller states found no place in their discourse.

"Not exactly," he said. "But then, he would be unlikely to admit his need of us, however strong that might be."

"But his need exists. We accept that?"

"Certainly."

"Then let Lorenzo force the pace in argument," Ferrante said. "To come to grips with the Medici is like trying to grasp a handful of mist at the best of times. If he needs us, let him say so."

Lodovico cracked a filbert with the handle of a jeweled dagger and pulled the shell apart delicately. "Much will depend," he said, "upon the outcome of the Castelmonte affair. Do you not agree?"

"I do. Perfectly. If Rome can hold Castelmonte and the upper Arno Valley, then we have the Medici at a disadvantage, to say the least. Since there is little doubt in my mind that Rome can do so, we may do well to leave discussion of any alliance with Florence until next summer. If Lorenzo needs us now, he will need us the more desperately then."

It was nearly midnight when Giuliano de' Medici nudged open the door to the upstairs library, holding a candelabrum and a ring with several keys. He was humming a tune, oblivious for the moment both to the sounds of revelry that filtered upward from hall and garden, and to the echoes of gaiety outside in the city's streets.

Resting the candles on the table, Giuliano crossed to where—between two rows of books—the triple-locked iron door of a strongbox was set into the wall at floor level. He knelt and was about to fit a key to the uppermost lock when his attention was caught by a still figure silhouetted against the dim light of a window at the opposite side of the shadowed room.

"Constanza?" he called softly. "Is it you?"

"It is, my lord."

"You almost startled me. I had thought you in your chamber and asleep." Dropping the keys to the floor beside him, he rose and walked to her, brushing at his knees. "What are you doing here, my lady? Alone, and in a darkened room?"

"Sleep did not come to me, Giuliano," she said, "as it has not for many nights. Therefore, I dressed and came here to watch happier people pass." She pointed. Lanterns gleamed in the alley beneath the palace wall, and snatches of song were rising from within a house on the corner of a small square to the right. "It is good to see festive people, my lord," she whispered.

He nodded and held out his hands to her, taking hers and cupping them protectively. "All of us mourn for Carla," he said. "Yet she was your sister, and the sharpest loss is yours. It is well enough to be a man and drown grief in thoughts of vengeance. Yours is the harder part, by far."

She turned and looked out of the window again.

"I am dry of tears, Giuliano," she said, her voice soft. "I have done little else these past weeks but weep." He moved closer, and she leaned against his chest.

"And yet," he said, "though yours is the greater grief, I feel it too, for reasons which are mine alone. For I rode to Florence behind her, Constanza, and laid her in our chapel.

And as I rode, the thought came to me unbidden that had it been you, I would no longer have wished to live."

He tightened his arm around her, and she moved to look into his eyes as though in search.

"You love me this much?"

"I do. I have loved you longer than I knew, being foolish and light-hearted. But so it is. When Carla died, I saw that I must not lose you."

"So much did Leonardo tell me this very morning," said Constanza, half to herself. "Death is but a long journey, he said. While we must weep, it should be as we weep when a loved one leaves us for many years. Not forever. He also said that mourning must cease with the arrival of new joy, and that my new joy lay in your love for me."

"A wise man. And did you believe him, Constanza?"

"I wanted to. But I wished to hear you say it too. Was that perverse of me?"

He shook his head. "No," he said. "God knows that I, too, hunger to hear you say that you love me. How could it be otherwise?"

"I love you, Giuliano. I had not thought to find you so kind, so gentle or quick to help ease my pain at Carla's death. I loved you before that, but—" she smiled fleetingly, "—in a different fashion, my lord. One which I do not seek to have you understand."

They stood in silence, looking out over the white city and the falling snow. A draft from the open doorway bent the candle flames and made the shadows dance. Giuliano stirred.

"We might forget the world," he said, "but I cannot do so. I came here to find some small coins to reward a troupe of tumblers downstairs. Lorenzo will believe me lost. Not far from the truth. But I must return."

Constanza released herself from his arms, her face glowing. "Then leave me," she said. "I am happy now, and I will sit here a while longer."

"No," Giuliano said. "Enough of darkness. Come with me."

"Is that what you wish?"

"It is. Shall I find my good friend Leonardo and have him offer you advice on the subject?"

Constanza laughed. "There will be no need to trouble him," she said. "I will come with you."

"Then give me your hand," Giuliano said.

The middle garden, serving chiefly as a means of passage between the halls and courtyard of the palace and the archery range for such as were willing to brave the wintry air, was deserted except for a group of five men who stood in shadows. From beyond the wall at their backs, the plangent notes of a *strambotto* sounded, drowning their muttered discourse in the soft cadences of lute and viol.

"The Count of Imola is for us," said Silvio Grimiani di Torino, Prince of Savoy. "I received a letter from him yesterday."

"It is not Riario's position which concerns us," Ippolito Pazzi said, "since we already assume his support. What we must know is the attitude of His Holiness."

"I cannot speak for His Holiness," said Silvio. "Nor can any man. What would you have me do—request an audience with him? Ask him whether or not he will give us his blessing if we commit murder on his behalf?" He brushed snowflakes from his hair petulantly. "Rome has always said one thing and meant another, and His Holiness has refined Rome's ambiguity to the point where it is impossible to tell what his views are on any matter at all, least of all a question of massacre. I cannot even tell what Rome wishes me to do about this damned artist."

"Leonardo da Vinci?" asked Paolo Pazzi. He grinned in the darkness. "Is he giving Rome the itch, as he gives it to you, noble prince?"

"Watch your words," snarled Silvio. "I have spitted better men than you, and upon less provocation."

"If you feel so heated," said Francesco Pazzi, "over a small matter of his paying too much attention to the lady Bianca

Visconti, then I suggest you use your sword upon Master Leonardo forthwith and cease inflicting your annoyance upon us. Eh, Bernardo?" He dug an elbow into the side of the man who stood next to him.

"Oh, by all means," Bernardo Bandini said. "By all means." He was a well-set man with reddish hair, whose chief employment was the casual running-through with swords of inconvenient persons on behalf of one patron or another. "I dislike his superior airs myself, and should be happy to support you, Prince Silvio."

"Too hasty," said Silvio. "I do not know whether Rome—"

"Of course. If you are uncertain of Rome's wishes, then there is no more to be said." Francesco Pazzi prodded Bandini in the ribs again, laughing. "It is always wise to consult Rome, even upon a question of unlacing one's doublet or blowing one's nose, I agree."

"Very well," said the Prince of Savoy.

Except for a few stragglers, the great hall was almost empty. Rigo Leone, as he had announced, had mounted horse and was on his way back to his cannon and the cruder delights of Pistrola. Leonardo, his hair tousled, sat alone in an inglenook by the huge hearth, charcoal and notebook in hand. Others yawned in corners or lay beneath tables asleep or drunk, to be eventually aroused by attendants and valets. But Leonardo seemed wide awake. He pulled several loose sheets from beneath his thigh—where he had thrust them for security—and held them out to Bianca Maria Visconti.

"And for how long have you been working thus?" she asked. "Six hours? Seven? I despair of you, sir. I had hoped for your company."

"That you are welcome to at any time," Leonardo said.

"And must I sit by you in this grimy fireplace in order to have it? How gallant of you! In any case, I should have been forced to push my way through a press of stupid women, or so I observed; and I did not care to do so."

"Very wise of you," said Leonardo. "However, do not imagine that this throng of beautiful ladies was fascinated by myself."

"I am sure it were not."

"It is simply that a man who appears to be doing something, no matter what it may be, is a powerful attraction for those who are doing nothing whatever."

"Of course. And now that they have all gone elsewhere, may I ask you to accompany me and speak with my guardian?" asked Bianca.

"I shall be happy to accompany you anywhere, and for any purpose. Where is he?"

"In the archery range. I warn you that he is very powerful and does not approve of you. He believes that you have been leading me astray, though I have assured him that it was far from being true. But he will not bite you."

"Then I will try not to be nervous," Leonardo said.

"And brush the soot from your sleeve."

"It is honorably acquired soot, and Milan is a city of smoking foundries. Il Moro will not object to a little honest dirt."

"And do not address my guardian as Moor in his hearing. Come."

"Little cousin," said Lodovico Sforza, "it is time you were abed. I thank you for bringing Master Leonardo to me. For the present, may I ask you to retire?"

If Bianca seemed prepared to offer some argument to this, her guardian's manner silenced it. When she had gone, he addressed himself to Leonardo, wasting no time with ceremony.

"Castelmonte," he said.

"What of it, my lord?"

"I do not believe Florence can take it," said the Regent of Milan. "Am I correct?"

"My lord," said Leonardo carefully, "my duty is at present to Lorenzo de' Medici, as you must be aware."

Lodovico Sforza eyed him for several moments, as though

in calculation. Then, "I am aware of it," he said, "and perhaps we misunderstand one another. I am not asking you to be indiscreet. Let me begin anew. Milan and Naples are considering an alliance with Florence; an alliance which, without consulting your patron, you must perceive that he needs. Do I offend your sensibilities thus far?"

"No. Milan would make Florence a valuable ally."

"Good. You are an engineer, you tell me, and hence, think objectively. Were you in my place, Master Leonardo, would you think such an alliance of advantage?"

"Beyond doubt," replied Leonardo promptly.

"You speak without hesitation, I notice."

"I have already considered Milan's position, with some care."

"Have you, by Hades? Then persuade me, since you appear to be surer of your ground, and Milan's, than I."

"Persuasion should not be necessary. Naples I discount, as being of little importance to Rome. It is the republics which His Holiness wishes to swallow."

Lodovico Sforza fingered the silk of the pavilion beneath whose shelter they stood. The archery range was bare and white, and the musicians had long since retired. Snow sifted into the footprints that dotted the lawn, obliterating them.

"Milan," he said brusquely, "is a duchy, not a republic. Where is your argument?"

"Milan, with great respect, is a duchy in name only. In all other respects, it is as much a republic as Florence, Genoa or Venice. The essence of a republic is that it is ruled by those who are strong enough to rule it, whether by popular acclaim or through seizure. Let us look at Milan in this light. Your brother, Gian-Galeazzo, is Duke. Does he rule Milan? No. You rule it, my lord. And my argument stands."

Lodovico pursed his lips. "I still do not altogether follow it, though I may grant your premise. What of Rome, then?"

"Rome's ruler," said Leonardo, "holds office through means other than purely temporal power."

"He holds it through the grace and will of Almighty God.

Well? Surely, a power stronger than . . . let us say, my own?"

"I would be more impressed if the Almighty did not, apparently, find it advantageous to work through the College of Cardinals," said Leonardo.

Lodovico Sforza blinked. "Why," he said cheerfully, "you are a damned heretic. But, proceed with your heresy."

"It is plain enough. His Holiness, not content with the authority of his spiritual office, seeks temporal power as well. More, he seeks gold, the fount of all temporal power. From whom will he wrest it? From those whom he perceives as controlling it, which is to say the republics. They are golden plums, my lord, from which His Holiness will squeeze what juice he can. If they are foolish enough to let him." Leonardo held up his left hand, and folded his fingers down one by one. "Florence first," he said. "Then Siena, Genoa. Mantua, it may be. Then Milan. After that, Venice, Savoy and the kingdoms of France. Therefore, he must be stopped—now. And therefore, my lord, it follows that you should make your alliance as soon as possible."

"And thereby provoke Rome?" said Lodovico Sforza. "I wonder."

"Rome will not wait to be provoked. She will, as always, divide and conquer. Make your alliance. There is nothing to be gained by waiting."

"I thank you for your counsel, engineer. But I think I will at least await the outcome of Lorenzo's fight for Castelmonte. Which brings me back to my starting point. Your guns cannot take it."

"I would not feel too sure of that."

"They have failed thus far."

"I admit it. Nonetheless, I will make you a prophecy, if it will ease your mind, and Milan's. The guns of Florence will take Castelmonte next spring."

"We shall see," said Lodovico Sforza. "We shall see. Meanwhile, I bid you farewell, Master Leonardo."

He strode away, the newly fallen snow spraying from his

boots as he crossed the lawn. Leonardo sat on the steps of the belvedere and plucked idly at the strings of a discarded lute. On the face of it, he thought, his prophecy seemed mere bravado. Doubtless, the Regent of Milan had taken it thus. What did he, Leonardo, artist turned engineer, truly know of gunnery? The calculation of angles and trajectories was one thing, practice was another. What made him so certain, then—and certain before he knew how he would set about it—that he could succeed where Florence's Captain-Gunner had failed?

Yet certain he was, as he had often been. Ideas swam in the reaches of his mind like fish in the sea, pale and fugitive, just as they did when he conceived a picture, seeing its essence before he could perceive its form—yet knowing that form to exist in some way he could not define. As it was with artistic discovery, so it was with science. His solution existed, and there remained only to grasp it.

He laid down the lute and walked from beneath the pavilion's eaves, following in Sforza's footsteps.

He had barely passed through the archway that opened onto the middle courtyard when his passage was barred by three figures.

"A moment, if you please, good fellow," said Silvio Grimiani di Torino. He stood easily, his feet slightly apart. At a discreet four paces behind him, Francesco Pazzi lounged in simulated conversation with Bernardo Bandini, who was propped against a torch standard, hand on hip. Leonardo slowly halted.

"Why, good morrow, my lord," he said. "Is there something I can do for you?"

"Nothing," Silvio said. "That is to say, the merest trifle. I have a question to put to you."

"It could, perhaps, wait until daylight?" Leonardo inquired mildly.

"I think not. It will not detain us long. It is simply that I have observed that you spend too much of your time in the company of the lady Bianca Visconti, a circumstance which I find odd and, on the whole, offensive. My question, then, is this. Why does a man such as yourself—a mere artist and the bastard, I believe, of a notary gotten upon some serving wench—how does he presume to thrust his company upon a lady so far above his station? I am sure that you can offer me a short and simple explanation, and we need then keep you no further."

Leonardo frowned slightly. Behind the Prince of Savoy, he saw that Pazzi and Bandini had turned their faces expectantly in his direction.

"Ah," he said. "I perceive, my lord, that I have been remiss. I confess that I had not considered the matter in the light which you now cast upon it. I am bound to say, however, that had I done so I doubt whether it would have disturbed me unduly."

"It disturbs me," said Silvio.

"I can see," said Leonardo, his voice suddenly low. "It might do so, though I am not sure why."

"Well," replied Silvio. "It is not necessary for you to know why. One sees that you have no sword, though we have noticed you strutting with one on occasion. One assumes, then, that you know how to use it; and, for the present, either of my friends here will be glad to lend you one. Between gentlemen, these matters are quickly settled."

"I am sure you are right," Leonardo replied. "However, I must point out a flaw in your reasoning. For here we have but three gentlemen upon the one hand. Upon the other, myself—the bastard son of a serving wench, as you have rightly described me. In general, I am at your service. But as regards your proposal, I am afraid that I find myself with better things to occupy me than to brawl with slighted princes. I suggest you return to your cups and your toys, and leave me to what concerns me." He laid a hand gently on Silvio's sword arm, as one pats a fractious child, and moved him aside. Passing between the two men a few paces farther on, he nodded to each of them and was gone.

Dawn found Leonardo in the company of Lorenzo de' Medici. As on a previous occasion, the two men sat in

Lorenzo's private and monastic retiring room, beyond whose window the sky promised sunshine after the night's snowfall.

"When do you wish to leave?" Lorenzo asked.

"As soon after Christmas as I may."

"Well. By then, you will, I expect, have attended to the roasting of my geese and my capons, if I understand your drawings of mechanisms for my fireplace aright. So, we shall be able to spare you." He smiled thinly. "It is unnecessary for me to point out that, in going to Rome, you cannot assume our protection."

"I do not seek it," said Leonardo. "I hope that Rome is unaware, as yet, of the nature of my employment with you. I go not as Florence's engineer, but as a humble seeker of truth."

"A dangerous commodity," said Lorenzo de' Medici. "If you should come across it in any quantity, have care." He drummed his fingers on the tabletop. "I confess, I am uneasy," he continued. "Will you not tell me what it is that you seek? Our libraries here are extensive, and it may be that your journey can be avoided."

"With respect, sir, I doubt it. The archives of the Church are a source of information I must examine now, since it is certain that I shall not be allowed to do so later. My mind runs upon the subject of gunpowder, a substance which your Captain-Gunner tells me is made in quite different fashion by different men, and whose properties differ according to its maker. These differences are vital, both to Captain-Gunner Leone and myself. Since the making of gunpowder is an ancient art, I must consult ancient records. Which means that I must consult Rome."

Lorenzo rose and crossed to the window.

"Very well," he said. "I did not appoint you my military advisor in order to question your judgment. You have my leave to go."

Eleven

Sunlight flooded the spacious upper-floor room of the Lateran Palace. Domenico Cardinal della Palla sat behind his writing desk and surveyed his young visitor with tranquil and inquiring eyes, his fingertips tented and resting on his lips.

It was probable that no more than two men—one of whom was himself—were aware that the Apostolic Chancellor was the most powerful personage in Rome. Certainly, his appearance gave no hint of the fact. Precise, calm and careworn, Cardinal della Palla at fifty looked like the teacher he had once been.

His power was of a peculiar kind—so peculiar that it had not even existed before he invented it. Its source and mechanism lay beneath his feet and those of his guest, and occupied, in terms of space, more than a third of the entire building. Its nature was both simple and, at the same time, complex. Della Palla's stock in trade was knowledge.

He had, in his youth, been handsome, and still possessed

the fair hair and piercing blue eyes of his northern ancestry. Over the treacherous years, his mouth had firmed with the need to conceal those secrets his mind had acquired, and a vertical furrow had eaten its way into the center of his brow—a furrow which deepened each time he listened, intently, to a message whose import lay not in the words but in the unspoken hints betrayed by a tone of voice, a moment's hesitation, a sudden blandness of expression on the part of its bearer. If he smiled seldom and laughed never, it was because he found little in the state of the Church to provoke amusement, much less joy. Daily, his two hundred clerks received and transcribed accounts of venery, fraud, treason, banishment and murder. Even the news of a marriage or of a birth of a son gave rise, not to good cheer, but to the calculation of a shift in advantage between one family and the next. The road of truth which the Cardinal had chosen to tread was severe and thorny. It had begun almost a quarter of a century earlier.

When the Spaniard, Alonso de Borja, had assumed, at the *habemus pontificem* of April 8, 1455, the title of Callistus III—thereby inaugurating a control of the papacy by the Borgia family that would last through many pontiffs—the man's first act was to promote his nephew Rodrigo, a student at Bologna, to the office of Apostolic Notary. The fact that the young man did not at the time possess a degree in canon law, he felt, was but a small disadvantage and one speedily rectified. He simply sent Rodrigo Borgia back to Bologna to obtain his doctorate. Unsurprisingly, Rodrigo passed his examinations a year later with high honors, presenting his teachers and his examiners with caps and gloves of the finest leather to mark his appreciation of their wisdom.

If there were those who felt—but were careful not to say—that the three hours each day, which the young Rodrigo Borgia had sacrificed from his hunting to devote to his studies in canon law, were perhaps insufficient to have justified his doctorate, one man disagreed with them. Domenico della Palla, although acidly and with a certain dry wit, wrote to

Callistus III and informed His Holiness that his nephew, when persuaded to discuss matters as dull as jurisprudence, showed a surprising grasp of his material and might—or so his tutor felt—eventually fill his position at Rome's Chancery with distinction in fact as well as in name.

Since neither Rodrigo nor his uncle intended that he should do anything so mundane, this letter from the twenty-six-year-old della Palla gave them some quiet mirth. But, ironically, yet with gratitude for an opinion he perceived as honest, Callistus summoned his nephew's tutor to Rome and offered him a position as secretary to his former pupil.

Della Palla, with equal irony, accepted.

Over the years which followed, the relationship between Rodrigo Borgia—now Cardinal—and his mentor slowly blossomed. At first, it was assumed as a matter of course that Domenico della Palla would play at politics with the same fervor as did the Borgias. He did nothing of the kind. His allegiances, it was discovered with surprise, were three: to God, to truth, and to the Church. The Supreme Pontiff, his family and his supporters all regarded this first as an affront, then as an amusing curiosity, and finally, in the roaring tumult of warfare with Aragon and the Turks, as an asset. Bribes without number were offered, including even the Bishopric of Valencia, once held by Callistus himself. Della Palla declined them all, graciously.

Seldom moving from the confines of the Lateran Palace, he seemed to do little but increase his staff of clerks and under secretaries, and the Borgias were on the whole content that he should do so. His advice before the sea battle off Mytilene gave Rome victory. His insistence that Venice would shortly conclude a trade agreement with the Ottoman Empire and could not, therefore, be expected to contribute to the Pontiff's proclaimed crusade against the unbelievers proved embarrassingly correct; and his unauthorized diversion of funds to Janos Hunyadi, the Hungarian *condottiere*, and his military advisor, Cardinal Carvajal, ensured the defeat of Mohammed II at the gates of Belgrade. Slowly but surely, then, while tramping the dusty corridors of the Lateran, Cardinal Borgia's secretary forged himself an empire founded upon the pens of his scriveners. Existing only in rank upon rank of specially constructed cabinets filled with a tide of documents, its range and power would have eventually surpassed the belief of those who refused to admit its existence.

As he had foreseen, he became indispensable. More than this, he remained neutral. Upon the death of Callistus III, the Borgias decided to elect the former satirical playwright and humanist, Aeneas Piccolomino. They did so. Pius II, as he had amusingly styled himself, proceeded to the Lateran Palace on a rainy autumn morning in 1459, was shown its bulging cellars, and retreated in awed haste before the evidence of so much industry. Two months later, for reasons he himself only dimly comprehended, he appointed Domenico della Palla to the Cardinalate of Santa Lucia da Vignola. His successor, Paul II, who had been expecting opposition to his Pontificate from the new Cardinal on the grounds that he, too, was an openly political Borgia appointee, was pleasantly surprised to find that della Palla gave not a fig for the mechanics of succession. And so Paul rewarded the Cardinal with the position which the latter had been seeking for years—that of Apostolic Chancellor.

Rodrigo Borgia, maker of Popes, was the only man in Rome who was less than intimidated by the paper empire in the Lateran Palace. He visited his former tutor and secretary often, complimented him without flattery, drank wine while laughing good-naturedly at della Palla's water carafe, and tried to make a friend of the Chancellor. He failed in this, as all men failed, but their relationship was comfortable. Della Palla, as always, had written only the truth in commending Rodrigo's intelligence to his uncle, Callistus III. Because of it, Cardinal Borgia prospered. He also listened, as few did, to what the Apostolic Chancellor had to say, and acted upon it.

Thus, when Francesco della Rovere became Pope Sixtus IV and ostensibly the most powerful figure in Rome, two men and two men alone could have told him (but did not) that Rome's true power lay elsewhere—in the Piazza di San Giovanni in Laterano—the Lateran Palace.

On this January morning, then, Domenico della Palla sat, conscious as always of the industrious army beneath him digesting the state of the world and thereby extending his reach, and watched the young Florentine who stood at the far side of his table with a leather-covered notebook under one arm. Before the Cardinal lay a letter. Since he knew its contents by heart, he had no need to consult it, preferring instead to study its author.

"Master Leonardo da Vinci?" he said.

"Myself," his visitor replied, "and at the service of Your Eminence."

"Please sit down, my son. And then tell me, if you will, in what precise way you hope that we may be able to assist you."

Leonardo sat in the chair the Cardinal indicated, transferring his portfolio to his knees. "My hope is, Your Eminence, to discover in the archives of the Church some learned works upon the making of gunpowder."

Della Palla drove the tips of his fingers against his lower lip, thoughtfully. He was accustomed to concealing surprise.

"Gunpowder," he said. "Yes. If I may say so, an odd preoccupation for an artist. May I say that I have admired your portrait of Donna Ginevra Benci? I will not, therefore, pretend that you are unknown to me." Leonardo inclined his head in acknowledgment. "Gunpowder, then," the Cardinal continued in a brisker tone. "I assume that this letter of yours is ironic in flavor, and that you regard warfare as the highest art form? An intriguing position. Why should you suppose the Church to have any material that might help you?"

"It is an assumption on my part, I agree," Leonardo said. "But I already know of the treatise by Albertus Magnus, the *Kriegsbuch Bellifortis*, and of course, the *Epistola de secretis operibus Artis* of Brother Bacon, all of which your libraries possess. I was hoping to find the original *Liber Ignium* of Marcus Graecus, though I believe the only copy to be at Nuremberg. Yet, there may be other sources."

"Your scholarship is impressive," said the Cardinal, "and I thank you for making it clear to me that you are far from wasting my time. Or yours, of course. May I ask what exactly your interest is in gunpowder?"

"It is philosophical," replied Leonardo.

"A careful answer. I accept it, for the present, though there are others who may not. Well, Master Leonardo, I will make some search of my own for anything I believe may interest you. Philosophical? I approve of that. From what aspect?"

"Specifically, then, Your Eminence, upon the vexed question of how the power arrives in the gunpowder during the making of it. For consider that charcoal, sulphur and saltpeter separately possess no power of explosion. How, then, does a mixture of all three come to have its force?"

The Cardinal's face remained as neutral as ever, though he was pleased by this.

"An excellent point," he said. "I shall ponder it while I am about your errand. Meanwhile, I have an errand of my own to inflict upon you, if I may. I should say rather that it is a request from my colleague, Cardinal Borgia. Since it will, in any case, take me until tomorrow to search for your . . . philosophical material, I am instructed to ask you to attend at the Papal Palaces for an audience with Count Girolamo Riario of Imola. Have you any objection?"

"None whatever. Have I not said that I am at the service of Your Eminence?"

"Then this afternoon will be suitable. Have you met the Count?"

"I have not had that pleasure. I have heard of him, of course. Who has not?"

Cardinal della Palla studied the artist's face closely. "Master Leonardo," he said finally, "it may be that we shall become better acquainted, through God's grace. I hope so. If things should fall out thus, it is also my hope that we shall, in time, learn to be candid with one another. In this spirit, then, I believe I must tell you that the Count of Imola has already seen *you*."

"Has he, indeed?" said Leonardo. "I thank Your Eminence. I must consider where he may have done so."

"Yes," said Cardinal della Palla drily. "In view of your philosophical interest in gunpowder, it might be worth considering the matter very carefully indeed. I expect to see you here tomorrow at this hour."

As he walked along the bank of the Tiber beneath the buried mausoleum of Hadrian, now Castel sant' Angelo, Leonardo found his thoughts not on the man he was about to see but upon the Cardinal who had interviewed him that morning. Since what had passed between them had been merely the courteous fencing which Leonardo himself enjoyed, and regularly indulged in, he was at a loss to explain a certain curious mental excitement which he had felt when talking to della Palla. And still felt, even now. It was true that the Cardinal was a man of massive learning; his position alone guaranteed the fact. Compared with the Cardinal's mind, the mind of the venerable Dr. Cino di Lapo Mazzone was that of a buzzing and importunate gnat. Yet there was more to Cardinal della Palla than learning, more even than wisdom—a quality so rare that one might spend a lifetime without meeting more than one or two men who possessed it. Perhaps, Leonardo thought, he was being overimaginative. Was there something, however tenuous, in the mind of Cardinal della Palla which called to his own? If so, he was aware that he had not, as yet, answered it.

He walked on, the river boiling past him. The walls of the Leonine City rose at his left, and he turned.

Arrived in the Borgia apartments, his destination, he was obliged to wait for almost an hour in a salon overlooking the San Damaso courtyard. At the end of this period, he was relieved of his sword by an impassive Swiss mercenary and ushered into a small room whose windows were all but obscured by heavy drapes. In one corner, seated in an oaken-sided stall, was Count Girolamo Riario.

Leonardo remembered with distaste what he knew of the man—and what he himself had seen from the gunners' ridge in the Arno Valley—and shuddered internally, despite himself. However, the Count was relaxed and charming. His legs, clad in parti-colored hose, were crossed. On his raised knee, he held a small gray cat and stroked it even as he greeted the artist.

"Welcome," he said. "Welcome to Rome, to whom all roads lead, sooner or later."

Leonardo bowed.

"And my thanks," the Count went on, "for allowing me some portion of your time here, which I am sure is very valuable. My good friend, Cardinal Borgia tells me you are here on some academic mission of deep importance, and I hesitate to keep you from it overlong. Stand forward in the center of the room, please, so that I may see you. Yes. I knew my memory did not fail me. Last November . . . was it last November? Yes. You were beneath my wall, were you not?"

"I was," replied Leonardo, coloring.

"My dear sir, think nothing of it. I wished but to see you to assure myself of the fact. I apologize for my somewhat hasty greeting that night. I did not know who you were, and my men discharged a few crossbow bolts in your direction. From which, I see, you took no harm. Had I known then what I know about you now, I would have been . . . less ungracious. I refer, of course, to your standing as an artist. Tell me," Riario said conversationally, "what were you doing there? I daresay you were upon some artistic pursuit."

"Quite so," said Leonardo. "I am at present painting an allegorical scene of battle for the monastery of Santa Cecilia, and to that end was making some studies in the field."

"But how admirable!" exclaimed the Count. "What industry! What devotion to your craft! To risk life and limb in the pursuit of excellence deserves the highest of praise. Why, as I recall matters, you were even feeling the texture of my somewhat battered wall, were you not?"

"I had not thought that you observed me so closely, my lord."

Riario lifted his hand from the animal on his knee and waved it airily. "It was but for a few moments," he said. "And in any event, it is all long past now. A scene of battle; you must allow me to see it when it is finished, though I am no artist. And you undertake . . . studies of this kind for every subject you paint?"

"Most surely. To set down the truth of things, it is necessary to understand them fully. One then shows not only the surface appearance but the reality."

The Count nodded.

"For example," Leonardo continued, "let us take yourself. You wear your armor jacket, even now. You sit in a corner of a room with drawn curtains. Seeing you thus, another man might say that you were withdrawn, reserved, that you sought to enclose yourself as do those crabs which live in discarded shells. Yet such is not my perception."

"This is presumption," said Girolamo Riario, frowning.

"Artistic presumption only."

"And what, then, do you see?"

For reply, Leonardo walked to the window and threw back the curtains, flooding the small room with light. He unfolded the cover of his notebook and returned to the middle of the floor. Intrigued despite himself, Riario rose from his chair and dropped the cat beside him. As Leonardo began rapidly to sketch, he came and stood behind the artist's shoulder.

"If I were to depict you," said Leonardo, his hand moving the while, "it would be thus. Not enclosed; not in the corner of some darkened room. But so—and so . . ."

Watching the flying charcoal in da Vinci's fingers, Riario with amazement saw himself emerging from the paper as a figure standing on the top of a hill, air and space all around; and dressed no longer in armor but in loose and flowing robes, as though inviting the very winds to caress him. He was momentarily stunned, and in that moment felt obscurely drawn, by something akin to gratitude, toward the artist—a man who, almost as though by wizardry, had perceived something of that inward nature he had so firmly thrust aside.

The moment passed, and he fingered his collar, his hands writhing. Freedom, his mind shouted at him, meant openness to attack. Had he not long since agreed with himself to barter freedom for security? What right had this Florentine, Rome's enemy and his own, to recognize his childhood bargain and mock him with it? A trap had been set for him, he now saw, and he had nearly fallen into it.

He reached across and tore the uppermost sheet away from the notebook, unfinished. In unreasoning fury, he was about to crumple it when he saw a brief irony in the artist's eyes and controlled himself. He sauntered back to his chair, holding the sketch as though studying it, his eyes and his mind rejecting its message. By the time he had seated himself once more, he was able to speak calmly.

"An interesting demonstration," he said. "I will keep your drawing, if I may. It shows that talent which all of us know you to possess. Well, well. I thank you once again for your time, Master Leonardo, and will keep you no longer. I hope your researches in Rome prove fruitful."

"I am happy to be able to tell you," said Domenico Cardinal della Palla in the Lateran Palace next morning, "that I have the answer to your question. It is contained in a treatise written by Brother Sfabalmaccio di Pisa in 1428, in which he clearly attributes the force of gunpowder to the accumulation of *vis naturae* or natural energy. He appends twenty-three different recipes for its manufacture. I am having the relevant passages copied out by my clerks, and will give them to you when they are finished. A most fascinating problem, and one which I am grateful to you for having brought to my attention."

Leonardo, who had risen from behind a small sidetable at the Cardinal's entry, now sat down again.

"I thank Your Eminence," he said. "It was good of you to put yourself to so much trouble on my account. May I see the manuscript for myself?"

The Cardinal walked to his own desk.

"There would be no particular objection, of course," he said, as though in faint surprise. "But why?"

"Because," Leonardo replied, "I should like to satisfy myself as to the extent of the learned friar's expertise in the matter of gunpowder. Is he reliable?"

Cardinal della Palla raised an eyebrow.

"I am not sure what you mean by that, Master Leonardo. His thesis bears the imprimatur of the Church, which means that he is the acknowledged authority on the subject. Therefore, your question answers itself."

"Nonetheless," Leonardo persisted, "I should very much like to read his opinions."

"By all means."

The Cardinal rose and left the room, to return a few minutes later with a sheaf of parchment tied with a ribbon. He placed this on the table before Leonardo, who thanked him for it.

"I will leave you to peruse it for an hour or so," the Cardinal said. "If my room here suits you, please feel free to stay while you do so. I have, in any case, to confer with my chaplain. Will an hour be sufficient?"

"It will be more than enough, Your Eminence."

"Kindly keep the sheets in their proper order. I have somewhat of an obsession with these things," the Cardinal said. He nodded and withdrew.

It was almost noon when he came back. Leonardo, intent upon the final page of the manuscript, did not notice him until the Cardinal had coughed discreetly. Then, carefully squaring the edges of the parchment sheets, he rose.

"Well?" inquired della Palla.

"I owe Your Eminence more than I can say for your indulgence," replied Leonardo. "Nonetheless, I must tell you that the conclusions reached by Brother Sfabalmaccio are inadequate. In fact, they are barely worth the paper they are written on."

"I am afraid that once again I fail to understand you," said the Cardinal.

"I have put it bluntly because Your Eminence was kind enough to suggest, the last time we met, that we should learn to be candid with one another."

"I did. Candor is one thing. I did not invite you to be sacrilegious."

"I intend no irreverence," said Leonardo. "But if I may give you an example of your friar's lack of knowledge. He nowhere implies that gunpowder made according to one or another of his twenty-three recipes will vary in strength according to its ingredients. I can assure you that such is the case. I must therefore assume Brother Sfabalmaccio to have been as ignorant as he is wordy. However," Leonardo went on good-heartedly, "I am fortunately, as you see, engaged upon a study of gunpowder myself, and will thus be able to report the true facts to you when I am finished. Your records may accordingly be set straight."

Cardinal della Palla, during this cavalier recitation, crossed once more to his writing table. He fiddled with various objects before seating himself.

"It is hard for me to know where to begin," he said finally. "The Church is already satisfied that she has the true facts."

"But suppose," said Leonardo gently, "that the Church is wrong?"

"Be careful."

"Of what? I fear that it is my turn to fail in understanding," said Leonardo blithely. "Why should the Church, in a practical matter of some importance, rely upon the opinions of a verbose and ignorant friar who says nothing except by way of retailing nonsense concerning vis naturae—a concept which is totally meaningless, as Your Eminence must perceive—when there is better information available to her?"

"*Your* information?" asked the Cardinal sharply.

"My information, naturally."

"Be very cautious, my son."

"Does the Church, then, believe that she can influence facts by denying them, or by accepting unsound views concerning them? This is not some learned and scholastic question. Nature is nature, and will not be denied. If His Holiness announces, like Joshua of old, that the sun shall stop in its course, will it heed him and do so?"

The Cardinal raised his hand. "I beg you to say nothing—even by way of philosophical argument—from the consequences of which not even I could save you. Your outlook, Master Leonardo, is heretical. Heretical, and thus extremely dangerous. Say no more, I pray you."

Across the width of the room, the two men exchanged an unblinking and steadfast gaze.

"My lord Cardinal," said Leonardo, "the time for swordplay in words is past and has been so since I parted from you yesterday. We have provoked each other into argument, and have known that we were doing so. You believe in the work of your Brother Sfabalmaccio no more than I do. You produced his treatise for me in order to try my mettle, and I have but replied in kind. The imprimatur of the Church gives him no more authority than would the cawing of rooks in an April treetop, and this too you know as well as I. As for danger, Your Eminence has pointed out to me what I already know, which is that I have accepted bodily risk in the very act of setting foot in Rome. And if my soul lies in peril, I look to Almighty God to save it. For what is God, my lord, if He is not truth?"

Cardinal della Palla held out his hand to receive the stacked sheets of parchment, and Leonardo gave them to the Apostolic Chancellor.

"Then go with God, my son," the Cardinal said.

"My dear Chancellor," said Cardinal Borgia after a late supper in his apartments, "Riario tells me that this man is military engineer to the Medici in Florence. Were you aware of that?"

"Yes, I am aware of it," della Palla replied.

Cardinal Borgia consumed a grape. "The Count's suggestion is that Leonardo da Vinci be assassinated before he can leave Rome, thus saving us all a great deal of trouble. I don't know how much merit there may be in his point of view?"

"The Count of Imola lacks patience," said della Palla, "unlike yourself. Given his very limited vision, I am not in the least amazed by his suggestion. It might, certainly, save trouble. And yet Rome is, and Rome will be, when you and I are dead; and therefore, haste is inappropriate. Furthermore, upon the short discussion I have had with Master Leonardo, he appears—albeit somewhat impertinently—to have a greater grasp of the subject of gunpowder than our own published authorities. A slight matter, I realize, but in the long term it should also be considered, do you not think?"

"I see. You are, as always, a model of restraint. Would you recommend protecting him, then?"

"No."

"You would not? I am a trifle surprised, I confess."

"He is in the hands of God," pointed out della Palla. "I am far from certain that we can offer him better protection."

Leonardo walked through a narrow alley in the Trastevere, on his way to the suburban inn where he had stabled his horse. The night air was wet and bone-chilling and the cobblestones slippery with ice, but neither darkness nor weather had so far dampened his spirits. If he had discovered little about gunpowder, his meetings with Cardinal della Palla had left him with an exhilarating feeling of well-being. No word of friendship had passed between them, and he knew that, upon reflection, the Cardinal might decide that his direct attacks upon the authority of the Church were threatening. Yet, in a curious way, this seemed to matter very little. What mattered was that they had recognized each other, for good or for ill, across the gulf of twenty-five years and more which separated their ages and the greater gulf between the Cardinal's temper as a cleric and his own as a freethinker. And the recognition of a mind akin to his own sang in Leonardo's blood. Glimpsing the slight movement of shadows farther down the street, he paused.

After loosening his cape, he walked on. At the foot of the slope, the alleyway emerged into a tiny square. As he approached it, the sound of sliding steel reached his ears. The piazza was deserted. The gutters, marbled with frozen snow, shone in the fitful glare of dying torches and the pale light of a quarter moon.

Of the three men who stepped into his path, Leonardo recognized only one. Francesco Pazzi, in padded tunic and velvet breeches, advanced toward him with drawn sword. To right and left, his unknown accomplices moved to the sides until they blocked the alley's mouth. Their ambush was well placed. Their victim, with a steep and icy slope at his back, could not turn and flee them. They were confident of success. Leonardo smiled.

"Well met, my friends," he said softly.

Francesco Pazzi made no reply but, instead, launched himself forward, his face twisted into a silent grimace of effort as he lunged. He had little need of finesse, and employed none. The murder of one man by three opponents was, as he saw it, a simple matter and rendered still easier by the fact that his target had not yet drawn sword.

Leonardo stepped backward a pace, and Pazzi's sword point flickered in the air a handsbreadth from the front of his doublet. Before Francesco could regain his lost balance, the artist swept the cape from around his neck with his left hand and swung it, entangling Francesco's head and sword arm in its folds, temporarily blinding him. He staggered aside, losing his footing on the treacherous cobbles in a wild and unsuccessful struggle to free himself from the wet and clinging camlet.

Leonardo dropped to one knee, drawing his rapier. Rolling, he removed himself from the reach of Francesco's blindly sweeping blade. The man on Francesco's right leaped forward in his support. Leonardo's weapon rose from ground level into the pit of the attacker's unguarded belly. His breath whistled, and he collapsed, carrying downward the rapier point which pierced him, losing Leonardo seconds in freeing it from the twitching body.

Seizing this advantage, the third assassin crossed in front of the flailing Francesco and hacked swiftly and clumsily at Leonardo's head. He missed his mark, but his edge bit deeply into Leonardo's right arm, near the shoulder. The artist continued his acrobatic roll sideways and pulled his sword from the fallen man on the flagstone. A warm gush of blood darkened Leonardo's sleeve. His third attacker saw this. Certain his victim was now disarmed and helpless, he moved in triumphantly for the kill.

Transferring his rapier from right hand to left, Leonardo swept it, razorlike, across the backs of his opponent's legs, hamstringing him instantly. As he fell, Leonardo reversed his weapon and drove the pommel with a terrible and anatomical accuracy at his temple. There was a soft crunch of breaking bone, and the assassin tumbled and lay with staring eyes beside his friend.

Leonardo got to his feet, pressing the side of his sword-bearing left hand against his torn and dripping sleeve. A vein had been severed, he knew. Francesco Pazzi was still on his knees, cursing sulphurously at the layers of cloth which hampered him. Leonardo placed a foot firmly on his chest and toppled him. As his face finally emerged, he was greeted by a rapier point an inch from the end of his nose. Sinister and dusky drops slid down the blade and fell, one by one.

"Go, Francesco," said Leonardo genially. "The streets of Rome are dangerous enough at night, in all conscience, and even a serving maid's bastard may prove fatal if provoked too far. Look about you, and think twice before you annoy me again. Good night."

Twelve

"Sir," said the Medici's surgeon, bending over the newly cleaned wound and examining it closely, "it will mend of itself, but things will go better and more swiftly if I sew the margins together."

"Then do so, by all means," said Leonardo. "But stand aside and allow the lady Bianca to see what we are about, if you please."

"My lady has no right to be here," said the surgeon, a stolid and competent man who was not in the habit of deferring to rank. "Madam, will you not return to your room?"

"Certainly not," said Bianca.

"There you are," said Leonardo. "Few of us have the opportunity to see what lies beneath the skin, except on the field of battle. Allow her to observe and learn, I pray you."

The surgeon, raising his eyes toward heaven, stood away. Leonardo, who was at present seated on a divan in his room at the Medici Palace, offered his arm to Bianca's gaze.

"It is deep," she said. "And what are those things that look like the ends of severed cords, buried in the flesh?"

"Vessels," Leonardo said. "They carry the blood. Observe

that they have sealed themselves—as part of the healing process."

"It must have hurt terribly."

"I was in no position to notice at the time," said Leonardo, "which is fortunately often the case. Have you seen enough?"

"Thank you, yes."

"And do you not feel faint?"

"No," said Bianca. "Should I?"

"Many people do. I confess that I have not yet discovered the reason for it. Sir, I apologize for delaying you. Please proceed with your stitching."

"I usually advise my patients to drink wine," the surgeon said. "Can I not persuade you to take a little?"

"No, I thank you. I have an admirable faith in your delicacy of touch, and the lady Bianca will distract me, I have no doubt." The surgeon rummaged in his bag for instruments. Leonardo turned toward Bianca. "How are your lessons?"

"Bad. It is exactly as you warned me," she said. "All my tutors bore me, and especially Brother Sigismondo. You cannot argue with them, for as soon as it looks as though you have the right of it, they become angry and take refuge in books and easy phrases. I detest them."

Leonardo laughed, gritting his teeth an instant later as the surgeon worked on his arm. "Did I not tell you to be polite to them?" he went on. "This is always the way of the foolishly learned. They cannot help themselves. I found something of the same attitude in Rome. And yet, not entirely. I may have discovered one wise man, for which it is worth traveling five hundred miles or a thousand, as you will also find out." He grunted involuntarily.

"I think you should drink some wine," said Bianca, looking at him. "If you imagine that you are impressing me with this show of determination, you are quite wrong."

"Unkindly spoken," said Leonardo, "and far from just. Tell me, have you noticed any change in our friend Giuliano of late?"

"If you mean that he now walks and rides without looking where he is going," said Bianca, "of course, I have. The explanation is simple, I assure you. He is madly in love with Constanza, and she is behaving in exactly the same manner. I think it very charming, though I am bound to say it makes them both a little dull. Constanza passed three paces away from me this morning and did not notice I was there. Poor things. I am afraid they are both due for a sad disappointment, though I would not dream of telling them so."

"Indeed?"

"Yes. Lorenzo will never let them marry."

"Will he not? May I ask, with the greatest respect, how you come to know so much?"

"By listening," replied Bianca tartly. "I have become a very good listener since meeting you. Lorenzo, I gather, wants Constanza to marry someone else. I consider it despicable, but there is nothing to be done about it. At least . . ."

"Go on."

"Nothing. I do not really see how anything can be done."

Bianca fell silent and remained so until the surgeon, having set two layers of stitches in Leonardo's arm, had sponged the last trace of blood from the skin and bound the wound. He bowed to Leonardo's thanks, and left the room. Leonardo prodded the bandage gingerly, and shifted the arm to test its mobility.

"A skilled craftsman," he said. "And now . . . let me see. I think we should not despair so easily, Bianca. You were going to make a suggestion concerning the plight of Giuliano and Constanza, were you not?"

"I *have* an idea," Bianca admitted, "but I don't think I shall tell you what it is."

"Come now," Leonardo said. "In matters of high policy such as this, discussion is always valuable; two minds are better than one. Perhaps not always, now that I come to think about it; but in this case . . ."

Bianca smiled. "Very well," she said. "I will tell you what I think."

Summoned by Lorenzo's page, Giuliano and Constanza found the ruler of Florence waiting at the door to the library, one arm outstretched, bidding them to enter. Giuliano thought him suspiciously affable.

"Good morning, my lady. Good morning, brother. I thank you both for attending me." Lorenzo's voice was silken and gracious, and Giuliano raised an admonitory finger at the sound of it.

"Listen, Constanza," he said. "My brother is using his policy voice this morning, which means that he wants something of us."

"Let us wait and see, Giuliano," she said. She led the way into the quiet room and took her seat at the table. "I will confess, Magnifico," she continued, "that I have been hoping for some time that you might wish to speak with us both. Do I guess aright, sir? Are we meeting to discuss our wedding plans with you?"

"We are, indeed," said Lorenzo, "in a fashion."

Giuliano said nothing. He was looking attentively at Lorenzo's face and did not appear to like what he found there.

"Has it been decided, then," Constanza went on, "that we need no longer wait for two more years?"

"My lady," said Lorenzo, "you know that I take most seriously my pledge to your father to serve as your guardian and to protect your interests in all things. You will also know that, before he died, your father gave to me all those powers which a guardian must have in order to satisfy Florentine law and custom."

"I know all this, sir," said Constanza.

"Nonetheless, while thinking of you, my lady, my duty is also to think of Florence."

Constanza looked toward Giuliano with misgiving, but he remained silent.

"It grieved me deeply, as it grieved us all," Lorenzo went on, "when your sister Carla was taken by the Pope's bastard general and slain so foully. I know you understand this. I have now to remind you that your sister's hand was pledged to the eldest son of the Duke of Ferrara. Shortly after Christmas, I received a letter from the Duke, who now requests your hand in Carla's stead. I called you here this morning to inform you of this fact."

Constanza's hands gripped the arms of her chair, though when she spoke her voice was low and controlled.

"I see."

"I will not conceal from you that your marriage to the young Count will bring certain . . . advantages to the republic. But it is also in your own best interests, since you will thereby eventually become Duchess of Ferrara. Weighing all this up, therefore, I have dispatched my courier to the Duke approving your alliance with his house in principle, though much remains to be discussed. I am not sure that this will be to your liking now, my lady, or to yours, brother. But you will see the wisdom in it as time passes. That is all."

Lorenzo rose, as though to signify that their meeting was at an end, and Giuliano rose with him. From her seat, Constanza looked up at both of them, her eyes brimming with tears.

"What kind of men are the Medici?" she breathed. "Have I no word in this? Am I a piece of merchandise to be offered first to this one, then taken away when that one offers more? Under your protection, my lords, my sister Carla is dead. Never mind! Here sits another d'Avalos sister. She is all but betrothed to a Medici, but never mind that either! The Medici will give her up, so long as it benefits the Republic of the Medici!" She rose then, and ran to the door. "You deal with my body too freely, my lords," she said, "and it makes me feel a whore. Pray excuse me." She whirled, and was gone.

Lorenzo walked to the door and closed it quietly.

"The lady Constanza speaks her mind," he said. "Not that I expected otherwise."

Giuliano nodded.

"You, in contrast," Lorenzo continued, "have had very little to say so far."

"True."

"Am I to hear no argument from you, then?"

"Would my arguments persuade you?" Giuliano asked.

"Probably not. But I had thought to hear a question or two."

"I have none to which I do not already know the answers," Giuliano said with asperity. "I know them because I know you. Ferrara wants the d'Avalos dowry rather than Constanza. Is it one hundred thousand florins? I forget. Possibly, now that Carla is dead, her marriage portion is added to Constanza's? It's a nice point." Sudden rage flooded his face. "And what will these florins buy you, Lorenzo? Ferrara himself, it goes without saying. Your own men in Ferrara's guilds, banks, and courts? One imagines so. Trade concessions, I have no doubt. Control of his army?"

"Very necessary," agreed Lorenzo calmly. "Did I not say that I must think for Florence? Within a few years, Florence will be fighting for her very life, Giuliano. You know this, and I cannot stand idly by even if I wished to do so. I need allies. With Naples, Milan and Genoa, I can deal in other ways. With Venice, I may not be able to deal at all. To obtain Ferrara I must also bargain, and it happens that what I have to offer him is Constanza d'Avalos—or rather, as you justly observe, her dowry. Come, Giuliano. You are no child. Are you angered?"

Giuliano was silent for a while.

"Have I said so?" he asked finally.

"You have not. But as you know me, so do I know you. It is unlike you to fence with me, for one thing."

"And if I were angered—and I do not admit it—what reason would I have, do you think?"

Lorenzo studied him. "It has crossed my mind, brother, since I am not entirely blind, that you have grown to care for this young woman since her sister's death, and think to keep her. I am not considering marriage contracts, but your feelings."

"Very observant of you," said Giuliano shortly. He got up again and headed for the library door. "However," he said, "I would remind you that I have not yet opposed the interest of Florence, or yourself. Good day, Lorenzo."

He found Constanza in the middle garden, wearing her great cape of blue velvet. As he approached, she turned her head from him, and he put his hand on her arm.

"Well?" she demanded. "Why did you say nothing?"

"I had nothing to say. I know my brother better than you do, Constanza. How many days and nights of planning has it taken him to untie the strands of our marriage compact? Had he consulted me earlier perhaps, I might have deflected him from his purpose, but I have seldom known Lorenzo to consult any man. This being true, what hope was there of altering the case with a few well-chosen words?"

"But . . . to make no protest at all, Giuliano?"

"Protest? He had already answered Ferrara. Only the weak protest after the fact. I am not weak, and neither are you."

"Ferrara!" She spat the name out, like a curse. "I will never marry that fat little princeling, I promise you!"

"Nor will I let you, my heart. Have we come so far together to be overset by a duke's policy? But it is not angry words we need now. We need the means to convince my brother, or to defy him, and neither will be easy. It will, I think, take time—as he has taken time." He held her arm, gently yet insistently, and she turned toward him.

"You have the Medici blood and mind, Giuliano," she said. "Tell me what we must do, and I will do it. I trust you, since I have learned to do so. And it is too late for me to unlearn."

Her voice was firm and full, and Giuliano's throat tightened as he looked at her. A delight to the eye, he thought. Black hair, smooth and shining, and roped now with tiny seed pearls; her skin olive-dark and soft, and those dark eyes, long-lashed. A generous face, animated and strong-willed. He knew he must go forward, but suddenly could not find the words to do so.

"It is bitter cold this morning," he said. "Do you not find it so? And sunlight is never as sweet for kissing as the moon; yet, let us kiss now, Constanza."

"And why not? I know of no better way to say that we love each other. I am sorry I spoke angrily to you, Giuliano. I wish it were moonlight now," she said. "And that we were alone together in some warm and secret place."

He drew his head back and smiled at her.

"A bed, perhaps?" he said.

"It might serve," she replied, looking at him steadily.

Despite himself, he was taken aback. He let her go. A suspicion, insistently merry, was beginning to form in his mind. He drew her to a stone bench and sat down beside her.

"I . . ." he began.

"Yes, my lord?"

"Well. To put it bluntly, my dearest heart . . ."

"Yes? I had not thought to find you tongue-tied, Giuliano, at such a moment," she said gravely. "Indeed, quite otherwise, or so I have been told."

"I have been speaking with Leonardo," he said.

"Have you, indeed?"

"His suggestion, you see . . ."

"Ah. More good advice from Leonardo. Well?"

"This is not exactly as I pictured things," said Giuliano with a touch of desperation. "It is true that I used to have some skill in affairs such as this—which seems to have deserted me now. But then," he added hastily, "I was never in love before this, as I am with you. As you know. And—"

"Giuliano," said Constanza, "If I wait to hear much more of this, I am very likely to freeze to death. If you cannot find the correct words for the occasion, let me help you. If we have a child, Lorenzo will be thwarted. You see? It is hardly complicated at all."

"I see that you also, Constanza, have been talking with Leonardo," said Giuliano.

"With Leonardo? Certainly not. That would be most improper of me," said Constanza indignantly, then laughed. "Oh, if you could only see how you look, Giuliano! Tell me, have I given way too easily, do you suppose? I should not like you to think my virtue too swiftly won, but it cannot be helped. Naturally," she added in a meditative tone, "I understand that one cannot always hope to succeed in such things at the first attempt, or even at the twentieth. Or am I wrong about that?"

"To whom have you been talking?" demanded Giuliano, his face crimson.

"Oh. To Bianca Visconti, of course. We discuss everything together. Did you not know?"

"The little vixen. I see. Since I am, then, outnumbered three to one—"

"Outnumbered? That is hardly gallant of you!"

"Supported, then. What you will." He held her lovingly, laughing with her. "Just the same," he said, "Lorenzo will be far from happy."

"Let him be unhappy, then. If he can play at politics, so can we. And I may say," Constanza finished, "that I had never until this moment imagined politics could be so joyfully played."

Thirteen

"And how did your researches go?" Lorenzo asked.

"Very well," replied Leonardo.

"You discovered what you were searching for?"

"Hardly. At least, not in Rome. But the ride there and back cleared my head."

"I must attempt the exercise myself sometime," said Lorenzo drily. He pinched the bridge of his nose. "Well?" he asked. "What now? Their wall is in better condition than it was last fall, so Giuliano tells me. How are we to proceed?"

"From theory to practice, as always, sir. I need the use of your archery range again. May I have it?"

"You may. Though I had hoped you might have finished your games there by now."

"By no means. I have a great deal of work to do and little time," said Leonardo. "And I have yet another request."

"Make it."

"You have a pair of small cannon on the roof of your eastern wing. May I borrow them?"

Lorenzo shifted impatiently in his chair. "For what purpose?" he asked. "They are toys to be fired upon occasions of rejoicing or proclamation, that is all. I do not see what use they can be to you."

"I am aware of their present function," said Leonardo. "However, I have examined them carefully. They were given to your father by no less a person than the great Milanese gunmaker Bertolo Bracci, and bear his name engraved upon them. Toys they may be, sir, but Ser Bertolo was the most renowned man of his time in his craft—and they are excellently made. Their bores are accurate to within a hairsbreadth, and are precisely what I need; it is no matter to me that their carriages are silver-chased and their barrels somewhat over ornate for my taste."

"Very well. Have your toys. I take it that you intend to perform more of your experiments with them?"

"I do. I need to know, for instance, a great deal more about gunpowder than I do already—a subject about which I found little in Rome to enlighten me and must, therefore, examine upon my own account. There are other matters, too. I will not hide from you that I am on the point of forming a new concept in my mind of great interest and far-reaching consequences."

"Large words," said Lorenzo de' Medici discontentedly. "I do not mock you, but *my* interest lies in Castelmonte and in Castelmonte alone. I trust you will remember that during the course of your experiments. And now tell me how you came to be wounded."

"It was a private matter, I believe," Leonardo replied. "A scrape with some friends of the Prince of Savoy, who seems—for reasons I know not—to have taken something of a dislike to me." He recounted the incident, Lorenzo de' Medici listening attentively while he did so.

"Perhaps you are right," Lorenzo said when he had finished. "And then again, perhaps there is more in it than you suppose."

"I hope not."

"Such is my hope too. At all events, I thank you for telling me the details of the affair. Even small and seemingly unimportant scraps of information are valuable to those who have to govern. We have little common ground between us, Master Leonardo, and yet, sometimes I think that in this we resemble one another. You are a man who attends to what others consider trivial, extracting kernels of knowledge from the shells of circumstance, and so do I, though for quite other purposes. Perhaps we are not as unlike each other as one might suppose."

"Perhaps," said Leonardo.

"Well, then. Use my archery range as you see fit. Borrow my toy signal cannon, if you wish. Try to avoid killing any of my courtiers with your experiments, though it is possible that I might be persuaded to turn a blind eye should some unfortunate mishap occur to the Prince of Savoy. But above all, remember that your experiments are of no consequence beside the fall of Castelmonte. The achievement of this end alone is the whole of your duty toward me. You understand this?"

"I am of one mind with you," Leonardo replied. "There is one more vital thing. I need the advice and assistance of Captain-Gunner Roderigo Leone."

"My Captain-Gunner? He is at work on his guns."

"I urge you to summon him."

"Then you had better know what you are about," said Lorenzo bleakly. "Should spring come, and I find my cannon in no fit condition for their appointed task because you have diverted Captain Leone from his duties upon some fruitless quest, then I warn you that your case will be hard indeed. You may go, Master Leonardo."

Arriving in Florence, Rigo Leone paid his respects to the Medici chamberlain and proceeded at once to the archery range. The snow had melted from the lawn, and he found Leonardo squatting by a contrivance somewhat similar to the framework he had been using to study the flight of arrows, except that this version was stronger and more compact, its angles bound with strips of brass.

He stood in the archway and took in the scene. The belvedere was now stacked with powder kegs, and the former target had been replaced by a wooden box, open-fronted and filled with coarse bags of sand. The artist himself was at present adjusting the barrel of a small decorative cannon, clamped, in turn, to the framework, with its muzzle pointing toward the distant butt. A burning slow match was clipped beside the gun's breech. Oblivious to Rigo's presence, Leonardo reached for this and stood upright, examining the lay of the cannon critically, the smoking match poised above it.

Alarmed by this display of amateur gunnery, Rigo shouted and strode forward.

"And what the devil do you imagine you are about?" he demanded on reaching the artist.

"Rigo! A welcome sight indeed!" Leonardo said. He transferred the slow match to his right hand which he was still using with caution, and held out his left to the gunner. "This confounded arm has had me fumbling for two days now. I am delighted to see you, my friend."

"‘"The fiend take your pleasantries," said Rigo, taking Leonardo's hand. "What are you doing with this damned peashooter, I should like to know?"

"Discovering its accuracy of aim, naturally, as I did with my mechanical crossbow last year. It is a superb piece of work, I find. Though since its maker was Bertolo Bracci, I am unsurprised. Watch."

"Watch? I do not care if it was made by Vulcan and St. Michael," said Rigo. "It is an unproven gun, and only a fool, or a scholar, would fire it."

"Not so," said Leonardo. "Bracci's proof marks are inscribed alongside the pan. See for yourself."

"And keep that pox-ridden match away," persisted Rigo, unheeding. "I have no wish to lose my head, even if you have." He examined the breech, sweeping away traces of loose powder with his fingertip. "Very well," he admitted grudgingly. "It is marked, which means very little. How many times have you discharged it?"

"Three. A beautiful weapon. Stand away, and observe."

Before Rigo could offer further argument, Leonardo applied the match to the powder atop the breech. Rigo backed away. The touchhole having little depth, there was a bare instant between the first fire spurt and the clanging detonation which followed. The framework rocked and a cloud of acrid smoke burst around the gun. When it cleared, both men could see that the barrel had split open for a full handspan along its length. The whining ball had chipped the top of the range wall.

"Most marvelous!" Rigo bellowed. "Marvelous indeed. Where are you hurt?"

"Nowhere, thank you," said Leonardo.

"A great pity. A wedge of bronze, properly lodged in your skull, might have served to let out some of your science and permitted a little common sense in. So much for your proof marks. Show me your powder."

"It is by your foot."

Rigo kicked at the small keg, rolling it with his toe until the letters burned into its side were uppermost. "Mining power!"

"I know that."

"Then why use it in a gun? Have I not already explained to you that powders differ? This kind explodes sharply, and is good only for rending rock."

"It was only a trial," Leonardo answered. "Though with unfortunate results, perhaps. I knew both from what you told me and from what I have read that powders differ in strength. Accordingly, their effect on the shot must differ also, but I confess that until now I had not realized some were strong enough to split a gun barrel."

"I can see that you need me here after all, or your learning is likely to cost you your life. Except, of course, that you now have no gun to play with."

"Not so," said Leonardo. "I have the second of the pair in the belvedere. Be kind enough to bring it here."

Rigo came back carrying the little cannon in one hand. It was no longer than his arm. "Let us put an end to this foolishness," he said confidently. "I see that you wish to study the principles of gunnery, a notion which has its merits. Now in Pontassieve there is an excellent cannon for your purpose, cast by Ghiberti. In length about four ells—"

"No," said Leonardo.

"And why not? What can you learn from this plaything here? The Ghiberti is quite a tolerable weapon and will throw a ball for two thousand paces and better as prettily as you please. I have been thinking of hauling it over to supplement my own two guns in the spring—"

"No," Leonardo repeated. "Save yourself the trouble. We shall not be using your guns in the spring."

The Captain-Gunner laid down the toy he was holding on top of the overturned framework between them.

"I cannot have heard you correctly," he said. "Again, if you will."

"You heard me well enough. Listen. Your guns are inadequate to the task in hand. Let me list their deficiencies for you. Firstly, they are heavy."

"They have need to be."

"Doubtless. But because they are heavy, they lack flexibility. You cannot move them."

"They are not supposed to be moved. How would I bring them to their point of aim, were I to shift them every hour?"

"Precisely. Also, being heavy, they sink in mire—a fact of which you are sufficiently aware, I imagine. Secondly, they are large, and cannot be hidden."

"And why in the devil's name should I wish to hide them?" Rigo demanded. "Will my enemy fly away with them in the middle of the night? Your arguments are ridiculous."

Leonardo tapped him on the breast. "Open your mind," he said. "We are not done with the tale yet. Three, they are costly; four, inaccurate—"

"They are not."

"Damnably inaccurate," continued Leonardo calmly. "Finally and in sum, they are ineffective. You have not yet knocked down Castelmonte's wall with them, nor will you in the spring. Come now, Rigo. Loving them as I know full well you do, will you yet refuse to acknowledge the truth in all this?"

"There may be some particle of truth there," Rigo said. "But these disadvantages you mention are but the normal facts of an artilleryman's life."

"Not all the facts," said Leonardo. "Not all of them."

In the library, five days later, Leonardo sat beside Lorenzo de' Medici and listed his requirements. Nodding to his clerk at each item, the ruler of Florence listened with impatience.

"Six cannon," Leonardo said. "I have the specifications here."

"Give them to Master Arnolfo when we are done," Lorenzo said. "They are details."

"Two hundred rounds of shot, cast and polished."

"Very well."

"Forty kegs of powder from the factory of Nencio Migliorini, the making of it to be supervised by myself."

"Ser Nencio is not likely to take kindly to your supervision, but proceed."

"Sundry other small items in metal of a mechanical nature, to be made here in the city at a probable cost of two hundred florins. Here is the list."

"Give it to Master Arnolfo. What else?"

"The hardest of all, sir. I need fifty men of Captain Leone's choosing, beginning not later than the first day of March and for two months thereafter."

Lorenzo knitted his brow. "Gunners?"

"The best of your gunners."

"When I must take Castelmonte as soon as the ground is firm enough to hold their siege cannon?"

"I know the gravity of my request," Leonardo said. "But I must have them. There are one hundred and ten men in Pistrola at this moment, many of them skilled."

"As craftsmen. Not gunners."

"Some of those we shall leave there will be gunners, though we shall take the cream," Leonardo said. "I cannot accept any man for my purpose who is not in the front rank of his profession. The less skilled will serve to move your siege guns from Pistrola to their firing position when the time comes to do so."

Lorenzo exhaled softly. "Upon your head be it, then," he said. "I will not hinder you. My task is to select men, not to obstruct them when selected; and I judge them—as I have told you—by the results they produce for me. You know the scale in which I intend to weigh your performance, Master Leonardo. You may have your fifty men, though the giving of them bleeds my artillery force dry."

Fourteen

"From Leonardo da Vinci, artist, to the Most Eminent Cardinal Domenico della Palla, Apostolic Chancellor at Rome: Greetings." The Cardinal glanced up from the letter at Rodrigo Cardinal Borgia, and cleared his throat. Then he continued:

> My Lord, Ever mindful of your kindness toward me at our last meeting, and of my undertaking to communicate to Your Eminence such results as I might achieve in my study of the composition and effects of Gunpowder; and mindful also that it ill becomes me, having spoken of the folly of the Holy Church Our Mother in placing reliance upon the work of one Brother Sfabalmaccio di Pisa concerning these matters, to delay in making good my promise to you at that time; I here submit to the regard of Your Eminence those conclusions which I have thus far been able to reach:
>
> i: the effect of powder varies notably as the proportions of its three components, viz: Sulphur, Charcoal and Saltpeter.

ii: that powder burns the most vehemently which consists of, 1 part of sublimed sulphur, 2 parts of willow charcoal, and 6 parts of redissolved saltpeter, and this powder is too powerful for use in cannon or bombards by reason of the rapidity of its conflagration.

iii: the less in proportion of saltpeter . . . .

"Enough," said Rodrigo Cardinal Borgia. "Impudently heretical. My dear Chancellor, if this is all your case, then I am bound to say that I favor the leaving of this young man to the tender mercies of Girolamo Riario."

"He is somewhat careless in both his speech and his writing," conceded Cardinal della Palla, placing the letter on the desk. "But I do not yet perceive heresy here. Has he not communicated these matters to us, thereby proving himself a good son of the Church?"

"I do not object to his information, but to his attitude and style of thought," said Cardinal Borgia. "Let me restate the case. I have here—" he lifted a piece of paper, "—a letter from an informant of Riario's in Florence. He confirms that Leonardo da Vinci is military engineer to Lorenzo de' Medici, a fact of which we were already aware; but he goes on to claim that da Vinci is now engaged in activities which are highly dangerous to Rome's cause. I admit that these activities, whatever they may be, are not described, since the writer clearly does not understand them. However, if we accept his view, then Riario is certainly correct in pressing for the . . . elimination of da Vinci. Since I knew you to have an interest in the young man, I thought it only proper to consult you."

"A kindly thought," murmured della Palla.

"In his defense, you have produced for me a letter from da Vinci himself, which you believe proves his possible future value to us. This I allow. Yet this same letter shows a disrespect for established authority which, if encouraged, will lead him one day to the stake; and your contention that he shows his good will toward the Church in no wise diminishes his present threat to Rome. My conclusion is that we may as well allow Riario to have his way, thereby saving the Church the trouble and expense of burning him in a few years' time. You see?"

"He may yet be saved from heresy," said Cardinal della Palla.

"By yourself?"

"Or by Almighty God."

"Upon which chance you propose to visit Florence and persuade him to see the light of reason?"

"If you have no objection."

"My dear Chancellor, I have not said that I object. All I have pointed out is that your letter from him makes no real case in his favor."

"And I suppose that it would be foolish of me to suggest that Your Eminence has little moral right to dispose of a human life in such a cavalier fashion?"

"Purely for the sake of argument," said Borgia with a faint smile, "may I remind you that I intend to do nothing whatever about him. The question lies in whether or not one should restrain Girolamo Riario from taking matters into his own hands."

"It was merely an idle thought," said della Palla. "The more idle since it seems that the Count has already attempted to murder him."

"Ah. There, your ground is stronger."

"I thought it might be."

"Although two dead men found in a gutter on the night of Master Leonardo's departure from Rome hardly constitutes proof of such an attempt."

"I am not seeking proof," said Cardinal della Palla blandly. "I presume that your knowledge of the matter is adequate."

Cardinal Borgia looked out of the window of his apartment at the wheeling pigeons.

"A most extraordinary occurrence," he said. "Here we have an artist, untrained—or so we may assume—in such affairs as swordsmanship, and he kills two highly skilled assailants and routs a third, singlehanded? I do not, I think, believe it."

"By which you mean that you do not believe it happened?"

"I know that it happened, though the man who remained alive has left Rome without telling his story. I am forced to conclude that Master Leonardo was helped. And yet, so far as you know, he came to Rome alone?"

"Quite alone."

"Therefore," said Cardinal Borgia, "we have Medici agents in our city upon whom he called for aid."

"Possibly. Probably, in fact."

"I meant, of course, agents of whom I am unaware. I would not have left such an incident without investigation, and have thus accounted for known Medici supporters. Well. The idea irritates me, and therefore, I would take it as a favor, my dear Chancellor, were you indeed to follow your own inclination and have a few words with Leonardo da Vinci. By whom was he assisted? And what, exactly, is he doing that makes Count Girolamo's agent so nervous? Your visit might prove well worthwhile."

"I will do what I can," said Cardinal della Palla.

"Excellent. I am delighted to find that, once again, we understand each other. Meanwhile, I shall endeavor to keep Girolamo Riario leashed."

Cardinal della Palla set out for Florence on a warm, rainy morning accompanied by a small entourage: his chaplain-confessor, his secretary, and eight men-at-arms.

Arriving at his destination in mid-February, he was received with distant courtesy, a circumstance which troubled the Cardinal but little, since he hardly expected to be *persona grata* in the republic. Indeed, his ostensible purpose being the fruitless one of attempting to persuade Florence to accept the installation of Archbishop Francesco Salviati in the See of Pisa—an errand which had been pursued with total lack of success by previous papal emissaries—he was somewhat surprised to find the citizens of Florence confining themselves to hostile glances whenever he passed through its streets.

He spent very little time with Lorenzo de' Medici in attempted persuasion, passing on from the topic of Archbishop Salviati's grievances with a haste which, while not unseemly, caused Lorenzo to wonder whether Rome had not abandoned hope in the matter. He spent rather more time, though inconspicuously, in the archery range. Leonardo and Rigo had now left this and were continuing their researches in the meadow beyond the brook. The Cardinal watched them from the archway in the rear wall of the palazzo grounds and pondered. He thought more deeply, and with a certain reserve, upon the frequent presence with them of Bianca Maria Visconti and upon her habit of linking arms with Leonardo at day's end.

As ecclesiastical custom and duty demanded, one of the first persons that the Cardinal visited in his rooms was Brother Sigismondo Carregi. He found the latter, after a few minutes' encouragement, so inflamed and vituperative concerning Leonardo da Vinci's freethinking habits and the manner in which—so Brother Sigismondo contended—he was engaged upon the spiritual corruption of Bianca Visconti, that the Cardinal invited him to unburden himself freely.

"It has, Your Eminence, become impossible to teach her," Brother Sigismondo complained bitterly.

"This is regrettable indeed. And are you sure that it is the influence of Master Leonardo upon her which is the true cause?"

"Beyond doubt, Your Eminence. She defies all authority, in the pretense that he has taught her to think for herself."

"And does she?"

"I beg your pardon, my lord?"

"I said, does she think for herself?" asked the Cardinal mildly.

"How would that be possible? She is a child."

"I see. How old is she?"

"Fourteen years of age, Your Eminence."

"And has Master Leonardo, then, a powerful intellect?"

"By no means," said Brother Sigismondo. "His philosophy is negligible, as Your Eminence may confirm by speaking with Dr. Cino di Lapo Mazzone, my colleague. He postures and plays, seeking thereby to impress those around him. Mentally, he is a butterfly."

"Most regrettable," said Cardinal della Palla. "Brother Sigismondo, I wonder if you would oblige me by writing down the substance of your complaints against Leonardo da Vinci, so that I may better consider them upon my return to Rome?"

"With the greatest pleasure, Your Eminence."

The Cardinal blessed him, and left Brother Sigismondo a gratified man.

The afternoon of Sunday, February 22nd, he sought out Leonardo da Vinci, finding him in a spaciously untidy attic beneath the roof beams of the eastern wing of the palazzo. The room was bare, well-lit and dusty, being littered with small lengths of timber, stained chairs, many-hued rags and pottery jars filled with oils and turpentine. On an easel rested a half-finished painting of a Madonna holding a striped cat. Leonardo himself stood framed in a window against a pewter sky, brush in hand.

"My Lord Cardinal," he said as della Palla entered, alone. "This is a visitation which does my heart good! I have seen you from time to time as I labored, but I hardly dared to hope that you would find time to speak with me."

"It was to speak with you that I journeyed here from Rome," said the Cardinal. "May I sit down?"

"By all means, if I can find you something that will not soil your robes."

"My robes are nothing. This will serve." So saying, Cardinal della Palla seated himself on the nearest chair, nodding toward the easel. "An interesting picture," he said.

"It is but a quarter done. Less. And uncommissioned," Leonardo said. "Today being Sunday, it would be inappropriate of me to continue my studies of warlike instruments, and I am thus able to please myself."

"A very proper spirit. Will you not also be seated, my son? There are things I must discuss with you."

"Of course." Leonardo sat down on a packing case, and crossed his legs. "What is it that you wish to speak of, my lord?"

"I came here," said the Cardinal surprisingly, "to ask you if there were anything you needed to confess."

Leonardo smiled. "My lord," he said, "I am a poor churchgoer, and it is a long while since I felt the need for confession."

"Indeed?"

"Moreover, my sins are of a peculiar nature, and not to be found in any calendar. Being a sinner, as all men are, I therefore take my sins to God, since He will not misunderstand them."

"The sin of pride is easily understood and is in all calendars," said Cardinal della Palla with some asperity. "Do not speak so glibly."

"My lord, I am frequently guilty of pride, I admit," Leonardo said. "But to look at the stars is to cure all pride. When I most lack humility, God seizes me by the neck and directs my gaze heavenward, thereby both correcting and absolving me."

"I see. You are stubborn, my son. What, then, of murder?"

"Murder?"

"Did you not kill two men, as you left Rome?"

"They would have killed me first, Your Eminence. I have asked God's forgiveness for it, but it was no murder."

"Then you did kill them?"

"I did."

"And you were wounded by them?"

"It is better now."

"I was not expressing sympathy. Were you wounded before killing both of them?"

"Yes. I am afraid that they had not been told that I fight equally well with either hand."

"So much for murder, then," said della Palla. He swiveled on the seat of his chair, robes in hand. "This painting," he went on.

"Yes?"

"A Madonna?"

"Yes, my lord."

"But with no Holy Infant."

"I intend later to paint the Infant in place of the cat. False starts are a part of . . . I do not know how to put this, my lord. It is hard to explain. The cat arrived there by accident."

A curious half-smile lit the Cardinal's face for an instant, though when he spoke his voice was as severe as before.

"It will not, in any case, serve for a Madonna," he said. "I advise you to leave the cat where it is, since—if my perception is not at fault—we have here another of your uncalendared sins."

"And what sin is that?"

"Carnality. No man, seeing this painting, is likely to be led by it into a state of grace. Far otherwise, I would say. The appearance of your model, if I may be blunt, is sexually suggestive to the point of concupiscence. Who is she, by the way?"

"No model sat for me, Your Eminence."

"You are fencing with me again. The face is that of the lady Bianca Visconti. Well?"

"It may be."

"It is. Must I wring confession from you as one wrings a cloth? Are your feelings toward this child carnal, my son?"

"If they are," said Leonardo carefully, "is that a sin? I doubt it. Were I to indulge in the passions of the flesh with her, the case might be different. My thoughts, however, are between myself and God, since they harm no one."

The Cardinal swung toward him once more.

"It seems," he said, "that there is a great deal which lies between yourself and God, Master Leonardo."

"That, too, is possible."

"To the exclusion of the Church. God's bride and mediator, if I may remind you of the fact."

"The fact? This is not a fact, as I understand facts," said Leonardo.

"Your contempt for the Church knows no bounds."

Leonardo rose and took a step toward the Cardinal in momentary passion.

"You are wrong, my lord," he said hotly. "Quite wrong, and I marvel that you have not seen it yet. My chief concern is for the Church, however foolish, ambitious and venal she may appear to me. Why should I labor to correct her, if not from love? If the Church is indeed prepared to accept her own imprimatur as the sole guarantee of truth, why should I care, unless from love?"

"We are back to Brother Sfabalmaccio again, I see," the Cardinal said.

"And shall return again. I have a vision, my lord, which troubles me from time to time. It is a vision of the future, of a day which neither you nor I will see, but which will come nonetheless. In it, I see a Pope in Rome, claiming before all his children that if God had meant men to fly, he would have given us wings; and therefore, that flight is impossible to us. And all the while he stands and claims this to be so, I see an impudent and heretical man, with wings, in the sky above his head, proving him to be speaking nonsense. On that day, my lord Cardinal, the world will see the Church for the foolish creature I now perceive her to be. I will not let it happen, if I have to shake her, as a terrier shakes a rat, and force her to recognize truth when it lies before her."

"Sit down," the Cardinal said gently. "My son, you have —or so I believe—some regard for me."

"I have."

"Then attend to me in the light of that regard. What happens to those who presume to drag the Church toward a truth of their own?"

"They are burned," said Leonardo promptly. "*Ecclesia non novit sanguinem;* the Church sheds no blood, being hypocritical, and, therefore, burns those who displease her. If you came here but to threaten me with fire—"

"I did not. I came to ask you to come with me to Rome," said Cardinal della Palla. "Your talents will be appreciated there. You may win fame and position; and more than all this, your passion for what you call facts can be guided, thus keeping your body from the flames and your soul from perdition."

Leonardo laughed. "What is the difference between being burned by the Church and being burned on the battlefield?" he asked. "It is the same death to which we all come but once."

"It is a death which can be better avoided in Rome."

"If you mean, my lord, that Rome will be at war with Florence in the spring, and that Rome is the safer choice of sides," said Leonardo, "then I thank Your Eminence, but must disagree. Florence, to mention but one thing, has myself."

"You rate yourself highly."

"As do all thinking men."

"I warn you again. You are walking a knife's edge."

"Then so be it," replied Leonardo. "All paths are dangerous in this world. If I displease Lorenzo de' Medici, he may have me killed tomorrow. Rome may have me killed next year. A score of days ago, I was almost dispatched by a bursting cannon. Therefore, I put my trust in God."

The Cardinal got up, sighing. "So be it," he echoed. "We are not yet friends, but neither are we enemies. I wish you well." Almost abruptly, he turned and left. As he passed out of the room and into the long corridor that ended at the narrow attic stairway, he was suddenly conscious of age, and did not know why.

Halfway to the stair head, he stopped. He remembered,

with an odd surprise, that he had been asked for no blessing, nor had he given one. His impulse was to keep walking. A man of such artistic nature and beliefs would not seek something which he must, in logic, regard either as a courtesy or else as a meaningless gesture. Yet della Palla knew that his duty was to bless, as always, to stand as a tree stands in the middle of a plain so that the lightning of God's grace might strike through him if it would, whether sought after or not and whether the speaker invested the words with meaning or with none.

He also owed the man in the room behind him a lesser duty. He had failed to warn Leonardo directly of the immediate danger by which he was surrounded, of sudden death at the hands of Count Girolamo Riario or of whatever human tool the latter might choose. That Leonardo had already escaped murder once did not alter the case. Rome might conveniently wish da Vinci dead, but it did not follow that Cardinal della Palla must acquiesce in that wish.

He turned and went quietly back to the attic. What he saw there stopped him on the threshold, amazed.

At the far end of the room Leonardo da Vinci, humming softly to himself, had returned to work upon his worldly Madonna. With his right hand he was oil-coloring what appeared to be a section of blue sky, seen through a corbeled arch. It would have been unremarkable except for the fact that with his left hand he was, at the same time, swiftly overblocking the outlines of the cat and transforming it into the figure of the Infant.

His eyes traveled easily between charcoal stick and brush, his head tilting slightly from moment to moment as he changed his viewpoint. The palette from which he selected his sky colors was clipped to the upper corner of the easel, and he would occasionally stop his drawing for an instant while he gave attention to the choice of a hue from it; but for the most part, both hands moved simultaneously, yet upon different tasks and in different directions, each stroke commencing near the picture's center and finishing toward its edge, to right or to left.

He stopped humming, and turned.

"My lord," he said to the advancing Cardinal. "I did not hear you return."

His mind in a whirl, the Cardinal questioned him.

"Do you always work thus?" he asked.

"Only in private, of late," replied Leonardo. "I have done so since childhood whenever I wished; but my master, Verrocchio, having described it as a mountebank's trick, and finding that it made my fellow apprentices uneasy, I desisted from it."

"But does it come naturally to you? To work thus, with both hands, together?"

"Yes. God gave me the ability when I was born, I suppose, though I do not know why." He put down his brush and took up his notebook, laying it upon the seat of a chair and squatting in front of it. Baring its topmost sheet, he wrote on it with his left hand, the letters of the script running from right to left and as though seen in a mirror. Changing hands quickly, he wrote a second line beneath the first, right handed. The script this time was normal. Picking up a second charcoal stick in his left hand, he wrote two lines simultaneously, each one running in opposite directions.

"But this is astounding," Cardinal della Palla said. "A miracle." He picked up the notebook and examined it closely. "And is there no difference, in ease or difficulty, between one hand and the other?"

"There is," Leonardo replied, "and it is another matter which I find hard to explain. I work best with my right hand when I do so carefully and with deliberation, upon tasks I have decided on before I commence them. When I am caught unawares by an idea—be it a swift glimpse of a picture or a half-formed principle in science—it is with the left hand that I set it down. Indeed, I do better with it when I do not attend to it too closely and allow it to move as it wills. Hence, when I use both hands together, as you must have seen me doing upon this painting just now, it is on the right that I concentrate my mind." He held his fingers out. "One might say that they are two different persons, these hands of mine," he said reflectively. "May I ask why you returned, my lord?"

Cardinal della Palla set down the notebook again.

"For a reason which I now think of smaller importance than I did some moments ago," he said. "I came back to warn you that the Count of Imola wishes you dead."

"Girolamo Riario," said Leonardo, still thoughtfully. "An unhappy man, and evil. He lives, I conjecture, in a coffin of his own making. The notion of his ill will costs me little sleep, Your Eminence, though I thank you for your warning."

"Even so," said the Cardinal. "Sleep in peace. For I see that God has blessed you with peculiar gifts and for some purpose of His own, and will therefore protect you."

Fifteen

Rigo Leone was patching the rectangular wooden target in the meadow with thin timber and bone glue. Discovering that his feet were freezing inside his boots, he swore. Leonardo, warming his hands at the brazier on which the glue boiler rested, looked up in time to intercept a glare which would have dropped a more sensitive man in his tracks.

"Suffer in silence," he advised, grinning. "I gave the same counsel to Matteo Barletta when he was undergoing privations in the cause of science."

"I wish him here now," Rigo said. "This playing of games was well enough inside the palace walls, where it was at least sheltered. Out here it is a different matter. Your bowman may have my job for the asking."

"He would not take it. He has but a low opinion of gunnery, and of gunners. Take heart, Captain-Gunner. Six more shots and we can retire for the evening."

"A total of some two hundred and fifty thus far," sighed Rigo. "And for what?" He removed his palm from the last wooden patch and brought the glue pot across to the fire. "I am beginning to think my mind is ill-suited to this science of yours, which is but mystery under another name."

"Remove the thought from your head. There is nothing mysterious in it. Science is the study of what is possible, and what is possible may be seen by all men. Now, what do you think of our toy cannon?"

"It is a very adequate little gun. Where does that get us?"

"It throws a little to the left, I fancy," said Leonardo.

"I agree. All guns have their peculiarities."

"And throws, perhaps, a trifle more to the left with one powder than with another?"

"As I told you it would. I trust we are agreed by now that powders differ."

Leonardo pointed at the target, patchworked with small plugs where the scattered shot holes in it had been repaired.

"And yet," he continued, "when one has settled on a particular powder and weight of ball, there is very little spread between the impact of one shot and the next."

"I have already admitted that it is a well made weapon," Rigo said. "I appreciate a true gun as well as any man, if not better. Allowing for its shorter range, it may even be the equal of my own two beauties in Pistrola."

"Good. Now tell me again how you would proceed with your siege cannon in the spring, were you to use them."

Rigo sighed. "Nothing I have seen here persuades me that I shall *not* be using them. Very well. I shall haul my guns over to that damned ridge, though I will choose a different position this time. I am not going to pound at a newly strengthened piece of wall, being no fool. I shall ask Agnolo how far we stand from whatever portion of the wall I select as target—"

"He is a good judge of distance?"

"The best. Better even than myself."

"Go on."

"Why, then the matter is straightforward. I aim my guns and fire some ten or twenty shots from each, adjusting them until both are delivering their shots in the same place. After that, I shall repeat last autumn's performance, though—God willing—with more success."

Leonardo stirred the glue idly with a piece of stick.

"But suppose," he said, "that you could predict, in advance of firing any shot at all, where your guns would strike? What then?"

"I would see no value in it," Rigo said, scratching his chin. "It would be interesting, I daresay. One does not want to spend hours in heaving cannon about to bring them to the correct point of aim. I do not see where this leads us, however. How many shots did I fire last year? Two thousand, and more. Five, ten or twenty shots spent in bringing my guns to bear are a small price to pay, with so much time at hand."

"And how if time were not available?"

"It always is. Time is what siege gunnery is all about. Time, and patience." Rigo glanced over Leonardo's shoulder, and nodded. "There stands your wench at the other side of the stream," he said.

Leonardo turned. Seeing Bianca Visconti, he raised a hand in salute. "And watch your tongue, gunner," he admonished.

"Surely," said Rigo. "No doubt, I am mistaken, and she comes here not for love of your company but merely to freeze while watching us fire shots at a board. Well, call her over."

"Not I," said Leonardo. "If she wishes to come, she will. I am not her master."

"She may stay away for all I care. Gunnery is no business for women, and she puts me in a terror lest I utter some mild and well-deserved curse in her presence," said Rigo.

It appeared, however, that the Lady Bianca had no intention of crossing the brook. Instead, she beckoned imperiously, walking along the far bank toward the footbridge. After some indecision, and with a frown at the look of amusement on Rigo's face, Leonardo went to meet her.

"And what brings you here, my lady?" he asked.

Bianca advanced one foot onto the planks of the bridge and

leaned against the rail. "Do not trouble to put on that stern look for me," she said, offering him a small bundle wrapped and tied in a silken kerchief. "I have brought you something to eat, that is all, and have no wish to distract you."

"Then I thank you and apologize for my lack of grace," Leonardo said. He took the kerchief from her. "Will you not come and share it with us?"

"No. Captain Leone will only glare at me as he always does. With the bribe of a pastry—you have two there—I hope to soften his heart somewhat, so the next time I come he may abate some of his ferocity. In any case, it is nearly sundown and very cold, so answer me. Yes, or no?"

Leonardo looked incredulous.

"Yes, or no?" she repeated, staring into his eyes and shivering a little.

"And how do you know that I love you, Bianca?"

"Oh, as to that," she replied calmly, "I have known for much longer than you, since I have no need to reason, or consider or conclude. Sometimes, I feel quite sorry for you, Leonardo. Answer me. Tonight?"

"Yes," said Leonardo.

Smiling, she laid a hand briefly on his arm, turned and was gone. Leonardo carried the kerchief back to the brazier, unwrapping it as he walked.

"Observe," he said. "There are rewards in teaching the young, particularly young ladies."

"Is that what you are doing? Teaching?" asked the Captain-Gunner. Then, as Leonardo started to withdraw his hand and its proffered burden, Rigo added hastily, "Not that I would ever dream of doubting you. As for my lady, may heaven forgive me if I have ever harbored an unkind thought toward her. A shrewd girl."

"And kind of heart," said Leonardo, glancing back at the retreating figure on the other side of the brook.

Bianca returned slowly along the path that led from the footbridge to the side gate of the palace, her fur-collared cape drawn closely about her neck. Following vespers, she was due to have a lesson in logic from Dr. Mazzone. It was one of her more unpleasant weekly trials, especially this evening, and she was happily conscious that by dawdling she might succeed in missing both service and lesson.

Dusk was closing in by the time she reached the shallow and broken steps that climbed from the water meadows to the gateway, winding between skeletal winter hedges and among stands of evergreen. At each turn in its familiar ascent, the rough stairway broadened into a circular bay, enclosing the base of a statue and surrounded by balustrades. As a friendless child, delivered into Medici care by her cousin-guardian Lodovico Sforza, she had learned her Latin not from the school books of her new tutors but from the inscriptions beneath these stone figures. Nondescript though most of them were, she had named them all, and now greeted them silently like old acquaintances and thought of the night to come. The anticipation was growing, warming her.

From behind a statute of Diocletian, the Prince of Savoy stepped into her path.

"An unseemly hour for strolling in damp fields, Bianca," he said. "I disapprove of this passion of yours for spying upon Master Leonardo da Vinci and his gunner colleague. You indulge it too frequently."

The note of peevish malice in his voice took her aback and she answered without thought.

"I spy on no one," she said.

"No? Perhaps not. In which case, you are too familiar with them, and I disapprove of that still more."

"Then it is a mercy that I care little for your approval," said Bianca. "Let me pass, if you please."

"Nor would Lorenzo approve of it, if he knew."

"You are more privy to Lorenzo's mind than one would have thought," said Bianca. "Let me pass, sir. It is no business of yours how I choose to spend my evenings."

"There you are wrong," Silvio replied. "It is very much

my business, since your continued attentions to this sweaty artisan are observed by all, and thereby make me a laughing-stock. We are not yet betrothed, my lady, but we shall be. Such is Lodovico Sforza's intention, and all at Court know it." He gripped both her arms now, pinching her flesh in deliberate spite. "For five days out of every six, and over more weeks than I care to consider, you have trotted at the heels of Leonardo da Vinci. Brother Sigismondo, who is supposed to be your instructor in matters of decency, may countenance it if he wishes to. I will not. Do you understand me?"

"You speak, sir, as though you owned me," said Bianca coolly, "which you do not."

"Evidently. It is, or so it appears, this artist who does so."

"He does nothing of the kind. Nor would he think of it, being possessed of a mind quite unlike yours. He is my teacher." She made no move to free herself from his grasp.

"Yes," agreed Silvio Grimiani. "And the whole palace wonders exactly what he teaches you—which is entertaining for them but mocks me. Well, madam, I can suggest better teachers for you, if that is your bent. Myself, for example. In but a short year or two from now, Bianca, you shall wear the saddle of Savoy, and I am a rider with many tricks to teach you. Study, then, to please me, since that is all which matters. Do well, and you will not find me unkind."

"Now," said Bianca, still without moving, "here is gentle courtship indeed! First I am a spy, and then something between a stable mare and a common whore. No doubt this is how love and marriage are viewed in the pigsties of Savoy, which is reason enough for me to stay away from them. Release me."

"I find you beautiful beyond compare, my lady, but lacking in respect. I am not done with you yet."

"Prince," replied Bianca sweetly, "I have had other teachers besides Leonardo. My Sforza cousins were rough company when they were boys, though they have grown out of it, as you have not. I learned early from fighting with them that the quickest way to discourage any man is to kick him between the legs. Therefore release me, or you will walk like an old man for the space of an hour or so."

Silvio let her go as though stung.

"What fashion of talking is this?" he demanded.

"Courtship, after the Savoy manner," said Bianca promptly. "Thus it is conducted. You may speak of riding me as a stallion rides a mare, and I may kick you where I please. Farewell, Prince."

She left him open-mouthed, and walked away—a little faster, perhaps, than she had intended, despite her assumed nonchalance—until she reached the gateway at the head of the path. Once safely inside the walls of the palazzo, she closed the wicket and leaned against it, her mind busy. The crudities of Silvio Grimiani as proposed lover or future husband were not, surprisingly, her chief concern. Another and sinister suspicion about the Prince of Savoy had arisen to trouble her, for men who speak in haste or in passion reveal—so she saw—more than they intend.

"Do I sound different to you, Leonardo?" she asked, entwining her knee with his in the darkness.

"No. Did you think that you would?"

"Yes," she answered. "And since everything else has turned out as I expected . . ."

"I am glad."

"Besides, *you* sound different."

"Do I? How?"

"It's hard to explain. For one thing," Bianca said, laughing, "you have not tried to argue with me since I came into your room."

"Perhaps I am growing in wisdom," said Leonardo. He lifted his hand from her breast and found a lock of her hair. "Every man must learn when the time for argument is over."

"I should hate to think that you were never going to argue with me again."

"Now that you have discovered how to stop me."

"I have always known how to stop you," said Bianca.

She decided to tell him of her suspicions about Silvio just before dawn. With her legs curled under her, she spoke without preamble.

"I think the Prince of Savoy is spying on you," she announced.

Leonardo broke his reverie. "Why do you suppose that?" he asked her, propping himself on one elbow.

"Because he was lying in wait for me last evening, near the top of the side path. Among all those statues, you know?"

Leonardo nodded.

"He seized me as I passed and tried to detain me. He was angry," Bianca went on.

"What caused his rage?"

"Nothing. Some nonsense which doesn't matter," she said hurriedly. "Among other things, he accused me of spying on you. I hardly paid attention when he said it, but a little later I began to wonder why he'd used the word, when I had obviously been doing nothing of the sort. Do you see? And then he had been watching me for a long time—at least that is what he said—because he knew how often I had come down to the meadow . . ."

"I assume, then, that it was your liking for our lowly company which annoyed him?" Leonardo said.

"Well, yes."

"Speaking for myself, I find it well worth braving the displeasure of the Prince of Savoy," Leonardo said gravely. "He had some few words to say to me on the subject, around Christmas, but we cannot all run our lives to suit Silvio's wishes. Go on."

"Perhaps I am being silly over this," Bianca said, "but I thought it a little odd that he should have been skulking in the bushes—or wherever he was—evening after evening, just to see how many times I was coming to make myself a nuisance to you and Captain Leone. Perhaps his jealousy kept him warm. He is that kind of person. But I thought it more likely that it was you he had been watching, to see what you were doing with that little cannon."

"It is possible. In which case, who would he be spying for?"

"He has always been as thick as thieves with the Pazzi family, because he wants a partnership in their bank. And the Pazzi have worked for Rome ever since Lorenzo lost a good deal of business to them a few years ago. So I think—"

"One moment," interrupted Leonardo. "How is it, little Madonna, that you know so much about the affairs of the Medici?"

"Oh, that is easy. Lorenzo has always favored me, ever since I came to Florence. He was furious for weeks, I remember. Naturally, he didn't say why, but I could tell. I found out all about it by asking Donna Francesca, who thought I wouldn't understand what she was explaining to me."

"Formidable," said Leonardo. "It seems to me that you must have been a scant eleven years old at the time. Florence's commercial secrets will be at risk for many a year with your sharp ears listening to them."

He spoke lightly, but was considering the facts as he did so. A great deal of what she suggested was possible, and more than possible. His experience in Rome supported it. He had argued to Lorenzo de' Medici that his fight with Francesco Pazzi was of a personal nature, a supposition which neither Lorenzo nor he believed. It was Lorenzo's concern, however, rather than his own if another interpretation were to be taken of the affair, and both of them had let it pass. There was now no doubt in his own mind that Cardinal della Palla was correct and that Girolamo Riario had been ultimately responsible for the attempt on his life, but it was difficult to regard the Prince of Savoy in any serious way as an agent of the Count. And yet, if Bianca's sense were not at fault, it might be so. Money greased many hinges, and a share in the Pazzi banking concerns . . . He became aware that Bianca was addressing him again.

"And do not patronize me," she said imperiously. Her face, turned down toward him, seemed angry.

"I spoke thoughtlessly and meant you no offense."

"If you find me childish, there are others who do not," said Bianca. "Silvio Grimiani, for one," she added as a wry afterthought.

"And which approach do you prefer?"

"Oh, you think that you are now going to reason with me, very coldly and logically, and crush me because you are better at debate than I am. And so you may be, but it proves nothing," said Bianca. "Do you tell me you have no true feeling toward me? None, I suppose. And much I care."

"I have said nothing of deep feelings," Leonardo pointed out.

"No. And I expect you will wear a long white beard before you arrive at doing so," she said, and wrenched at the sheets.

Despite himself, Leonardo burst out laughing. "And you will be a matron, past middle age, I suppose?" he said. "Come now, Bianca." The first light touched the ceiling and walls.

"Do not say it!"

"You are—"

"If you tell me how old I am after last night," said Bianca, more calmly, "I promise you I shall scream. And there is another thing. Since you know me for a good listener, shall I tell you what rumor says of you? That you mostly prefer boys to women. What have you to answer to that?" Bianca felt him tense.

"I have heard the rumor myself," he replied judiciously.

"Oh! And is that all?"

"Except to point out what you already know. What are sexual pastimes at the Medici court or any other, but an excuse for strutting display and the cackling of idiots? Love is a toy for idle and rich people who are also, as it happens, notoriously stupid and lack all occupation which might otherwise bring meaning to their lives. You know this to be true. Fetch me a pretty woman or a pretty boy, both equally stupid, and I will send both away. Do you suppose nobody scratches at my door of nights? Since I am known to have no mistress, naturally they say I am a taker of catamites. It is said, in particular, by those ladies who might otherwise fancy themselves in my bed."

"Your conceit," Bianca said, "is astounding."

"Whether I am conceited or not has nothing whatever to do with the case. Do you deny anything that I have said?"

"No. But you are beginning to debate again. You were doing much better a few moments ago."

Leonardo sat up.

"My lady," he said, "this is neither debate nor quarrel. If love is to be a mere plaything for the wealthy and vicious, then it is worth neither my time nor yours. I will play no such games with you. You claim that I treat you like a child. Perhaps I do so because it is, for the present, better that I should. Do you understand me?"

Bianca surveyed him, her chin in her fists.

"Perhaps, I do," she said. "Give me your hand."

He reached out to her, and they remained companionably silent for a time.

"Tell me, then," said Bianca.

"What?"

"When they scratch at your door, do you never open it?"

"Never," said Leonardo with feigned sobriety.

"Your nights must be somewhat dull." Her eyes were shining with amusement. "How do you spend them?" she teased.

"In reading books, or stargazing. What else is there to do?"

"Giuliano returns from Milan today," said Bianca, "and therefore, I imagine that Constanza might give me a different answer. However, I am content."

Constanza slipped along the quiet and moonlit gallery like a shadow. At the door to Giuliano's chambers she halted, stealing one last look to right and left. The palazzo slept. Lifting the latch and opening the door just wide enough to admit her, she entered.

"Giuliano?" she whispered. "Giuliano? Where are you?"

Silence. "Giuliano?" she called softly once again, and crossed the marble floor of the dressing room to stand in the arched doorway to the bedchamber beyond it. There, illuminated by the gentle glow of candles, stood the great canopied bed, and she contemplated its crimson expanse, her hand on the rough stone of the pillar at her side. Room enough and more for the two of us, she thought, no matter how we may sprawl. She smiled to herself at that, and her heart quieted. She felt, suddenly, the warmth of a thousand mornings to come when she and Giuliano would awaken to the new day, bodies fitted in the sleep of a good marriage, replenished by a thousand nights of love given and received.

She sat on the edge of the bed, palms caressing the velvet texture of the spread. This will cover us on cold nights and we shall talk of the Court and of our children, she told herself, and we will plan visits to my aunt in Modena and my friends in Ravenna and of the new dresses that I shall wear and a thousand things besides.

The fat candles gleamed steadily, reflected in an oval mirror that hung upon the wall opposite her. I shall dress by that mirror, there, she thought. Giuliano will watch me, and I, knowing it, will watch him. She rose and went to the glass, studying her face with a small and critical smile of greeting.

This will be your first time, she said to her reflection silently. The first. Let me remember every moment of it for ever. It will hurt, they say. But the pain passes and the pleasure comes soon. Will I also remember how I shiver now? I feel so full.

Her thighs tightened, informing her of what she barely understood as yet, and she felt a kind of heat flood her, as though from some internal and secret midsummer. She lifted her hands to cup her breasts, and her face, returning her gaze from the dark mirror, seemed to swim out of focus for an instant.

Then the door of the outer room clicked softly and she turned. Giuliano came through the arch into the bedroom; the draft of his entry stirred the candle flames and sent shadows dancing across the tapestries. Within his embrace, she murmured, "Where have you been, my lord? Almost I had begun to wonder if you had suffered a change of heart."

"Nay, my Constanza. I have but been to my strongbox, which is in the library. I went there for this." He opened the fingers of his cupped right hand to show her a ring—a heavy, gold band crowned by a perfect oval ruby with an encircling fence of diamonds. "Our wedding ceremony will come in God's time, my heart," he said. "But we are wed this night, and this shall be your marriage ring, though none know it but ourselves. I brought it with me from Milan."

"Where you have tarried too long for my comfort, Giuliano."

"And too long for mine. I suspect that Lorenzo sent me there in order to cool my passion. He reckoned poorly, if so. Not an hour has passed without my thinking of you and of this moment."

"As I have thought of you, my lord. Though I have no ring to give you, which shames me."

"No matter. You have captured a far-sighted husband. I chose one for myself as well. Look." In his other hand, he held a pair of miniature golden serpents, twined together in perfect symmetry and with eyes of ruby to match the stone he had given her. "The emblems of wisdom," he said. "Wisdom of the heart, not of the mind."

Constanza laughed happily and slipped the ring onto his finger. Impulsively, she bent to his hand, and felt his answering lips on her hair.

"Let us go to bed, Giuliano," she said, "since that is what we are here for. I am immodest, I know; and yet, I care not."

Wordlessly, he guided her to the bed. She watched his face while, confidently, he undressed her until she stood naked, and as softly white as shadowed ivory. When he left her side to quench the candles, she reached out and touched his arm.

"Leave them alight," she bade him. "Have I not said that I am immodest? I want to see you. I must learn, and shall learn less in darkness." She began to unlace the points of his doublet, her hands as confident as his own had been. He looked at her, and felt passion rising within him. The artless grace of her body as she moved fired him, and he wove his fingers into the tumbled and midnight strands of her unbound hair. "Yes," she breathed. "This is what I need to remember, every time I see you so. How much a man you are, and how I feel when I see that you want me." She stood close to him, tracing her fingers slowly down his chest. "I have never touched a man before, as you know. You must teach me, since I am a virgin and unskilled. I pray that I may please you, Giuliano."

He took her face in his hands and kissed her. "There is little need for me to teach you anything, Constanza, my bride," he said. "All that a loving woman should know, you know already. It is, as love is, within you for the finding. And as you pray to please me, so I pray to please you, though I may cause you pain in doing so."

"I am prepared for it, and welcome it. Teach me."

For a long while, she let herself drift, surging now and again with the touch of his hand and his mouth. And when it occurred to her to please him in all the ways he had shown her, she felt him respond. As the pain came at last, her body arched to meet it and him, in a softly exhaled cry that turned the sharpness at once into the promised joy. For a while, they lay still, and still connected, breathing in unison, the rhythm of loving echoed in the slow rise and fall of their breasts. She spoke into his ear.

"How long will it be before we can do this again, Giuliano?" she asked. "Will it be soon, or must our bodies rest now?"

Startled, he raised his head. "There is something, after all, that I can teach you," he said. "You did not know? That we can do this again, tonight? Now, if you are not tired."

She leaned up and bit him softly on the lips. "No, I did not know," she replied. "You see? I am no virgin now, it is true, but it seems that I am still no wife, either. Will you show me more, my husband?"

Sixteen

. . . received of Maestro Gian Giacomo Portinari of Arezzo 6 cannon, these being for the new artillery and very fine, in weight 280 pounds each one and bound with iron straps. Remember to speak with Maestro Gian Giacomo concerning his means of slowly cooling metals after casting them . . . and from Ser Nencio 300 lbs of powder, milled and corned according to our speech together . . . the spikes to hold the wheels to the carriages must be in bronze or in marine alloy, since iron will rust and is sometimes friable under pressure. . . .

Show that the effect of the shot in going forwards must be equal to the effect of the cannon in recoiling, and that the backward travel of the cannon must be unhindered, which is contrary to the practice of our gunners. Is it possible to propel a cart by ejecting fire or stones from behind?

. . . I shall have to cut the screws for myself. Scarpellino is a good workman but cannot understand them . . . and

> those parts of the carriage in which they work must likewise be made of bronze. . . .

"*Quid vobis videtur?*" asked Pope Sixtus IV. "I borrow here the language of the Consistory, since the question is one of some importance. Something must be determined, and quickly."

"I see no reason for haste, Your Holiness," said Cardinal della Palla. "A man's life is at stake."

"We are aware of the views of Your Eminence," said the Pontiff. "However, they are but one factor among many. We must beg you to confine yourself to military reality, since your colleagues will undoubtedly do so."

"I have learned to be a realist," replied della Palla. "Your Holiness need have no fears on that score. I had rather be here to argue the case than elsewhere. My question remains: Why must a decision be taken now? I seek only for information."

"For reasons of war," said Girolamo Riario, at his left.

Della Palla turned his mild blue eyes toward the Captain-General's face, dwelling briefly upon what he seemed to see there.

"Nothing else?" he inquired.

"As His Holiness points out," interrupted Cardinal Borgia, "we shall be discussing only matters of war here." Della Palla looked at him in turn.

"Very well," he said. "Would it be improper to ask what your position is?"

"I take no position," said Cardinal Borgia comfortably. "Surely, you are aware of that by now, my dear Chancellor."

"What, then, of Leonardo da Vinci?" asked Sixtus, apparently of the room at large. "He has refused the Most Eminent Cardinal della Palla's invitation to bring his talents and lay them at Rome's feet. This argues that he is indeed working directly for the Medici, as claimed by the Count of Imola and confirmed by His Eminence Cardinal Borgia. More than this, he represents Florentine thought at its worst and most reprehensible—Neoplatonic, heretical and humanistic. Do I hear any dissent from this?"

"None," said della Palla. "Except I had thought, with respect, that we were confining ourselves to things military, in which case his style of thought is irrelevant."

"Not if it shows antagonism toward Rome," said the Pontiff. "Riario?"

"He will prove a thorn in our side at Castelmonte," said Riario. "Kill him, and have done with it."

"Borgia?"

"There is a good deal to be said for the Captain-General's point of view," answered Rodrigo Borgia. "However, I will hear the opinion of the Apostolic Chancellor. All human life is precious in the sight of God, and only God may call a man to final judgment."

"Enemies are killed in war," said Riario impatiently, "and he is a fool who hesitates overlong in thoughts of final judgment. Rome is at war. Leonardo da Vinci is Rome's enemy. The conclusion speaks for itself."

Sixtus fingered the lobe of his ear.

"Defend him," he suggested to Cardinal della Palla.

The latter leaned back in his chair. "Leonardo da Vinci," he pointed out, "is hardly likely to take Castelmonte single handed. We were informed that he was studying the art of gunnery, and so he is. He came here openly seeking information on gunpowder, and—equally openly, if tactlessly—transmitted some of his own conclusions on the subject to me. In this, at least, he has shown himself a good son of the Church. I see no danger here. I have watched his gunnery studies myself. The weapon he is using is no longer than my arm. It is, in point of fact, an ornamental cannon used chiefly for firing salutes. I assure you that its effect on Castelmonte's walls would be non-existent, and I see no danger here, either. He is an artist, a philosopher, a somewhat conceited young man and a butterfly."

"Who says so?" asked Borgia.

"That he is a butterfly? It is the opinion of those around

him," said della Palla innocently. "Notably, of one Brother Sigismondo Carregi, who is tutor to the lady Bianca Maria Visconti and himself a theologian of renown in Florence. Most fortunately I have a letter from Brother Sigismondo, amply confirming this view. He denounces Leonardo da Vinci bitterly, but as a danger to nobody except the lady Bianca, with whom—according to Brother Sigismondo—he flirts continually, his experiments being aimed largely at impressing this young lady—and the Court at large—with his own brilliance. Well. I see no terrible danger to Rome here, and no reason for seeking the hasty death of a man who may, when all is said and done, be of service to God one day through his undoubted talent as an artist."

"That is all very well," said Riario, "but my correspondent—"

"Your correspondent in Florence?" said della Palla. "The Prince of Savoy, if I am not mistaken? My dear Captain-General, if Leonardo da Vinci is paying court to the lady Bianca Visconti, he is without doubt also annoying the Prince, who intends to marry her one day. I hardly think that Silvio Grimiani's opinions are free from bias."

Sixtus IV cogitated in silence, while Cardinal della Palla offered up a brief prayer for absolution; his own testimony, he was aware, had carried bias almost to the point of distortion. Finally, the Pontiff delivered judgment.

"We have decided," he announced, "to proceed as follows. Cardinal Borgia will send a letter to Florence forthwith, commanding—not requesting—this young man to come to Rome and place his artistic talents at the service of the Church. He is to obey immediately. If he does so, then we may regard His Eminence Cardinal della Palla's assessment as correct, and need not trouble ourselves further. If he does not comply, whether it be of his own will or because our errant son Lorenzo de' Medici will not release him from service, then we shall accept the position of the Captain-General, who will at once proceed as he sees fit. My Lord and Your Eminences, I thank you."

Snows softened and melted. Meadows and bottomlands were soggy with new water, and everywhere brooks ran full to their banks. Only in the higher peaks and in the deep slashes on mountainsides did the winter snow stubbornly persist.

With spring Rome's messenger hastened to Florence—His Grace, the Bishop Manfredo Romolo-Paro, Apostolic Prothonotary and Nuncio Extraordinary, member of the Curia, and aide to His Eminence Cardinal Rodrigo Borgia.

Lorenzo received the prelate, and the pontifical decree he bore, with courtesy. "We shall send for Master Leonardo at once," he said, "and the command of His Holiness shall be that of Florence."

Thus, a bare hour after the withdrawal of the bishop to prayer in a chapel of the Cathedral of Santa Maria del Fiori, Lorenzo de' Medici and Leonardo faced each other across the table in the library. The ruler of Florence extended the papal summons.

"It seems," he said, "that Rome has urgent need of your services. Read."

Leonardo scanned the ornate scroll.

"Evidently," he said. "I am here commanded by God, by His Church, by the Supreme Pontiff—twice—and by Cardinal Borgia; and also, your assent being presumed, by yourself. These are a great many commands to one poor Florentine artist . . . almost overwhelming in their weight. Well, though it pains me, I cannot go."

"Naturally," said Lorenzo. "But allow me to point out the difficulties. If I do not relinquish you to Rome, then I defy Sixtus and the Church. Since I am already doing so in the archbishopric of Pisa and at Castelmonte, this is a small matter for me. But if you defy Sixtus your position may be dangerous. Both he and the Count of Imola have long arms and claws of iron. Let yourself be gripped by those claws, my friend, and your days of experiment are over."

"They are over in any case, sir. At least for your purposes."

"Do you think so? With what result?"

"If my studies are now confirmed by trial in the field, then I have invented a new warfare," said Leonardo simply. "And one which has never before been contemplated in man's history."

"Hum," said Lorenzo, looking at him closely. "And how is this warfare waged?"

"With cannon. You cannot have supposed differently, after all that I have been doing in your meadow and your archery range. I have designed new cannon for the Medici; that is the long and the short of it."

"Which you need to test in the field?"

"Exactly."

"Will they give me Castelmonte?"

"By God's grace, sir, they will."

"Then test them. Where had you thought of doing so?"

"In the marshes outside the city."

"That will no longer serve. And you are now going to demand from me your fifty gunners, I have no doubt. In March, you said, and it is March now."

"I am grateful for the excellence of your memory."

Lorenzo motioned impatiently with his hand. "It will be necessary for you to disappear," he said. "You, and your new cannon, their powder and shot, and my fifty gunners and Captain-Gunner Roderigo Leone. Let me think. Have you any objection to mountain terrain?"

"None whatever, provided I can have a practice range of some three thousand paces," Leonardo said.

"Then I have an answer. There is a hunting lodge of mine in the mountains between here and San Marino, unused these many years. Behind it—I will give you a map of the region—you will see a notched ridge, with a path that climbs steeply to the notch; beyond the ridge is a valley where I used to play as a boy. Few know of its existence save for Giuliano and myself, yet it lies less than twenty-eight miles from this room. You will be safe from prying eyes there.

Take your men and go. I suggest that they travel in small groups, gathering only at the lodge."

"I can arrange it. The idea is admirable, and we are ready to leave at once."

"You had better leave sooner than that," said Lorenzo with an ironic smile. "By which I mean that you have already left, since I propose to inform Rome's nuncio that such is the case. Moreover, since you are close friends with my brother, I am sure he will lend you both his horse and a cloak. Do you follow me?"

"Perfectly," Leonardo replied. "I have vanished even now."

"Good. The ground in the Arno Valley will harden within some eight or ten weeks. Whether your trials have been crowned with success or not, you will return at once to Florence whenever I send for you. At once, you understand? Castelmonte—"

"I know. Sir, we have here not one paradox, but two. For though I stand here in your library, I have left Florence; and, though we seem to be doing nothing, yet the siege of Castelmonte has already begun."

"You should not be here, my lady."

"I know that. The tally of my sins grows longer every day." She took her seat in the window. "However, since you are no longer in Florence, having left for I know not where some hours since, there can be little harm in my entering your apartments. They are empty, are they not?"

"And who informed you of all this?"

"Constanza."

"And who told her?"

"Giuliano, of course. He has lent you his cloak, I see. How long will you be away?"

"I do not know, Madonna."

"Well. At least, I do not need to ask you for what purpose you are leaving, since I already know that much."

"With respect, Madonna, I doubt that you do, since nobody is aware of my purpose save myself."

"More conceit. You have devised a means of aiming guns not by trial and error, as hitherto, but by mathematics. I admit that I do not understand precisely how."

"My lady," said Leonardo, "every day you amaze me, since you perceive what has entirely escaped such learned men as your tutor and the worthy Dr. Mazzone. Lorenzo would have been well advised to ask you to guard your tongue long before this. I ask you to do so now."

"You have no need to ask it, Leonardo *mio*. And as for my perception, how could it fail to be better than that of others?" Bianca said. "I have had, you see, an excellent teacher."

"And I an admirable pupil."

"That is understood. Nevertheless . . ."

"Yes, Madonna?"

"Will you not kiss me before you go?"

Seventeen

It was strange, Leonardo thought, how poorly men's childhood memories served them, particularly in matters of size. He sat outside the smaller of the two caves, his back resting against the side of a gun carriage, and surveyed the pocket valley which sloped gently away from him. A narrow rill of snow water meandered along its floor, to vanish where the stony path entered it between two pillars of rock. Lorenzo, he recalled, had assured him that it was at least three thousand paces from end to end. In fact it was barely a quarter of that length. Well, it would serve. A thousand paces was the maximum range he intended to work at when the time came, and they could achieve eight hundred or so here by siting the guns carefully.

What he needed this morning was to dispel the air of skepticism—if not of incipient mutiny—which the fifty men about him almost palpably exuded. He could hardly blame them. Urged blasphemously onward by Rigo, they had taken an entire day and the better part of the previous night to wrestle the six guns up the steep and zigzag path from the lodge in the foothills below, with no knowledge of why they were engaged upon such a backbreaking exercise. They had asked, of course, both continually and colorfully. To each question, Rigo had offered the advice that their breath might be better saved for climbing, and met their scabrous suggestions for the alternative disposal of their burdens with invitations to fall out of line and be beaten to a pulp by their Captain-Gunner.

They had gained the valley head, and the caves which they now occupied, well after midnight. The debris of their prompt collapse lay all about Leonardo this morning: bags of flour and salt fish, lanterns, canvas and rope for bivouacs, boxes of candles, mallets, spikes, a small anvil, sacks of charcoal, three barrels of last season's apples and a single discarded boot—hurled into the darkness by young Tesoro di Veluti, whose head upon arrival had been as sore as his feet. Leonardo noted, however, that the powder kegs, shot and other appurtenances of the cannon had been carefully stowed within the larger cave. Rain or snow might be allowed to soak all else, but their professional equipment would receive greater care, under Rigo's command, than would the gunners themselves.

"Good morrow, friend engineer," said Rigo, arriving with a platter of bread, cheese and olives, which he handed to Leonardo. "Tell me how you wish us to proceed. We shall be ready for your instructions in an hour or so, after I have broken a few heads in reducing the disorder here."

"Exactly as I outlined to you," Leonardo replied. "The first four or five days are to be spent in learning to dismantle the guns and reassemble them, neither procedure to take longer than a slow count of ten. Eight men to each gun, with two as runners or replacements. Four men in each team to carry the barrel; three more for the carriage and its wheels, the wheels to be removed from the axles or not as occasion and terrain demand; one man to carry the powder, the shot, the sponge staves and the slow matches. They must learn to move fast and silently, bearing these things."

"Before firing a shot?" said Rigo. "That will come hard, Leonardo."

"It will come harder yet if they enter battle while they are still falling over each others' feet," Leonardo pointed out.

"Quite true. Nonetheless, if you will accept some advice from me, I would, in your place, show them some purpose in sweating off their winter wine bellies," Rigo said. "You have succeeded in convincing me. *They* remain unconvinced, and therefore surly, and I had rather they saw the light. We have grown to understand each other somewhat, you and I, so forgive my bluntness. We are not now dealing with machines and mathematics, but with men."

"So we are," said Leonardo. "Let us give them some theater."

By ten in the forenoon, the ground was unlittered, and three storage tents had been raised. The gunners—in a silent group—were gathered about one of the small cannon at the valley's head, between the mouths of their caves and the stream. Five hundred accurate paces away, a wooden target was propped against a rough triangular base of poles—a door to an abandoned hut, stolen opportunely from behind the hunting lodge at the commencement of their climb to the high basin they now occupied.

Leonardo da Vinci was pouring gunpowder into a small brass measure. He tapped the side of the cup, settling the grains.

"One of these measures goes with each gun," he told the assembled men, "and each to its own. Do not confuse them. They differ slightly in amount—by half the weight of a hazelnut, it may be—but they differ." Several of the gunners nodded, among them Agnolo Fulvio and Scudo. Care in measuring powder was a concept they already knew.

Leonardo now moved to the cannon. It was a bare four and a half feet long, and weighed perhaps one-hundredth as much as the guns they were used to. Yet its appearance was familiar. The trunnions at either side of its barrel rested in notches, so that cannon and carriage could be quickly dismantled. Likewise, the wheels were spiked to the axles with removable pins. Aside from these features, its sole peculiarity lay in the fact that its breech rested on a curved block which could be raised or lowered by means of a screw, this screw being part of the carriage itself. As the thread turned, a pointer on the screwblock moved past a series of marks engraved on the carriage, thus showing the degree of elevation of the barrel. By tilting both screw and block backward, the gun's breech could be disengaged from them, allowing it to fall and rest on the oaken carriage tree so that the muzzle—as Leonardo now demonstrated—pointed steeply skyward for loading purposes.

He tipped the measured powder into the barrel, following it with a leather patch and then with the four-pound, polished iron ball. Then, reaching into the front of his tunic, he produced a narrow, brown cylinder, the length and thickness of a goose quill. It was tapered at either end.

"This is your fuse," he said, showing it to them. "It is merely powder, twisted into a roll of paper and sealed with Arabian gum. You will have little time to fill the breech hole with loose powder to serve as a train, as you are used to doing. The same end may be achieved with this, and more quickly . . . thus." He inserted one end of the quill into the touch hole, pushing it home until only an inch or two of it protruded. Lifting the breech and lowering the muzzle, he swung the range screw forward once more, and then allowed the breech to settle itself in the curved upper surface of the traveling block.

"Ready," he said.

Turning his head, he looked down the valley at the distant rectangle of wood. From this distance, it appeared no larger than a man's thumbnail. He knelt behind the cannon and shifted the carriage fractionally, aligning the barrel so that it pointed neither to one side nor the other of this diminutive mark.

"Who will undertake to strike the target board?" he asked, still kneeling.

Agnolo Fulvio at once stood forward and crouched beside him. Looking along the top of the barrel, the Lieutenant-Gunner sighted along the two filed notches, one at the swell of the breech and one cut into the rim of the muzzle. Sitting in the notches was the distant target.

"I have seen these sighting marks before," said Agnolo, "upon Turkish cannon. How many shots will you give me?"

"One," said Leonardo.

"With an untried gun?"

"The gun will shoot as truly as any you have handled," said Leonardo, smiling, "and better. You have my word on it."

"That may be. I still do not know how it carries," Agnolo said. There was a murmur of agreement from his colleagues. "What is the range, do you say?"

"Five hundred paces."

"Give me three attempts, then, and I will do it."

"One," said Leonardo.

"An impossible task," Agnolo said. "No man can do it. My first shot will either strike short or else fly above and beyond the mark, unless I have the luck of Satan. My second will serve to determine by how much I must raise or lower the barrel in order to increase or shorten the range by a given number of paces. Once I know this, my third shot will strike home. Eh, Scudo?" He looked at the big gunner for confirmation.

"He is right," agreed the latter. "That is the way of it."

"Stand aside, then," said Leonardo, "and observe how mathematics may replace both your first shot and your second."

Agnolo rose to his feet. Rapidly, Leonardo turned the range screw until the pointer attached to the block rested upon the mark corresponding to five hundred paces. He got up, dusting his knees.

"Give me a short space of time," he said, "and then fire. One shot is all that is needed."

"How much time?" demanded Agnolo. "And for what purpose?"

"Why," Leonardo replied, "so that I may check upon my calculations." He turned to Rigo. "Perhaps, you will accompany me?" he asked.

"Where to?"

"Down to the target, of course."

Rigo, who had opened his mouth in order to deliver himself of some comment, shut it again as the artist strode away.

"Fire when I raise my hand," ordered Rigo. "And remove that look from your face, or I might mistake it for impertinence."

Agnolo bowed deeply. "To command, Captain-Gunner," he said. "He is your friend, and doubtless you know what you are doing."

Several minutes later, Leonardo and the Captain-Gunner were standing at either side of the propped door. A short distance from them, the brook pattered its way between snow patches and over sunlit pebbles, heeded by neither of them.

"Closer," suggested Leonardo.

"Why not directly in front of it?" Rigo snarled. "Theater is all very well, but I had not imagined being asked to lay my head on a block."

"Take courage," Leonardo advised him. "Though I admit that I have less to lose than you do. If this should fail, your gunners will probably tear me limb from limb, so I may as well be decapitated before they have the chance to do so. Give the signal."

Rigo raised his hand.

A puff of white smoke bloomed from the center of the group of men clustered at the top of the valley. The whipcrack of the cannon's detonation reached their ears almost at once. They caught a glimpse of the shining ball in mid-trajectory an eyeblink before the target between them shattered into matchwood. Splinters flew, one of them driving deep into the fabric of Rigo's sleeve. He plucked it out with a grunt of relief, his eyes following the ball which, spent and misshapen, was rolling away in the direction of the stream. The men were beginning to pour downhill toward them, some waving their caps.

"Well, Sir Gunner," said Rigo, "I like a confident man, to be sure. The next time you take it into your head to make a point, however, I shall be glad if I am elsewhere."

At dawn a day later and some twenty miles away, Silvio Grimiani di Torino allowed his great black horse to pick its way through the rubble-strewn courtyard of a ruined abbey. Below him, the roofs of Fiesole glistened damply in the gray light of the day's coming. Farther away, the Arno River made its presence known in the drifting banks of mist which the bitter night had breathed upon its surface. Indifferent to the cold, Silvio watched the wooded trail that slanted up the hillside from the sleeping town. Riding close to the old and broken wall he was invisible, he knew. His charger snorted, steam curling from its nostrils, and the reins in his hand slapped gently against its neck.

Four of us, he said to himself. Three, if the truth were told. Paolo Pazzi would be worthless; so much was already clear. He had spent too many hours hunched over his figures—a clerk, not an assassin. His brother Francesco would have been better for an undertaking such as this, even taking into account his failure in Rome. But old Jacopo had insisted that Paolo should accompany them, thereby learning—as his father ironically put it—some of those aspects of commerce which were not to be found in ledgers and bills of lading.

Well, there was likely to be little for Paolo to upset. Benno Foscari, and his stiletto, would be worth two men; so would Mario Bandini, who was vouched for by his more notorious elder brother, Bernardo. The latter, like Francesco Pazzi, had other fish to fry. Two professionals, a scrivener, and himself, Silvio thought. It was enough.

He had spent three days in scouring the countryside for news of Leonardo da Vinci's whereabouts. Roderigo Leone was said to be with him. Tales of mysterious night time comings and goings abounded. Silvio supposed that such was the way with rustics, who had—God knew—little enough to excite them. He had learned nothing specific until his arrival at the Medici hunting lodge. The place was crumbling, but was still occupied by an aged caretaker and his wife, to whom Silvio had offered a simple choice—speech or death. The old woman had cursed him, but her husband had proven less stubborn. He had taken the Prince of Savoy outside, pointing up the steep and hidden trail to the notched ridge that commanded the house. Leonardo da Vinci, he insisted, was even now up there upon some errand with a thickset companion. The caretaker had then lapsed into mumbled and incoherent pleas for mercy. Satisfied, Silvio had allowed him to rejoin his toothless wife.

Doubtless, he would have been less complacent had the retainer informed him the artist and Captain-Gunner were accompanied by fifty armed men. Since this intelligence had not been sought by the prince, however, the crafty old man had seen no reason for adding it.

In the ruined courtyard above Fiesole, Silvio strained his ears, hearing the sound of approaching hooves. He blew into his cupped hands and awaited the arrival of his accomplices.

"I see a difficulty," Rigo said.

"There are several," admitted Leonardo cheerfully. "What is yours?" He was tossing a handful of pebbles, one by one, from where he sat onto the path beneath them. It was late afternoon, and the weather was fine. The gunners were preparing their evening meal outside the caves at the upper end of the valley; Rigo and Leonardo had taken a stroll, and were now perched on the summit of one of the rock pillars which guarded the entrance to the glen from the head of the track outside. The hunting lodge lay, minuscule, seven hundred feet below them; from its door, a wider road descended across foothills streaked with snow toward the distant plain.

"It concerns the measurement of range," said Rigo, rubbing his neck. "Your piece of theater this morning was admirable in its effect, but for all of that, Agnolo made a telling point. We are not troubled overmuch by estimating the distance of our targets, since hitherto we have done so by guesswork and by means of our sighting shots. Your new method does not allow this, if I am correct in my reasoning."

"You are."

"And you were careful to pace out the distance between your cannon and its target before you fired. You had need to do so, since otherwise your approach could not have succeeded. Am I also correct in this?"

"Quite correct."

"Then how," asked Rigo, "do you proceed when you do not know your range beforehand? That is my difficulty."

"Rigo, my friend," said Leonardo, "your perception is acute and your point crucial, the more so since we shall eventually be firing our cannon at night."

"At night! This grows harder to fathom by the minute."

"Sit closer."

Leonardo unfolded the cover of his notebook, took charcoal in hand and began to draw.

"Let us suppose," he said, "that we take a long staff, and lay it on the ground before us with its ends to left and right. So. Now upon either end of this staff, let us mount two notched strips of brass, like the arm of a pelorus, or like the sighting notches which you saw filed into the barrel of our cannon up there. We first set our eye to this one, here at the right, and align its notches upon the target . . . thus. Without moving the staff, we proceed to its left-hand end and do likewise with the notched arm there. Both arms are now pointing at our target. Do you understand?"

"Yes. It is as though we had aimed two small guns at the same mark."

"Exactly so. Now you may readily see that, although both arms are aimed at the same place, yet they point in slightly different directions, since they are set apart by the length of our staff. In fact, they point inward toward each other, though but a small degree. Very well. The nearer the target, the greater will be their inclination toward each other . . . thus. And by measuring this angular inclination inward, which I can do by means of a graduated wheel mounted beneath one of the arms . . . thus, and . . . thus, I can compute the distance of the target from where my staff lies. Once you perceive the nature of the device, it is easily done."

"And you have built it?" asked Rigo.

"I have built it, and it works with sufficient accuracy for our purpose."

"And at night? What then?"

"That also I have considered . . . what is it?"

Rigo, interrupting him, laid a hand on his shoulder and pointed.

"Look," he said. "Below us. There, by the side of the lodge. Riders."

Leonardo stared downward through the tops of the pines. "Four," he agreed. "And coming this way." He lowered himself, slowly, until he was lying prone on the rock's surface; Rigo had already done so.

"Here is trouble, then," said Rigo. "It is too far to see who they may be, and they will be among the trees soon. Friend or foe? What do you think?"

Leonardo, reaching into a leather pouch that was chained alongside his notebook at his waist, brought out a small cylindrical object and held it to his eye. "The Prince of Savoy," he announced matter-of-factly. "And Paolo Pazzi. The other two I do not recognize, but your question is answered."

"Now, by the Passion," cried Rigo, "what is this? I took you for long-sighted at Castelmonte last year, but this passes all belief! Show me what you have there."

Leonardo handed the metal cylinder to him. It was the thickness of two fingers, and a little longer than it was broad. "You have seen eyeglasses before, have you not?" he inquired mildly.

"Not of this sort. Eyeglasses are flat, and worn by old men and lawyers. How is this thing made?"

"With two glasses, at a short space from each other, as you see," replied Leonardo, "the rear one being ground in the opposite sense to the one in front. I hit upon the principle by accident when playing with a pair of such lenses, and mounted them myself."

"A miracle," Rigo proclaimed, peering through the tube. "They are gone," he added. "But they must be climbing toward us. I can even see their tracks. My friend, this will make you a rich man. I would pay—"

"You need pay nothing," Leonardo said. "Accept it, as a gift from one artilleryman to another. Only be so good as to keep it concealed; let others think, as you thought of me, that you have keen sight and no more."

"I thank you. What am I saying? I cannot thank you sufficiently."

"In God's name," said Leonardo with a smile, "let us have less turmoil over a piece of trumpery through which to gaze at the moon. It will take me but a few days to make another. Meanwhile, if you will drag your attention back to more immediate matters, shall we decide what to do about Silvio and his friends? I confess, I am beginning to tire of them."

"Of course. Well, it will take them a half hour and more to reach the head of this track."

"Then I will await them here," said Leonardo, "and you collect together a small group of such as may feel the need for exercise. Then we will see what they are about."

It was Benno Foscari who saw him first. He signaled the others to silence with upraised arm. There was no need for him to point at their prey. Two hundred paces ahead, and clearly visible through the pine trunks which flanked the final curve of the trail's ascent, Leonardo da Vinci was sitting on a log in the center of the path, his back to them. He appeared to be sketching, evidently making use of the remaining daylight.

Silvio reined in beside Foscari.

"An easy matter," he whispered. "But where is the gunner?"

"Either behind us, or else around that bend, where those twin rocks hold the path," Foscari replied softly. "For I see no horses. Is that the entrance to the valley you spoke of?"

"I imagine so."

"Then they are encamped in it," said Foscari. "You may depend on it." His horse pranced, but there was sufficient wind in the trees to hide any small noise they might be making. They would be seen before they were heard, if they were reasonably quiet. "How important is the gunner in this affair?" Foscari asked.

"A side dish. If he appears, kill him. If he does not, well and good." The Prince of Savoy beckoned to the two riders behind him. "Paolo," he said, "keep to our rear. Cry warning if you see Captain-Gunner Leone; otherwise, do nothing. Is it understood?"

Paolo Pazzi nodded, hoping that his relief was not making him shamefaced. He had little stomach for what he knew was about to happen, whether fighting or simple murder, and he was grateful for the proffered chance of returning to Florence in neither triumph nor disgrace.

Even as rearguard, he was incapable of fulfilling his duties, though this mattered little under the circumstances. Pulling his horse aside, he kept his eyes not on the trail below him, but upon Silvio Grimiani, who—flanked by Benno Foscari and Mario Bandini—now advanced up the last stretch of the path toward the unsuspecting artist's back.

By the time they had halved the distance to their intended prey, Mario was conscious of faint unease. Was the man deaf? Breeze or no, he should surely have become aware of their deadly purpose by now? He had heard that painters often became immersed in their work to the exclusion of all else, and certainly it seemed true of this one. Surveying the scene from a professional point of view, Mario Bandini could find nothing amiss. Twenty paces beyond the seated artist, the track turned sharply to the right, presumably entering the upper valley. There was nowhere for him to run except away from them. If he did so, it would be a simple matter to ride him down, and Rigo with him, should he be anywhere around.

At thirty paces from his back, Silvio Grimiani halted. He drew steel, his teeth set in the remembrance of past slights, both real and fancied.

"Artist," he called, menacingly.

Leonardo da Vinci turned, rising to his feet in a single fluid movement. There was a look of dangerous amusement on his face. At the same instant, as though signaled by Silvio's rapier, men appeared from all around the Prince and his companions. From behind boulders and trunks of trees they arose, and from around the corner where the track vanished between its guardian rock pillars—dark, leather-clad men, their skins powder grained, bearing daggers, iron spikes, clubs and short swords.

Benno Foscari, his stiletto already in hand, saw defeat at once and spurred his horse desperately. The animal reared and plunged forward for a step or two. Rigo Leone seized its bridle, sweeping his thigh against its forefeet and heaving simultaneously at the leather. Foscari, badly seated, had a second to marvel at the gunner's enormous strength as the horse toppled, whinnying. After a brief moment of soaring flight, he crashed into the side of a rock. Rigo, a gutter brawler by nature, promptly and unceremoniously kicked in the side of his skull.

Paolo Pazzi, terror-stricken, watched the first instant of this ambush from his distant station among the pines. In offering himself as bait for their trap, Leonardo had ordered the gunners—much to Rigo's disgust—to refrain from violence until Silvio Grimiani had made his intentions clear; and moreover, no time had been available to cut off their opponents' retreat by closing the trail farther down the mountainside. Their chief concern, in any case, was to prevent penetration of the valley.

Pulling his horse's head around, therefore, Paolo was able

to see Mario Bandini wrenched from his saddle by the gigantic Scudo, who clamped the crook of an arm about his neck and bent the assassin's head inexorably forward until his spine snapped like a rotten twig. Shaken, Paolo spurred his horse into stumbling flight and was gone.

The Prince of Savoy cast a glance in the direction of his rearguard's retreating figure and twisted his face into a sneer. Ringed by men and blades, he still sat his charger, whose bit was held by Leonardo da Vinci.

Rigo Leone, idly casting Benno Foscari's stiletto into the air and catching it again, came toward the group and grinned carnivorously at the artist.

"What do you say?" he asked, gesturing at the Prince with the weapon. "From ear to ear?"

Leonardo shook his head and retrieved the rapier which Silvio had thrown to the ground in surrender.

"We gain little by silencing him," he pointed out. "His friend is already lost to us, and news of our whereabouts must therefore reach Rome's ears before long. Well, it was bound to happen sooner or later, and matters little. Let him live."

"This is folly, Leonardo," Rigo said. "Leave aside, if you will, the fact that this princeling would have slain you unarmed, and that nothing stands in the way of our doing likewise to him. Our whereabouts may no longer be a secret, but outside this valley nothing appears of our purpose. Would you hold him prisoner?"

"Yes. For Lorenzo's mercy."

"Then you risk a great deal, for there is more that he will see. Let us cut his throat like the dog he is, and hurl him down over that cliff."

"No," said Leonardo. "For one thing, there is a matter I have to discuss with him." He addressed Silvio Grimiani. "Prince," he said, "will you give us your word to seek no escape? It is that, or death."

"I give it," said Silvio. "Keep your peasants from me."

"Then dismount," Leonardo told him, "and keep a civil tongue."

They housed him—under continued and vehement protest from Rigo Leone—in the smaller of the two caves. There, after the evening meal, Leonardo visited him. He found the Prince in ill humor.

"These are no conditions for a prisoner," the latter said at once.

"They are the same as our own. Better, in fact, since you have privacy," Leonardo said.

"Your swinish companions may live as they choose," said Silvio, "and you also. I am of different breeding."

"I would be the last to deny it. Have a care, Prince; I may throw you to them yet."

"You would not dare," said Silvio. "Not if you hope for mercy from Rome, whose cause I serve."

Leonardo, who had brought with him a low stool, set this down and sat upon it. He trimmed the candle, which was their only light, and moved it until it stood equidistant between them.

"Oddly enough, I do not walk in constant fear of Rome," he said, "though I am pleased to hear you declare your allegiance at last. Let us, then, discuss the nature of your service to Rome. In particular, let us talk about a certain camisado which took place in the autumn of last year."

"I do not follow you," said the Prince.

"I think you do," Leonardo said gently, studying his face in the glow of the candle. "I think you do. I mean the foray in which the lady Carla d'Avalos was taken from your custody by the defenders of Castelmonte, thereafter to die most foully at the hands of the Count of Imola. You recall it?"

"I do. What of it?"

"I have been wondering, these last five months," said Leonardo, still conversationally, "how much you were offered by the Count for betraying her?"

"What is this talk of betrayal? I betrayed no one," said Silvio. "Giuliano de' Medici himself can testify that I fulfilled my duties as escort as well as could be expected, numbers being against us. Your suggestion is infamous."

"No," replied Leonardo. "No, I am afraid that will not answer. Giuliano told me, certainly, that you were fighting with their rearguard when he arrived upon the scene. He also believed that the attack had been part of a chance foray, perhaps by a party from Castelmonte breaking siege in search of supplies. This notion was never challenged, and Giuliano, of course, was too distressed to draw the correct inference from what he had seen. It was, he said, a camisado; and men do not wear shirts over their armor unless their sally is of deliberate purpose and one which involves recognition by friends in the darkness of night. Had their encounter with your party been accidental, as was claimed, they would have been plainly dressed. It follows that it was not by accident, but by design, that they came upon you. By whose design? By yours. It was you who insisted that the lady Carla and her companions should leave Pistrola at midnight, rather than wait for Giuliano's escort the next day. It was you who led them past Castelmonte, rather than by the longer and safer route through the hills. Therefore, you betrayed them, and sent Carla d'Avalos to her death. Did you suppose," he continued, his voice still soft, yet terrible now, "that I had spared you as prisoner for Lorenzo's justice in the trivial matter of my own attempted murder? I did not. It is for the life of Carla d'Avalos—a woman helpless, and no part of your miserable contrivings for Rome and against Florence—that you will answer, to Florence and to God. You may keep the candle by you, Prince. It would be a needless cruelty in me to consign a man with your craven soul to darkness."

He left the Prince of Savoy white-faced and made his way out of the cave. Rigo joined him by the side of the stream.

"A snake, Leonardo," he said. "Tread on him swiftly, my friend, lest he bite your heel, for I see from your appearance that you know him to be evil. Meantime, I will set a guard over him."

"He has given his word," said Leonardo. "Let him keep it, if he hopes to take one small step toward salvation."

"I would not give you a pinch of dust for his word."

"Nor I," said Leonardo grimly. "Therefore set your guard, but not too closely. He cannot outrun you, when all is said."

"There, by God, you speak truly," said Rigo. "Get some sleep, engineer, and I will order things as I see fit."

Shortly after midnight, Giunta di Lenzo, who had drawn the unwelcome task of sitting outside the cave which housed the Prince of Savoy, heard him groaning within it. He got up.

"What ails you?" he demanded.

"Bring me a candle, as you are an honest man," said Silvio. "Mine has expired."

"Then sleep," said Giunta. "I am not your servant."

"No, good fellow," Silvio said. "I cannot sleep, since I must pray for my soul. Do not leave me without light, I beg you."

"A pest on your soul," the gunner replied. Nonetheless, he fetched a candle from the nearest store tent, a bare ten paces away. Returning with it, he entered the cave, his hand outstretched. The Prince, stationed immediately inside the entrance, struck him on the head with a stone and stepped over his unconscious body into the open air. Flattened against the granite, he waited for five long minutes; then, satisfied that the remainder of his captors were asleep, he dropped to his knees and began to crawl.

Halfway down the valley, he rose to his feet again. The night sky was covered by clouds, and he walked swiftly toward the rocks at the valley's exit, secure in the knowledge that he could not be seen and that, even should the alarm now be raised behind him, he could be lost among the trees outside before any pursuit could reach him.

They heard him coming while he was still a hundred paces away from them.

Kneeling in the damp grass beyond the twin rocks he was approaching, Rigo grinned invisibly and blew on the end of his match, shielding its tiny glow with cupped palms. His four companions, crouched by their cannon, held their breath in alert anticipation. The cannon itself, standing on the surface of the outer trail and loaded with small shot, was pointing into the valley, its muzzle exactly covering the gap between the natural pillars at either side of the path.

Silvio Grimiani dropped lightly from the bank he had been following into the track, his feet sliding almost inaudibly on the loose stones of its surface. He recovered his balance, peered into the blackness that surrounded him and then walked confidently into the gateway which led to freedom.

Twenty paces away, Rigo touched the match end to the fuse.

The shower of sparks startled the Prince of Savoy, bewildering him for an alarmed instant or two before he realized its import. He half turned, screaming. His shout, merging with the brief thunder of the gun, was torn asunder with the rags of his body, fading amid the crashing echoes from the nearby rocks into a dreadful patter of unseen fragments of cloth, metal, bone and flesh.

Rigo Leone fanned smoke away from his face with his cap.

"Say a Hail Mary over the pieces," he suggested to nobody in particular. "We cannot hope to collect them all. Tomorrow, we shall build a dam and divert our stream down this pathway. I am, as all men know, fastidious, and I do not care to live with carrion scattered about my doorstep."

Eighteen

Francesco della Rovere, Pope Sixtus IV, in robes trimmed with purple, sat before a sunlit window in nervous discontent. His state of mind was occasioned neither by robes nor sunshine, but they formed a subtle part of it. For his dress was Lenten, and Lent was drawing to a close. The fine weather announced the arrival of spring, and with spring, must come decision.

His Holiness was unprepared for decision as yet, and therefore, he fretted, the more so since his nephew, the Captain-General and Count of Imola, had requested an audience. He would arrive soon, and would—so Sixtus knew—press for an immediate opening of the season's campaign. To this, Sixtus had no objection, having laid his purely military plans well in advance. The Count would also press, however, upon other matters—matters more tenuous, more liable to go awry, of dubious ethical standing and, worst of all, of questionable utility. The trouble with Riario, Sixtus reflected, was that as a weapon he resembled a hand cannon—noisy, potentially terrifying yet liable to backfire.

Somewhere, a bell chimed softly. His chaplain rose from a table and crossed to the door of the suite. He returned, to the Pontiff's faint surprise, with Rodrigo Cardinal Borgia.

"We are delighted to see Your Eminence," said Sixtus after the formalities of greeting, "but unfortunately, we are shortly expecting our beloved nephew. At noon, perhaps . . ."

"The Count of Imola has been called elsewhere upon military matters, and asks your forgiveness," said Cardinal Borgia. "If Your Holiness will graciously pardon his absence, I am come in his place and upon his errand."

"Then please be seated." Sixtus smiled. "We confess to some relief, and welcome Your Eminence unreservedly. Along with our relief, we confess to both curiosity and, if you will accept it in a spirit of charity, a little suspicion. Your Eminence is notably more persuasive than the Count, and we take it that your errand is one of persuasion."

"To the very slightest extent," said Cardinal Borgia. "I will not conceal from Your Holiness that it was thought that mine would be a more delicate touch."

"So I feared. But proceed."

The Cardinal settled himself. "May I summarize for Your Holiness?" he said. "Leonardo da Vinci, upon the orders of Lorenzo de' Medici, is in the Apennine Mountains. An attempt—the second attempt—upon his life has miscarried. The Prince of Savoy is believed to be dead. Two of his companions certainly are. The one man who escaped this affair reports that Leonardo da Vinci is accompanied by Captain-Gunner Roderigo Leone and a large force of gunners. All this confirms what we have long presumed to be the case—that Lorenzo de' Medici plans to resume the siege of Castelmonte soon and that da Vinci is for this purpose devising new weaponry."

"Of what nature?" asked Sixtus.

"That is the difficulty. Since none of us possesses the mind of Master Leonardo, and since the escaped man did not see what he was doing, his work remains an unknown factor. We may guess that he has built a larger and more formidable cannon with which to pound Castelmonte's walls, Florence's guns having proved inadequate to the task last year."

"It is very likely," said the Pontiff. "Go on."

"The point is," said Borgia, "that whatever is being planned clearly concerns gunnery and must, therefore, take time to deploy. Nonetheless, your Captain-General is anxious that no surprise be sprung upon himself, the Count della Rovere of Castelmonte, or the Duke Federigo da Montefeltro in—let us say—six weeks from now. They have allowed for a preliminary bombardment of two months' duration, as was the case last autumn. They do not wish to find themselves suddenly faced with a gun which, because of its size and power, could reduce their wall within—again, let us say—one month. Since his task is to hold the Arno Valley until Rome's armies need to pass through it, this is a reasonable attitude upon Riario's part."

"We accept it as such. Well?"

"Riario feels that Florence's designs—of whatever nature—should be flushed into the open as soon as possible, so that he may lay his plans accordingly. Therefore, he proposes to force their hand."

The Pontiff's eyes immediately narrowed in caution.

"By what means?" he demanded.

"We have with us in Rome," said Borgia, obliquely and carefully, "the man who escaped Leonardo da Vinci's ambush. He is Paolo Pazzi." The Cardinal paused.

"We know what is proposed by the Pazzi family," said Sixtus IV at once. "We cannot be a party to it. An attempt on the life of Lorenzo de' Medici himself—"

"Your Holiness does not need to be a party to it," said Cardinal Borgia. "That is why I am here, and not the Count of Imola."

Sixtus perceived the force of this argument. Had Girolamo Riario been sitting before him now, their discourse would undoubtedly have been unpleasantly direct.

"Then let us state it in terms," he said. "Under no circumstances will we countenance what is planned by the Pazzi family, useful though it would certainly be in the present context. Is that clear?"

"Perfectly. Save for one thing, Your Holiness need trouble yourself no further."

"What thing?"

"A trifle," said the Cardinal. "As . . . let me consider how best to put it . . . as a token that Rome's displeasure will not be extreme, should anything untoward occur that might force Florence to reveal her plans, the Count of Imola requests that the young Rafaello Cardinal Sansoni-Riario, his nephew, be sent to Florence from Pisa to attend High Mass on Easter Sunday. That is all."

"Thereby ensuring that we do, in fact, lend countenance to violence? By no means. We must refuse."

"Your Holiness speaks too hastily, which is perhaps understandable. By sending the Cardinal to Florence, the Church will, on the contrary, demonstrate her innocence of any design upon the persons of the Medici. The Cardinal," added Borgia reflectively, "is but seventeen years of age, and a youth of admirable purity."

Pontiff and Cardinal regarded one another for a long while. Sixtus saw his dilemma only too clearly. If he refused to agree, Borgia would set out the details of whatever conspiracy was being planned in Florence against the Medici and invite him openly to forbid it. Should he then do so, any failure in the spring campaign could be laid directly at his own feet. The Cardinal, expertly as always, had left him only one possible course. He took it.

"For the protection of the Church, and as a sign of our continuing love toward the ruling family of Florence, no matter how far they may have strayed in our esteem, we shall so ordain. Take care, Your Eminence, that no harm befalls the Cardinal Sansoni-Riario," Sixtus said, "who is as dear to us as he must be to the Count of Imola, his uncle."

"And what of my word?" asked Lorenzo de' Medici coldly. He was furious, as they could all see plainly. Even

Bianca, who had endured his rage more frequently than her companions and had learned to survive it without harm, was somewhat paler than usual. Lorenzo's temper, however, was more than matched by that of his brother.

Giuliano released Constanza's hand and stepped forward.

"What of it?" he demanded in reply. "Has anything been signed between the Ferrara and the Medici? I doubt it. Let the Duke find another woman to marry his son."

"You speak like a child," said Lorenzo. "Doubtless he will do so; how does that assist me, or Florence?" He turned to Constanza. "Let me hear it plainly from you, my lady. You are with child?"

"I am, my lord."

"By Guiliano?"

"My lord," said Constanza, "I will allow you a certain displeasure in the news, but do not insult me. If you have made promises, so have I. No doubt you believe yours to be the more important, but do not expect me to share your opinion."

Lorenzo put his palms on the table and pushed himself to his feet.

"Displeasure?" he said. "Take care, my lady, that I do not visit my displeasure upon you. I do not take kindly to being thwarted."

"Then I suggest you quarrel with me," Giuliano said, "since the offense was mine. It is time that you and I came to a reckoning, Lorenzo. You have my loyalty and my service, because you are best fitted to rule and I to follow. When they have plotted against you, I have taken your enemies as my own. If you have the interests of Florence at heart, so do I. But the love which I bear for the lady Constanza is not at the disposal of your contracts and seals. If that is not plain enough for you, then I know not how to make myself better understood."

The two men glared at each other across the width of the table.

"Come now," said Giuliano with less animosity, "will you admit that half your anger is caused not by what you must tell Ferrara, but by your having been cozened by us? We have defied you, yet we took the only path that was open."

"They are right," said Bianca. "They—"

"Will you be silent?" thundered Lorenzo. "I perceive your hand in this, madam, in any case. And were I to look farther, I daresay I could lay some portion of blame with another, by which I mean Master Leonardo da Vinci. None of which, I may add, finds favor in my sight. Well." He rubbed his jaw.

"Not everything which happens here is Leonardo's doing," said Bianca, correctly observing that the worst of the storm was now over.

"I commanded you to be silent."

"I am very sorry."

"As for the two of you," said Lorenzo to Constanza d'Avalos and his brother, "I would be within my rights were I to banish you from Florence. It has been done before. However, what is done is done, and Ferrara is unlikely to rejoice at having a Medici bastard wished upon him."

"Sir, your style of speech is offensive," Constanza said.

"Possibly. Do not assume that because my forgiveness seems likely, I have become soft. I have not."

Constanza laughed. "We are to be forgiven, then?"

"In time," said Lorenzo. "For now, give me your hands, both of you."

"I will do better," said Constanza. She came around the table and kissed him heartily. Giuliano extended his hand.

"Touching upon this question of bastardy," he said, "may we now announce our betrothal?"

"You had better."

"And your blessing?"

"Unwillingly wrung from me, but that also," said Lorenzo, relaxing, at last, into a smile. "Easter approaches; a suitable time for rejoicing, I think. However, we had better first seek the approval of the lady Bianca, without whom it is clearly impossible to move in matters such as this. Come here, little one. It is seldom these days that I have the opportunity of being embraced by two ladies of beauty and determination at once. I had better seize it, so that I may later remind myself that my authority is not always as powerful as I fancy it to be."

On Easter Sunday, the twenty-sixth of April, the city of Florence awoke to a warm and cleansing thundershower which left the streets and squares sparkling in the later sunshine of midmorning. Through these precincts, in bannered guild processions or as informal groups of relatives and friends, the Florentines walked in cheerful concourse, made joyful by the close of the Lenten fast. In costumes which matched their gaiety of spirit, they greeted one another on their way to church to give thanks both for the Risen Christ and for the official commencement of spring. Children splashed in the remaining puddles, to be cuffed without rancor by their elders; soldiers swaggered beneath arcades in their scarlet doublets, with harness burnished to a fine gleam for the benefit of the passing ladies; with robes gathered, clerics bustled by in twos and threes toward the ecclesiastical duties awaiting them.

There were those, however, who saw this Sunday with different eyes. For them, it was to be a day of fulfillment, the climax of a plot so foul in its impiety that one of the original parties—the disaffected mercenary Gian Batista da Montesecco—had found it too strong for his stomach and had withdrawn from it. He was not known to be squeamish. Its purpose, the dual assassination of Lorenzo and Giuliano de' Medici, troubled him not at all. He was grimly familiar with political murder. What he recoiled from were the place and the time of its intended execution.

Others were not so delicate. In the Villa dei Pazzi, the brothers Paolo, Francesco and Ippolito conferred with their father and the hired killer Bernardo Bandini. They found nothing objectionable in staining the marble of the cathedral with Medici blood.

"Vengeance," Bernardo said. "And I care not where I take it."

"Nor should you," said old Jacopo Pazzi. "Your brother lies dead in the mountains, slain by these tyrants and their hirelings. We offer you payment for his death. What do you say?"

"That I am your man," replied Bernardo. Paolo gripped his arm, and Ippolito offered him a cup of wine.

Archbishop Salviati, still smarting from the continued denial to him of the See of Pisa, was more cynical in his approach to the matter in hand. Having lost Montesecco, he had replaced the soldier with two priests from his personal entourage, Stefano di Bagnone and Antonio Maffei di Volterra.

"Pray for their souls as you strike, sirs," he said, "and shall not your prayers be answered? If the Medici die in church, they will be so much closer to heaven when they do so. *Requiescant in pace*, my friends. We do them a service, beyond doubt."

Young Rafaello Cardinal Sansoni-Riario, innocent of all complicity in this scheme of cowardice and sacrilege, rode to the Cathedral of Santa Maria del Fiori on a white palfrey. He had been told by prelates older and wiser than himself that Florence held little love for the Church he represented, and he had begun his ride in a fit of nerves. He was surprised to find himself welcomed on every hand. His downcast eyes were seen by the Florentines as evidence of a pleasing humility, and they were far from vindictive. Confronted by a Legate Extraordinary who, far from showing the conceit common to princes of Rome, seemed, on the contrary, to have nothing whatever to say upon any subject, the nobility had taken him to their hearts and the townspeople followed suit. He had, in addition, been given a rose by the lady Constanza d'Avalos at the steps of the Medici Palace, a gesture which left him scarlet with embarrassment. Not knowing what to do with this offering, he bore it through the streets in one hand, the reins of his pony in the other, and this picture of simplicity he presented won him smiles wherever he went.

He was greeted at the Cathedral by Lorenzo, whose groom

led his mount away, and by Giuliano, who asked the blessing of His Eminence upon the forthcoming union between the lady Constanza and himself. Archbishop Salviati watched this amiable scene with satisfaction, observing that the practical purpose of the young Cardinal's visit had been served no less than the symbolic. Both Medici brothers were attending Mass in recognition of his presence.

Half an hour later, toward the end of the first portion of the service, the Archbishop was seen to rise, genuflect, and leave the Cathedral. His departure caused a brief stir of whispered comment. Those nearest to him drew the conclusion, from the pallor of his face, that he had been taken ill.

That they were wrong became plain almost immediately.

For the signal to proceed with their violent plan, the conspirators had chosen one of the most solemn moments of the Mass—the elevation of the Host before the eyes of the faithful. Tactically, if in no other sense, their timing was admirable. As the officiating priest raised his hands with their sacred burden, he held the attention of every person present. From high above him, sounded the single chime of a bell.

At once Francesco Pazzi and Bernardo Bandini, thrusting aside those who stood between their victim and themselves, attacked Giuliano de' Medici. With daggers produced in haste from beneath their cloaks, they stabbed him repeatedly and viciously; so viciously that Francesco, aiming his fourth downward stroke at the reeling man in an insensate ecstasy of rage, missed him and drove his blade deeply into his own thigh.

In the same instant, the two priests from Archbishop Salviati's entourage hurled themselves at Lorenzo. Their assault was hurried, nervous, and pathetic. Stefano di Bagnone, jostled by his accomplice, achieved an ill-aimed stab wound in the muscles of Lorenzo's neck before the ruler, who had turned his head in the other direction at the sound of Francesco Pazzi's first shout of passion, realized the full import of what was occurring. The nearest of Lorenzo's friends, the poet Angelo Poliziano, pulled him backward and sprang between him and his assailants, warding off their blades with a cloaked arm and drawing his rapier. At once, the priests dropped their weapons and fled, amid the cries of the now alarmed congregation.

Of these, only those closest to the short lived drama had more than an inkling of its actual nature. Panic spread among the rest, borne by the rising clamor. Many of the worshipers toward the back of the crowd became seized by the notion that the great cupola of Brunelleschi's Duomo itself was about to fall in upon them, and within moments the nave was a maelstrom of surging and fear stricken humanity.

With blood gushing from his neck, Lorenzo was hustled by his supporters toward the sacristy. He fought with them like a tiger, trying desperately to reach his younger brother; but Giuliano de' Medici, his body torn by a dozen wounds and more, had dragged himself some fifty paces away and already lay sprawled and lifeless at the end of a hideous trail of red. Beyond him, at the foot of the altar steps, could be seen the figure of Cardinal Sansoni-Riario. He had stumbled in the course of an appalled flight for sanctuary and, with his gorgeous robes twisted about his knees, was now huddled and sobbing in terrified outrage.

Thus, in the space of time between one breath and the next, were altered irretrievably both the course of the war between Florence and Rome and the fortunes of those who were caught up in it.

For the Pazzi family and their associates, the alteration was immediately disastrous, since their conspiracy was as inept politically as it was vile.

Archbishop Salviati, at the head of two hundred armed men, was sweeping toward the Palazzo della Signoria, the city's council chamber, as the confused exodus from the cathedral began. Buoyed by an optimism the source of which was known only to himself and God, his intention was to take Florence's center of power without further ado.

In this ill considered task, he failed. The Signoria's defenders, under the leadership of the Gonfaloniere della Giustizia, beat back his attacking force with rocks cast from the windows and with swords deployed upon the stairways. Within minutes, the attackers found themselves surrounded by swarming and enraged Florentines, livid at the news of their favorite's assassination. Before his rebellion was fairly under way, the Archbishop was hanging, partially dismembered and writhing, from a window of the very building he had hoped to capture and occupy. By the time he was joined in his death agony by Francesco Pazzi, similarly mutilated, nothing remained of their *coup d'etat* save for the screams of their followers as they succumbed to the vengeance of the mob.

Jacopo Pazzi, together with his sons Paolo and Ippolito, fared no better. Alerted by the single chime which had announced the death of Giuliano, they rode from their mansion at the head of a demisquadron of horses, raising a shout for liberty from the Medici yoke. Like Archbishop Salviati, they had misjudged badly the temper of Florence and paid dearly for doing so. They were met, in the Piazza San Giovanni, by the spectacle of Archbishop Salviati's men in attempted flight from a crowd which outnumbered them by ten to one and had no thought at all of seeking liberty from a ruling family which, far from being tyrannical, was universally held to be just, competent and benign.

Barely half of their cavalry escaped to the countryside. The rest were pulled from their saddles and slain on the spot. Paolo and Ippolito Pazzi rode for Castelmonte and safety with the Count Giovio della Rovere. Their father was captured during the afternoon. He was dragged back to the city, tortured and—at the close of a smoking and bloodthirsty evening—executed. Days later, his moldering body was dug from its rough grave by Florentine urchins and pulled through the streets at the end of a rope before being thrown into the Arno.

Constanza d'Avalos stood, motionless, as she had been standing for five hours. Giuliano's body, covered in a cloth of purple and gold, rested upon a table—strewn with spring flowers—between her still figure and the altar of the Medici chapel. Brother Sigismondo had come and gone.

"My lady," said Lorenzo de' Medici, "I do not pretend that we are close, nor that we have been brought closer by this terrible thing. Let others feign such sentiments; we cannot serve each other thus. I offer you what is mine to offer: revenge."

He was behind her, nursing his shoulder. She did not turn.

"I care nothing for your revenge, my lord," she said.

"I did not suppose that you would," Lorenzo said. "Not now. You are as you are, and I am likewise myself—a harsh man, as befits my calling in this world. Think about it, nonetheless. You may come to desire it, as I do."

He left her and mounted the stairway to his suite. Exhausted both from his wound and from a fury which he could control only by the exercise of an iron will, he called his secretary to him as soon as his doctors had left the room. The message he dictated was brief and to the point, and a travel-stained messenger brought him his reply toward nightfall on the following day. "*Set your siege*," Leonardo da Vinci had written. "*I follow your courier within the hour. Both justice and warfare now demand the fall of Castelmonte. I promise you that the taking of it shall be swift.*"

From the city's easternmost turret, the view across the valley was clear, and menacing.

Federigo da Montefeltro, Duke of Urbino and commander of Castelmonte's defenders under Rome's Captain-General, stood with the captain of his wall, Guido Falcone di Riccomano, and surveyed the panorama spread out before them. Except that the golden light of last autumn was now replaced by the fresh sunshine of an early spring, the scene was a familiar one. On the summit of the ridge immediately opposite them, the two great Florentine siege cannon stood again in their positions of the previous year, having appeared there overnight. Men were gathered about them, hauling them into final alignment. Again the tents of Toscanelli's infantry had sprung up along the lower slopes of the ridge, while on their right flank, the picket lines of the Medici cavalry stretched away into the middle distance.

Montefeltro turned his gaze skyward, eying the clouds that drifted in convoy overhead.

"What is your assessment?" he asked.

Guido Falcone considered his words before replying. He

was a tall, squarely built man whose aquiline nose befitted his name. Like his superior, he was a professional soldier, born of a line of distinguished mercenaries; his mother had been Swiss, and her ancestry was displayed in his skin and his fair hair, now thinning at the temples. When summer came, his face would redden and peel.

"Firstly," he said, "Roderigo Leone is not with them."

"I see that," Montefeltro said. "But let me hear your reasoning."

"Their guns are resting on grass," said Falcone. "That is their primary error. Captain-Gunner Leone would have spent several days in laying a foundation of rock and timber; the ground is still far too soft for them to hold any degree of accuracy. I will grant them twenty shots, at the most, before they are forced to move. What puzzles me further is that their point of aim appears to be exactly the same as it was last year, and they can hardly fail to be aware that we have strengthened our wall. It is a hasty piece of work, however you look at it. Therefore, it is not Captain-Gunner Leone's."

"Then he is still in the mountains," said Montefeltro, "perfecting this new weapon of which we have heard so many rumors."

"I suspect so." Captain Falcone pursed his lips and expelled air from between them explosively. "It will be a bombardment," he announced. "You may depend upon it. They mean to throw their missiles high, thus clearing our wall and damaging our inner defenses. I know these so called engineers. Martini thought always of mortars and the lobbing of rocks over the perimeter walls of his opponents. A pointless exercise. At Rapallo, he tried to use missiles that were stuffed with powder and burst at the end of their flight, though it seems to me that he killed more of his own gunners than the enemy in doing so." He tapped the side of his head. "They are always too clever, and this da Vinci will be no different."

Montefeltro smiled. "Your opinion of military engineers, then, is, on the whole, a poor one?" he said.

"Sir," replied Falcone, "when I hear that my opponent has an engineer in his employment, I rejoice at the news. Why? Because I know, of a certainty, that he will spend months in the building of escarpments, counterescarpments, redoubts, towers, tunnels, bridges and similar pieces of foolery. When he finally makes his assault—which is to say, when his engineer and his military commander have all but come to blows with one another—his men are worn out from shifting earth and stones and are easy meat for the defense. Your engineer, sir, is well enough employed while he sits with quill and paper. But in warfare, he sees a God-given opportunity for inflicting his fantasies on others, to the detriment of their purses and their backs. You have spoken with the Count of Imola. When does he say that Rome will march this way?"

"Next week."

"Then, sir, I care not what our friends opposite are doing nor what new weapons they bring. If Rome's army marches next week, it must be here within ten days from now; and if our wall cannot withstand Florence until then, we may as well jump from the top of it here and now."

"Set your siege," said Leonardo.

"So you advised in your message. I have already done so. Where are my gunners?"

"They are on their way."

"On their way? Why are they not here with you?"

"Because they are marching directly to Castelmonte. They will reach it tomorrow night."

"I see. Very well."

Lorenzo de' Medici, his neck bandaged, sat behind the small table in his private and cell-like conference chamber overlooking the palazzo gardens. His wound would have kept a lesser man confined to bed, but the ruler of Florence, driven by a rage for vengeance, would no more have received his advisor there than he would have considered appearing publicly in his nightshirt. He was dressed for campaigning in soft leather tunic, breeches and boots. He could turn his head only with difficulty, and his face was sallow. Leonardo studied him.

"Sir," he said, "your neck is poorly bound. May I suggest—"

"I did not summon you to act the physician," put in Lorenzo.

"By no means. Nonetheless, I see that you intend to ride your horse," said Leonardo. "Is this so?"

"Very likely it is. What of it?"

"Then, sir, your head must be braced so that it will not easily move, or you will tear open your wound. I can design a support of armature wire that will achieve this for you, if you will allow me to do so."

"I thank you for your solicitude, Master Leonardo, but you distract me. Did my gunners leave the mountains at the same time as yourself?"

"Perhaps some few hours later."

"They are the same distance from Castelmonte as from Florence," said Lorenzo. "That being the case, why will it take them until tomorrow night to reach their destination, since you are here now?"

"Because," Leonardo said, "they are carrying your guns—the Medici Guns—with them. They will have requisitioned wagons, but even so, their progress must be slower than my own."

"A moment," said Lorenzo, raising his hand. "Let me understand you aright. These guns you speak of are the same six that you took with you to the valley?"

"They are."

Lorenzo, his eyes hard, pushed his chair fractionally backward.

"I would not care to suppose you were jesting with me," he said. "I have read your original specifications. These cannon weigh, as I recall, some two hundred and eighty pounds each?"

"That is correct," said Leonardo calmly.

"And were designed only for purposes of experiment and practice? We seem to be at odds here, Master Leonardo."

"They were designed for practice," Leonardo replied, "but hardly for that alone. Our practice is done, and we shall now wage war with them. Did you suppose differently?"

"*With small cannon?*"

"Even so."

"I cannot believe you. I had supposed, indeed, that by your science and with the help of the knowledge you had gained from your trials with them, you would be able to use my big siege guns to better effect. Do you tell me I was wrong in this? In God's name, what nonsense have we here? What damage can a four-pound ball inflict upon such a wall as Castelmonte's?"

"Sir," said Leonardo, "I pray you, for the sake of your own ease of mind, suspend your disbelief. With the coming of these small cannon, as you term them, your great guns are surpassed; and the nature of warfare from this day onward is changed entirely for all the centuries to come."

Lorenzo de' Medici laughed shortly. "I care nothing for the centuries to come," he said, "and therefore, let us have this truthfully. Will they give me justice for Giuliano and for Carla d'Avalos? Will they give me Castelmonte, that foul city?"

"They will. And when they do so, shall it be—as we agreed—the full and final discharge of our bargain together?"

"*If* they do so. In how long?"

"In one day from the time of their arrival there."

Lorenzo laughed again, mirthlessly. "I agree to your terms," he said. "Also, I will watch your guns—and you."

"In that case," said Leonardo, "you had better permit me to construct you a neck brace, and save yourself discomfort."

During the afternoon of the following day, the two heavy guns on the ridge bellowed their first challenge to the citadel across the river. It was a loud challenge, but—in the absence of Florence's Captain-Gunner—ineffective.

Lorenzo de' Medici and Leonardo, on horseback, examined the terrain from a smaller ridge, opposite the postern gate and a quarter of a mile upriver from the point where the road crossed and led to the main portal of the city. In the shallow basin beneath them, Guido Toscanelli was attending to his supply lines. Barely a tenth of his mercenary force was present as yet, together with some two hundred Florentines. There was, after all, little need for urgency, since several weeks of bombardment must follow before any large force of field troops would be needed for an assault. He had invested Castelmonte and could hold his siege with what men he already had. More to the point, his main force was encamped twenty miles to the south, awaiting the appearance of the army of the Church of Rome.

Lorenzo, silent, was fretting, though his neck and shoulders seemed more comfortable than before. Leonardo followed his glance.

"Have no fear," he said. "One hundred men, at most, will be all you require."

Lorenzo made no reply to this. Leonardo dismounted, and began to unfasten from his saddle roll a curious contrivance of wooden poles, hinged in three parts. Allowing his horse to graze quietly, he set up his rangefinder and lay on the ground behind each arm in turn, adjusting these with great care. Then he sat up, opened his notebook and began to write figures in it.

His calculations showed that the distance from where he sat to the postern gate was three hundred and sixty paces.

He turned over the top two sheets of the notebook, consulting some previous drawings and comparing them with what he could see now. Beyond the gate lay the defile, he knew; beyond this again, the vineyard where Toscanelli's assault force had perished last autumn, and then the inner gate which gave onto the alleyways of the city itself.

This inner gate, he noted, was invisible from the ridge they now occupied, since it lay in dead ground behind the outer wall. While this added to his difficulties, he had made allowance for the fact in his plans and was undismayed by the problem it presented.

"I wish to dismount," said Lorenzo. "Assist me, if you please."

Leonardo rose to his feet and, forming a step with his interlaced fingers, enabled his patron to descend painfully from his saddle.

"I thank you," said Lorenzo. "And now show me your purpose."

Leonardo held out the notebook for his inspection, pointing away to the left.

"There stands the main gate," he said. "We cannot see it from here since it faces northwest and is beyond the bend of the wall. For the same reason, your siege guns cannot bombard it, nor is there any position from which they could succeed in doing so. We knew this, of course, last year."

"Well?"

"Inside the main gate," Leonardo went on, "there is a small open space and then a covered lane which leads to the square." He added a rapid sketch. "This lane is angled at its center, so as to provide neither a clear line of fire between the gate itself and the square, nor a straight path for skirmishers. This is a common and sensible arrangement, as you are aware. Behind the square the streets climb steeply, thus . . . to the top of the hill; at the summit stand the inner keep, the palazzo and the building which you can see beside them—the monastery of San Piero Maggiore. All of these we can ignore, together with the hilltop and its immediate surroundings, if the main gates are opened and we succeed in taking the square."

"I will agree," said Lorenzo.

"Very well," said Leonardo. "Our scheme is a simple one, and ancient in conception. We propose to take the postern, make our way to the square and hold it. Then we shall open the main gates from inside and admit your attacking force."

"Excellent thinking," said Lorenzo ironically, "but a possibility foreseen by those who built Castelmonte. You cannot take the postern. You know what lies beyond it, and its name?"

"Of course. Its supposed invulnerability forms part of our plan."

"And how will you take it?"

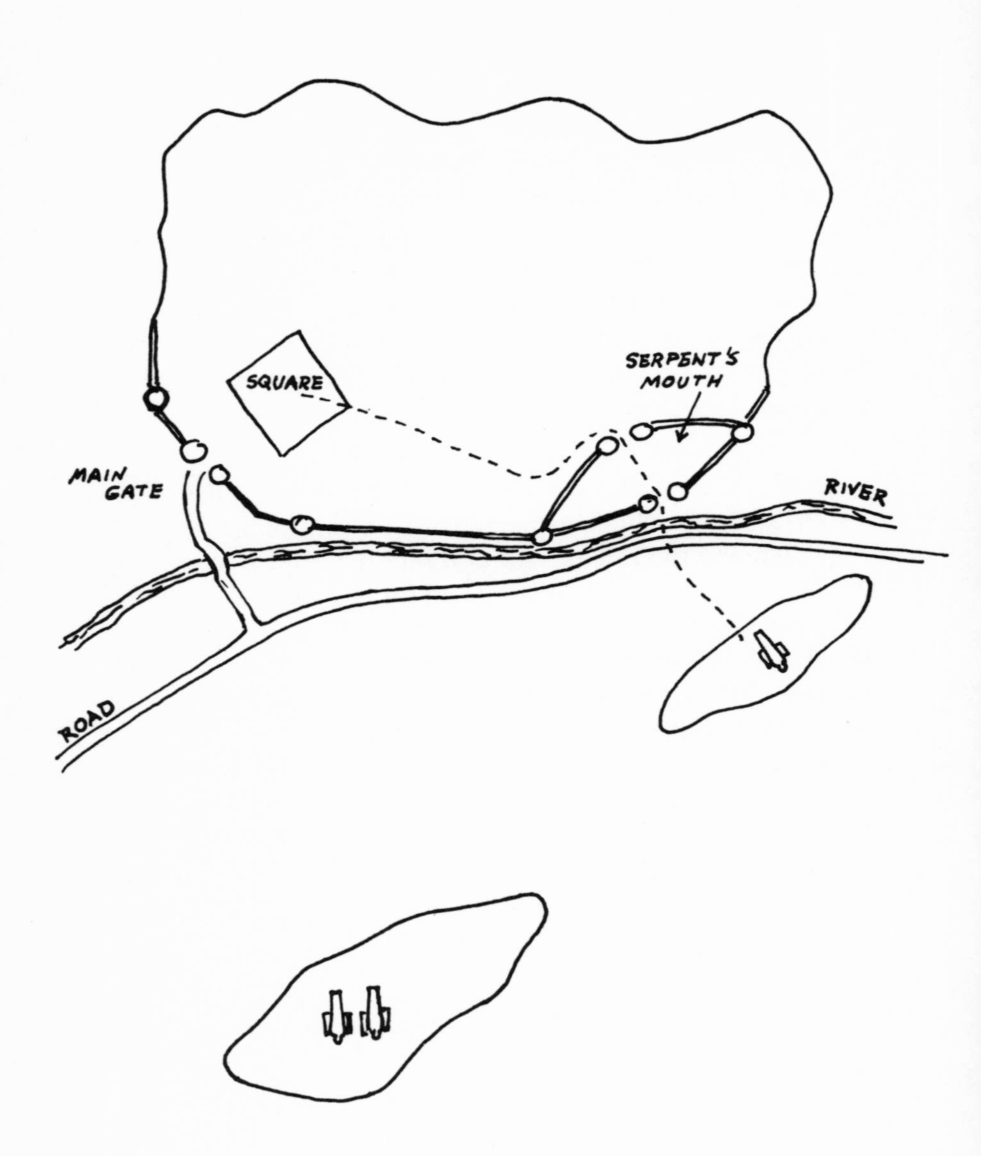
SQUARE
SERPENT'S
MOUTH
MAIN
GATE
RIVER
ROAD

"With the Medici Guns."

"I will concede that you may, after some time, be able to breach the outer postern," said Lorenzo. "What then?"

"We shall then take the vineyard and the inner gate."

"You propose to take your cannon *inside* the citadel?"

"Yes. Did I not tell you yesterday that the nature of warfare was about to be changed forever? Guns, sir, are no longer immobile and unwieldy. Therein lies my entire strategy."

Lorenzo scratched irritably at the bandage where it emerged from the collar of his tunic.

"I do not know with what speed you can carry your guns," he said, "and I must, perforce, believe that you are no fool. However, your gunners will be cut to pieces in the vineyard."

"With respect, sir, nothing of the kind will occur."

Behind them, on the larger ridge to their left, one of the two great siege guns roared again. Lorenzo half turned, and swore.

"A diversion," said Leonardo. "Let us, by all means, continue with the obvious, if only to keep the minds of Federigo da Montefeltro and the Count of Imola occupied. I presume that Rome's Captain-General is within the city?"

"He is. He has been there since before my brother's murder, in which I know his to have been the guiding hand. Were I forced to choose between Girolamo Riario and the Pazzi, I would take him." Lorenzo raised his fingers to his shoulder again. "God grant that I may be given him," he said softly. "God grant it so."

Twenty

By the third hour past midnight, Lorenzo's impatience was ill concealed. Earlier, a foot soldier had brought two plates of fish from the camp below. Lorenzo had declined the meal, and Leonardo da Vinci had eaten both. Hour by hour, twilight had faded into darkness, and now a quarter moon illuminated the river and the city, from which little sign of life had been seen since early evening when the trumpet had sounded and the guards—posted in each turret—had changed duty. Throughout the long night, Lorenzo's eyes strayed toward the tethered lines of dozing horses at their right. Leonardo knew that he was thinking of Giuliano, who should have been moving among the pickets exchanging greetings with knight and farrier, and would do so no more. The artist also knew that, if he wished to offer comfort, he had none to give that would turn the scales by a hair against the service he was about to render his commander in chief and, therefore, kept silent. Only the wind in the grass, the clink of the bits in the horses' mouths and the occasional call of one man to another in the valley broke the night's stillness until a sudden axle creak on the track that climbed behind them to the small ridgetop caused both men to stare, alerted, into the blackness.

The gunners, led by Rigo Leone, were barely thirty paces away when they became visible; fifty men, in dark clothes and with their faces smeared with mud, and beyond them, two open carts. The Captain-Gunner saluted Lorenzo, who lifted a hand in acknowledgment, and then turned to Leonardo.

"We rested at Pistrola," he said.

"Good. I trust that you left your wagons hidden outside the village," Leonardo replied.

"We did. Nor were we dressed as you see us now. We gave out that we were but returning to our duties on the ridge over there, though few troubled to ask us. Why should they?"

"Why indeed?" replied Leonardo. "Well, I see no reason for delay, if you are ready. Whose guns remain here?"

"Those of Marco di Carona and Giunta di Lenzo," said Rigo. "And Balestraccio has broken a bone in his foot. He has changed places with Piccio Berignalli of Marco's team, since he can still load for you. Otherwise, we are in good order."

"Then let us commence," said Leonardo.

Rigo spoke into the night. "Move," he said. "One."

There was an instant stir about the wagons. Sacks were thrown aside, revealing the dull barrels of the Medici Guns.

"Two," said Rigo.

Wheels and carriages were grasped and lifted to the ground.

"Three."

Men seized sponge staves, powder kegs, shot.

"Four," Rigo said. "Five."

The cannon slid toward the wagonsides, tilted, and were lowered. The carriage bearers were already in position, six paces between each team.

"Six. Seven. Eight."

The teams stood partially ready. Two of them were assembling their weapons, fitting the barrels to the wheels and carriages; pins dropped into place; range screws were swung forward.

"Nine," Rigo said.

Forty of the men rested easily, their drill complete. The remaining ten had unhitched the horses from one of the wagons and were pushing it steadily toward the ridgetop. They positioned it on the right flank of their formation and rejoined their comrades.

"Well," Rigo said, "I suppose it will serve." He grinned at Leonardo. "Marco and Giunta have already loaded, so that in fact we are somewhat slower than I would like. What is your first range?"

"Three hundred and sixty."

"Then they are yours. I retain command of the assault crews. Is it acknowledged?" asked Rigo.

"By all means."

Lorenzo de' Medici cleared his throat.

"I congratulate you," he said, "upon your demonstration. Your men are well trained indeed, and it does all of you credit. And now, if you will help me to horse, I shall go and take some sleep before tomorrow. Good night."

Leonardo detained him gently.

"Sir," he said, "it appears that we misunderstand each other yet again. This is no mere demonstration of skill with which to seek your approval. Spring is somewhat advanced, and dawn comes early these days. We take the city before it does so."

Lorenzo turned, moving his head and shoulders carefully.

"You intend gunnery at night?" he asked. His voice contained less surprise than it had done of late. "Perhaps, you will be shooting at the moon, since it is the only target to be seen?"

"We shall have our target shortly," said Leonardo. "It is true that you cannot make out the postern gate from where we stand, but that is a small matter. We can strike it."

"Can you? And how will you know whether you have succeeded in doing so or not?"

"We do not need to see where our shots strike," replied Leonardo, "and were we now in the darkest pit of Hades, your gunners could still fight. All we await are your instructions to proceed."

Lorenzo de' Medici looked from side to side, striving to pick out men and weapons he could barely perceive. Only their outlines and a faint shine of moonlight upon scoured metal revealed their presence. Abruptly, he slapped his glove against his thigh.

"Give me my city," he said. "And God go with you all."

Leonardo walked over to where the two assembled guns stood, their crews at the ready. He knelt behind each in turn, and set the range screws to three hundred and sixty paces. Rigo strode in the opposite direction, joining the four teams that were to make the assault. They carried the parts and accessories of their weapons—eight men to a crew—as they had been trained to do. When he saw Leonardo stand up once more, silhouetted against the starlight, the Captain-Gunner signaled to the two men who belonged to no team, and who now stepped forward. Each of them carried, in a waterproof pouch, flint, steel and a length of slow match. A knowledgable observer would have called these slow matches peculiar, since each was fully two inches thick and made from heavy rope soaked in a solution of niter.

"Go," said Rigo. He slapped them on the back in farewell, and they set off down the face of the ridge toward the river. Within ten paces, they had melted into the darkness and disappeared.

"And what now?" asked Lorenzo.

"Our target team is fording the river," said Leonardo. "Can you not see them there, against the moon's reflection?"

"I believe I can. What is their function?"

"To provide a target, as their title implies."

"You intend to shoot at them?"

"If they do not stand aside quickly enough when their task is done," rejoined Leonardo, "we shall do exactly that. Fortunately, they are aware that such is the case, so that I have no great fears for their safety."

Across the stream, the two advance gunners, unseen and soaking wet, pressed themselves close beneath the arch of the postern gate. The overhang hid them from the guardhouse above.

Both unwrapped their small burdens, finding them dry. One man nodded, therefore, and struck flint against steel, while the other pulled from his belt a fine metal spike, testing its sharpness with his thumb. A spark caught amid the loose strands at the end of one of the matches and was quickly blown to a spitting redness, soon turning the entire width of the rope into a brightly glowing ember. Its bearer centered himself carefully in the doorway and positioned it against the planks. His companion drove the spike through the strands of cord, working the point well into the grain of the wood with repeated twists of his fingers. They would have liked to make sure of it by giving it a few blows with some improvised hammer, but they dared not do so. Even the struck flint had sounded, to their nervous ears, like the clash of cymbals.

When he was satisfied that the spike would hold, the gunner who had driven it tapped the other's arm and stepped with him from beneath the doorway. One on either side, they slid around the side columns of the arch, hunched themselves into what protection they could find and looked back across the river. They could see nothing against the blackness of the ridge.

In silence, they awaited the shattering of the night.

Leonardo saw the glowing head of the fuse as soon as it was fairly alight but said nothing; it vanished almost at once, screened from him by the body of the man who held it. A minute later, it reappeared, pinned in the center of the invisible archway as though hanging, disembodied, in the void. To right and left of him, Marco di Carona and Giunta di Lenzo were already swinging their guns to the point of aim, and once again, he knelt briefly behind each barrel in turn, seating the tiny and distant spot of fire exactly in the muzzle notches.

"Ready," he told them. "Rigo?"

The Captain-Gunner, standing with two assault teams at either side of him, raised his left arm. In his right hand, he held, as did several of his companions, the weapon of his choice for fighting at close quarters—a six-foot length of stout chain, the bulk wrapped around his forearm. He looked toward the wagon to his right. One man from each crew had left his fellows to push the vehicle, whose flat bed carried, for the moment, the powder bags, sponge staves and shot.

"Go," said Rigo.

The long wagon, propelled by strong arms at each wheel, began to roll down the slope. It gathered speed, and was followed by the charging assault teams. Seconds later, its hurtling splash into the river announced the making of an improvised bridge for their crossing. The powder men hastily unlashed their burdens and were clear of the boards as Agnolo Fulvio reached its nearer end, carrying a pair of wheels and with boots pounding. No shout had as yet broken the stillness, and the wash of the cart's entry into the water could be heard plainly from the top of the ridge.

Rigo crossed himself, lifted a hand again at Leonardo in unseen salute and ran downhill after his men.

"Fire," said Leonardo.

Agnolo Fulvio reached the postern gate some five paces in front of the others. The grass of the bank was trampled, and his foot slid on a loosened piece of turf. He stretched down a hand to preserve his balance, and it seemed to him that, in the instant of lowering his head, the door in front of him exploded into fragments. The twin cannon cracks from beyond the river and behind him rang as one. He imagined that he had seen the flash of the balls, passing within inches of his head, but was uncertain. Half of the postern door, torn from its hinges, fell slantwise across the mouth of the arch, and a rebounding timber struck him heavily on the shoulder. He regained his footing, took another two steps and kicked the obstructing door section inward to clear his path as the four men who carried the barrel of his gun arrived at his back, their breath rasping in their throats. His powder man clapped him on the arm to signal his presence, and Agnolo threw himself forward into the hollow blackness of the tunnel's mouth.

Cipriano, the last man to cross the wagon bridge with Rigo, threw the wheels of the gun he commanded onto the bank and followed them, stepping delicately and without apparent haste. He was held by his companions to be a dandy, which meant that he washed himself twice daily; they also called him a cold-blooded fish. They had called him other things in the past, since his family were haberdashers and inclined to give themselves airs; he had once been handsome, but now displayed a broken nose in witness of the battles he had fought for acceptance.

His present task, a dangerous one, allowed him several seconds of grace as compared with the other three assault crews, and he took advantage of these by refraining from working himself into a sweat. Rigo overtook him, two steps from the shore, in a flying leap whose momentum carried the Captain-Gunner a quarter of the way up the bank. Cipriano climbed after him, reaching the small flat area outside the postern in good order and scarcely out of breath.

Three of the crews had vanished into the mouth of the defile beyond the shattered door. Cipriano's two carriage bearers raised their load, and he fitted the wheels to it, pegging them securely in place with the metal spikes he also carried. The four men who held the barrel lowered it into position, its trunnions slotting into the tops of the carriage wings, and Cipriano swung forward the range screw and block. The gun was already charged with powder, and his loader now tipped a double handful of small shot into the muzzle, following this with a patch and then ramming the handle of the sponge stave home to seat the olive-sized missiles in the breech.

The screw was set at pointblank range, the duty of Cipriano's crew being to cover the defile beneath the guardhouse from outside.

Since, in order to do this, they were forced to remain unprotected below the guardhouse windows, and hence were sitting targets for both the defenders immediately above them and those who might man the walltop at either side, Cipriano's icy calm was a necessary ingredient in their task. His crew watched him as he took the match from his loader; his face, briefly lit by its glow, was impassive. He made a small and nonchalant sucking noise with his lips and teeth. Around and above them, a confused uproar was beginning to swell. Cipriano di Ser Giacomo Giachetti di Lucca paid it not the slightest attention as he blew gently on the end of his match.

Three hundred and sixty yards away, on top of the ridge, Leonardo had seen his fiery target disappear, blown inward with the shards of the postern door, and grunted with satisfaction. He could make out nothing else. In the deep shadow at the wall's foot, the attacking gunners were but deeper shadows still. His guns had recoiled so he had no guarantee that they were aiming as before, but for the moment it mattered little. He reset the range screws, elevating both barrels slightly so that they would now rake the face of the guardhouse, and told his crews to reload. In a short while, he would need to fire another precision volley. Until this next target was presented, he would, meanwhile, give the outside assault group what covering fire he could.

Inside the gatehouse, confusion reigned.

The watch commander, Ridolfo Peruzzi, had been alerted by the splash of the wagon as it plunged into the stream, but had, from that point onward, been able to make no sense of what he saw. Dark figures had crossed the river, using the wagon as a bridge. They were heavily laden, but the nature of what they carried was unclear. While he strained to see what was happening, the flash and roar of cannon had come, not from the northern ridge, but from directly opposite him, to be echoed at once in the rending of what he knew—though could hardly believe—must be the oaken door beneath his feet.

"At night?" he exclaimed. "In God's name, it cannot be possible!" He rallied himself. Whether he could credit his eyes and ears or not, he was under attack; so much, at least, was plain. "You, and you," he ordered, "to the roof, with arbalests! Nofri, Alessandro! Find Captain Falcone. Tell him we are assaulted, and have lost our gate to cannon fire. Say also that we have dropped our portcullis." He turned as more of his men thrust into the room from their sleeping quarters behind it, and gestured toward the supporting ropes that slung the heavy iron grille from the roof beams. "Lower it!" he snapped.

Feet were clattering along the passage below him. He counted his men. With the departure of his messengers and crossbowmen, fourteen were left to him. He watched the foot of the portcullis being fitted into its slot between the floor timbers, heard the rasp of its massive and swift descent and the crash as it met the stone surface of the tunnel.

His defenses secured for the moment, he crossed again to the window of the room and leaned out. It was his last action in life. A four-pound ball, traveling six hundred and fifty feet in each second of its flight, tore a section of masonry from the wall beside his head, half decapitating him instantly. Chips of flying stone filled the air. His body, hurled backward like a doll, collapsed across a bench amid breaking crockery and the shafts of tumbling pikes.

Aghast, his men looked at one another. The walls shook under the impact of yet another ball from Leonardo's guns. Oil dripped from a swinging lamp, and a helmet fell with a clang. From the defile below, no further sound could be heard.

"They have taken the vineyard, then," said Guaspare di Piombino, the dead Ridolfo's second in command. "Down, then, and counterattack!"

"And the guns?" he was answered.

"They are not our concern," said Guaspare. "Our task is to hold the gate, as always. Lanterns, and follow me."

He ran down the winding stairway that emerged into the defile. His detachment followed, stumbling out into the passage, bewildered. At their right, their upheld and flaring lights revealed the portcullis, and beyond it, barely visible, the deadly circle of a cannon's mouth. Hardly one of them recognized it for what it was in the terrible instant before Cipriano addressed them from the shadows.

"Farewell," he said, and held match to fuse.

The gun's enclosed bellow turned the passage into a reeking and smoke-filled charnel house.

As the gunners strained their backs to raise the iron grid which barred their progress, propping it with the fallen door bolt, and stooped to haul their cannon beneath its lower edge, even the most hardened among Cipriano's crew were thankful that there remained no light to show them what nameless things they strode through—and kicked aside—before they reached the open air of the vineyard.

Leonardo knew by the muzzle flash of Cipriano's gun that their immediate task had been completed. He tapped Giunta and Marco on the shoulder.

"Rest," he said. "And load with care for your next shot."

Lorenzo spoke from behind him.

"What progress do they make?" he asked. "I confess that I can see nothing whatever."

"They have won the Serpent's Mouth, sir. All four cannon are now within the wall. Next, they must take the inner postern at the far side of the vineyard, which we shall break for them as we did the outer. It will be a difficult shot since even in daylight the inner gate cannot be seen from here. But I dare not rely upon Captain-Gunner Leone to shatter it himself since he must use his guns for close fighting and the vineyard provides no level ground for their placement. It can be done from here, by calculation, once they provide me with a range mark."

"By calculation?"

"Sir," Leonardo said, "when you and I are long dead, the time will come when men shall fire guns by calculation only, at targets which they never see. There is nothing marvelous in it, I assure you."

"I am becoming accustomed to marvels," said Lorenzo. "Meanwhile, these guns of yours . . ."

"They are yours, sir. What of them?"

"Nothing. I find myself," Lorenzo said, "at a loss for words."

Twenty-one

Sitting in the small room overlooking Castelmonte's main gate which served as his command post, Captain Guido Falcone was in ill humor. Like Ridolfo Peruzzi, he was unable for the moment to comprehend the events he had just observed, and he had been further annoyed by the hasty reports of these same events delivered by various of his subordinates—no two of which agreed.

The two soldiers from the postern gate, now standing uneasily before him, were proving to be of no greater assistance.

"It was a gun," Nofri said.

"Sir," dissented Alessandro Gambacorte, "this is not so. There was—"

"Silence!" Falcone roared at them. "You have brought, I take it, a message from your commander?"

"Yes, sir," said Alessandro.

"Then deliver it, and nothing else."

"Yes, sir. Sir, we are to report that the postern is under attack and the outer door is broken by cannon fire. A party has forced the tunnel and is now in the vineyard. The portcullis has been lowered. That is all, sir."

"Thank you," said Captain Falcone. "Dismiss."

"Sir," said Nofri again, desperately, "I will swear that they had a cannon with them, beneath the very gatehouse itself. I looked back over the parapet as we left to report to you."

"Dismiss," repeated his captain.

The two soldiers saluted and went out. Reaching for his burgonet, Captain Falcone could hear the two arguing forcibly in the corridor, and smiled to himself. He left the room by another door and crossed above the gateway to its counterpart in the right hand turret. Here, he found Federigo da Montefeltro staring from a window. The Duke turned to greet him.

"Well, Guido?" he demanded. "Six shots, and they have now ceased fire. Seven, perhaps, though I have seen but six muzzle flashes. What news of the postern?"

Falcone repeated the message he had received, and then hesitated.

"And?" prompted the Duke of Urbino.

"One of the men who brought me this report, sir, believes that he saw another cannon on this side of the river."

"Unlikely," said Montefeltro. "In God's name, for what purpose?"

"Precisely, sir. May I offer my views?"

"Please do so."

"Then, sir, I do not think we need cudgel our brains in order to make sense of the situation. They have fired six shots, as you say, from the ridge at our left. In addition, there has been an explosion at the postern itself. Now it is true that I have never, until now, seen artillery used at night, but it is quite certain that they can be achieving no accuracy with it. I suggest that they are harassing our parapet, more or less at random, in order to give cover to an attacking party. This party has destroyed our outer postern door by means of a mine set directly against it, which accounts for the seventh detonation you heard. It is this mining party and their equipment which the gatehouse messenger saw. His conclusion was false but understandable."

Montefeltro considered this for a while. Then:

"I accept your conclusion," he said. "A mine seems likely. It would seem that we have here an engineer who is not wasting his time."

"I admit it," said Falcone. "I will go further. Their assault is damnably well planned, coming well before we might reasonably have expected it."

"And our answer?"

"Why, sir, I see no reason for proceeding beyond the ordinary. It is evident that their attacking force has penetrated as far as the vineyard, having taken the gate house by surprise. But the portcullis is now down. With this in place, it is obvious that three men alone could hold the passage against any further assault. Those who have already entered can be dealt with in the usual fashion. I shall send reinforcements both to the postern and the inner gateway. That will be the end of the matter, since they cannot escape. As for this talk of cannon having been brought across the river, it is moon madness, and nothing more."

In the vineyard, things were proceeding according to the practiced pattern which Rigo Leone and Leonardo had worked out between them.

From the inner mouth of the defile, a fairly steep and uneven path led across the vineyard and upward, to end at the inner gateway at its farther side. To right and left of this path, the gun crews of Agnolo Fulvio and Scudo had deployed, and their weapons were now assembled and ready to fire. Cipriano di Ser Giacomo Giachetti di Lucca had emerged from the tunnel to join Guccio Berotti, who commanded the third assault group. Guccio's cannon was already charged with small shot, and Cipriano's loader was sponging out his barrel before doing likewise.

None of them had been troubled by the arbalestiers who

had gathered on the gate house roof and the top of the wall to either side of it. The moon had disappeared behind a cloud, and the vineyard was therefore a black arena against which neither the clothing nor the faces of the gunners were visible. Their movements could be heard, and a single stray bolt had whanged metallically off the barrel of Scudo's gun, cutting open his cheek; but since they were not even on the path—whose position could be guessed—the crossbowmen behind them could loose only haphazardly, and did so with little success.

As soon as Cipriano's crew had reloaded, both his gun and Guccio's moved forward and up the path. The creaking of their boots provoked a brief rain of crossbow bolts, none of which took effect. Passing between the teams of Scudo and Agnolo Fulvio, they took station at the sides of the track about twenty paces from the inner gatehouse, and turned their muzzles slightly inward so as to cover the gate itself.

The two men who had formed the advance target party for Leonardo's guns on the ridge now prepared to repeat their task, with a slight difference. They approached the wall to the right of the inner postern with lines and grapnels, and were followed by the loader from Guccio's crew, who carried a sponge stave with its tip soaked in oil. With them, also, came one man from each of the rearmost guns. They were to give the target bearers what support they could during the vital minutes it would take them to perform their dangerous function.

A murmur was now arising from within the turret above the inner gateway. The six guards inside it, whose lookout duties were usually negligible, were peering cautiously from their embrasures and conversing with each other in low tones, trying to make some assessment of their position.

Their first instinct, upon hearing the tumult at the outer postern, had been to emerge from their post in a body. In this, they had been restrained by their leader, whose orders were plain. The gateway itself was to be held in case of assault, since behind it lay the streets and alleys of the city itself; and the fact that within living memory no enemy had survived the vineyard to attack it made—in his view—no difference whatever. The destruction of the outer postern had told them nothing useful, save that the vineyard was probably occupied by the foe. Therefore, they must remain where they were until instructed to the contrary and, more particularly, until reinforcements arrived.

They did not hear the soft clink of the grapnels at their flank, and by the time they became fully aware of Rigo's target bearers and their supporters, events had overtaken them. Thankful that some positive line of action had at last presented itself, they now rushed from the gatehouse onto the parapet, armed with swords and halberds. The clouds had drifted clear of the narrow moon, but two men, unseen, were already on the roof above their heads. The remaining three were crouched—for what reason, the defenders could not fathom—behind the low curtain wall that faced the vineyard.

Reason enough burst upon them at once, though only one of them survived the moment of knowledge.

One of the crouched men shouted. From halfway across the vineyard below, Agnolo and Scudo swept the parapet with a murderous hail of small shot, killing five of the guards instantly. The sixth, partially screened by the breastwork, staggered to the open rear of the wall and fell, screaming, twelve feet into the alley at its foot.

The attackers rose. Two of them kicked open the door to the gatehouse but found it empty. The third man, jumping nimbly to the top of the curtain wall, passed the oil-soaked sponge on its eight-foot stave to the pair on the roof. Taking flint and steel in hand again, one of the attackers ignited a pinch of tinder, blew it into flame and held it to the sponge, which flared into a brightly blazing torch. The second target bearer stationed himself in the center of the roof, took the flaming stave from his comrade and held it at arm's length above his head.

"There is my second target," said Leonardo.

He was already lying prone behind one swiveling arm of

the rangefinder, which lay, as before, upon the grass some little way from the guns. As the distant torch rose into view above the top of the outer wall, wavered and then steadied, he took his sight on it and then rolled swiftly to the other end of his device to set the second arm.

"A light," he called, and sat up. After reading the marks at the base of either arm and working his brief calculations beneath a lantern held by Giunta di Lenzo, "A little more than five hundred paces," he announced. "Set your guns, therefore, to four hundred and ten paces."

Giunta moved away.

"I understand—if but dimly—the nature of your contrivance," said Lorenzo de' Medici. "But why four hundred and ten paces, rather than the true distance?"

"That is easily answered," Leonardo said. "My sight was taken on the flame of the torch, but it is not the torch I wish to strike. Since I could not see the inner postern gate itself, I asked one of your gunners to stand on the roof above it and hold a burning sponge as high as he could reach. He is doing so now, as you see. But the center of the door must lie some five *braccia* beneath his feet, and hence ten braccia below the flame. Do you see?"

"Yes."

"Very well. My experiments have taught me that toward the end of its flight, a ball from one of these cannon will fall in height by one braccio in every nine paces. Accordingly, in order to strike ten braccia beneath the flame, I must shorten my range by ninety paces, which gives me four hundred and ten."

"And you believe this firmly in your science?" asked Lorenzo.

"Sir," replied Leonardo, getting to his feet, "science will stand of its own accord, whether I offer it the prop of my belief or not; and what was a fact yesterday will remain a fact today."

"Ready," said Giunta.

"And now forgive me," Leonardo said. "I must not keep

my torch bearer standing exposed any longer than is necessary." He rushed past Lorenzo to the guns.

"Sir," said Guccio Berotti to Rigo, who was standing beside him, "why do I not take out this door myself? At ten paces, it is a simple matter even with small shot."

Rigo ignored him. "Agnolo," he called. "Scudo?"

From the middle of the vineyard behind him his gunners signaled that they had reloaded. From the other side of the inner gateway, hammering footsteps and the clash of carried weapons told of the arrival of a party of reinforcements from the city.

"How many?" Rigo asked his men on the parapet.

"Twenty," replied a voice from the night above. "Perhaps more."

Rigo turned back to Guccio.

"There is your answer," he said shortly. "Hold your tongue, then, in patience."

Before his eyes, the torch flame, blown by the softest of night winds, danced in the muzzle notch of the cannon. Leonardo patted its breech and rose, releasing the pent-up breath from his lungs.

"Fire," he said.

Tesoro di Veluti, his hand on a wheel rim of Cipriano's gun, was looking over his shoulder and saw the glinting arc of the shot in their flight overhead. "One," he counted, as the sound of the volley reached his ears. "Two."

The door burst asunder, one leaf of it ripped from its supporting post, the other slamming backward into the archway and rebounding from the wall. Unseen voices yelled their dismay.

"Fire," said Rigo.

From either side of him, the guns of Cipriano and Guccio belched forth torrential death. Scudo and Agnolo reached the head of the vineyard path, their cannon loaded but disassembled. They were running awkwardly, since each of their teams was still a man short. Rigo addressed the other two crews.

"Leave your guns," he said, "and fight." He charged the now broken entrance to the city, unwrapping the chain from his forearm.

Not all of the reinforcement party had been killed or crippled by the cannons' blast, though the archway echoed with the shrieks of those who had been thrown back by the doors' inward disintegration and immediately decimated by ten pounds of scattered and hurtling death. The gunners who had just fired their broadside fell on the remainder milling about the small piazza behind the gateway, stunned by the sudden descent of the incredible upon them. Rigo Leone accounted for three of them within as many seconds, flailing them to the cobbles with his chain. Back-alley fighters to a man, his men joined him, opposing sword and halberd gleefully with fists, boots and iron bars. Into the midst of this melee, a few moments later, came the crews of Agnolo Fulvio and Scudo. They assembled their guns with what haste they could and then looked eagerly about for opponents. They found few, their comrades having beaten down all the defenders except for two terrified crossbowmen. One of these, brought to the ground by a sponge stave accurately thrown between his feet, impaled himself upon the point of a bolt he was carelessly holding. Scudo felled the other with a cannonball, tossed as though it were a pebble from a distance of fifteen paces.

On the roof of the gatehouse, Tomasello Cennini drew his palm away from the wound in his shoulder and wiped blood across the front of his shirt. His fallen and still flaming torch lay beside him. His companion knelt by him.

"How bad?"

"Bad enough," said Tomasello. "Wave the torch."

"What?"

"Pick up the plague-blasted torch," said Tomasello pleasantly, "and wave it in the air, misbegotten and stinking son of a pig. I had no time to give the signal."

His friend complied, raising the flaring sponge above his head and swinging it to and fro in a wide arc.

"Thank you," Tomasello said.

"And what of you?" demanded the other, lowering the stave once more. "We cannot leave you here."

"And why not? Even your worm infested mind must perceive that no dog of Castelmonte is likely to find me up here," replied the wounded man ungratefully. "Go to the devil."

Across the river, Leonardo da Vinci had seen the fall of the torch and had guessed that its bearer was now wounded or, possibly, dead. It was a hazard that he had been forced to accept, but it left him in ignorance concerning the success or failure of his volley. He was relieved, therefore, to see it rise once more into view and move steadily from side to side in the prearranged signal which told him that the inner postern had, indeed, been destroyed. Giunta and Marco, seeing it also, cheered wildly. Gunners and engineer embraced, slapping each other on the back.

"By God," said Marco di Carona, "I swear that until this minute I had not believed it possible! At five hundred paces, and in the dark? It is a thing to tell one's grandchildren, and they will not believe it either."

"Yet it is true," said Leonardo, "and I thank you, my friends, for your patience." He disengaged himself with some difficulty and went over to where Lorenzo de' Medici stood by his horse.

"It would appear," said the latter, "that you have earned your hire, Master Leonardo."

"Not yet," said Leonardo, "but I will agree that the Medici Guns, at least, have proven worthy of further study. Sir, you should now collect what force you may require. God willing, we enter Castelmonte at first light."

Twenty-two

Rigo Leone looked about him, ignoring the huddled and silent bodies. The piazza was roughly semicircular in shape, and alleyways radiated from it like the spokes of a wheel. He counted nine of them, though half he could immediately discount; they led either to the right or straight ahead of him, and, therefore, away from his objective.

The four men who had been on top of the wall came out of the archway at his rear, having descended the gatehouse stair.

"Tomasello?" he inquired.

"Wounded. He will live," came the laconic reply.

"Well enough," said Rigo. "From which of these streets did the reinforcements come?"

Scudo's loader pointed. "From that one," he said. It was the alley that ran closest to the bank of the wall itself. Rigo nodded.

"Good," he said. "We will take it, then, since it seems likely to lead us most speedily to our goal. Number your crews."

"All present," Agnolo said.

"Present," said Scudo.

"Present," said Guccio, "but Stefano has a cut on the arm."

"How is it, Stefano?"

"It is dead, sir, but it is my left. By God's grace, I can still carry my share."

"Very well. Cipriano?"

"In order, sir."

"Then move out," Rigo said. "Wheel your guns, unless we come across a stairway. You are reloaded, Cipriano?"

"With ball, sir."

"Take the rear."

Quietly, except for the chatter of their wheels over the cobblestones, the gunners rolled forward.

A hundred and fifty paces farther on, Rigo raised his hand. They stopped, and at once heard the sound of footsteps atop the wall that lay close at their left hand. Motionless, they waited in the shadows. A body of men went by overhead at a run, heading for the gatehouse. When they had passed, Rigo motioned again, setting a faster pace. The quarter seemed deserted. The defenders had taken the opportunity presented by the winter truce to rid the city—at least temporarily—of its civil population. A mistake on their part—as things had turned out—thought Rigo. He remembered the legend of the geese which had raised the alarm and saved Rome, centuries ago, and grinned to himself as he strode past the unlit doorways.

The second reinforcement party, whose arrival at the inner postern had been delayed by the fact that they had reached it along the walltop rather than by the streets of the town, searched the gatehouse and its surroundings with some care. They found little to enlighten them. To his good fortune, they missed the wounded Florentine on the roof, who held his breath when the head of an archer appeared briefly in an embrasure a mere arm's length from where he was lying.

Their leader, one Mariano di Gaddo, turned over a body crumpled against the curtain wall of the parapet and frowned.

"How is one to make sense of it?" he said. "They have been torn to pieces." He crossed to the rear of the wall and spoke into the darkness of the piazza. "What of the others down there?"

"A hand to hand fight," one of his men called up to him. "And those beneath the archway have been killed by cannon fire."

He came down the stairway. "What nonsense is this?" he demanded. "Cannon fire?"

"Most certainly," replied his subordinate, extending a hand toward him, palm upward. "I know small shot when I see it, and if we cast about, I will wager we find the ball that has shattered this door. Did not Nofri speak of a cannon, back there at the main gate?"

"Nofri is a drunkard," muttered Di Gaddo.

"Perhaps. But in this he was right."

"And where is this cannon now?"

"How the devil should I know? I draw my conclusions from what I see, and that is all."

Di Gaddo cleared his throat and spat.

"Back," he decided. "There is nothing to be done here." Being no fool where immediate tactics were concerned, he told the two archers in his party to string their bows and walk the alley. Then he climbed the stairs again, collected the rest of his men and set off on the return journey along the wall.

The alley forked, one arm continuing behind the wall and the other directly ahead. Estimating that this latter route would take them to the main square, Rigo Leone chose it for his assault force. Three of his gun crews rolled beyond the corner and were out of sight when Di Gaddo and his men reached the small turret which straddled the angle of the wall.

Cipriano's team, however, had paused at the fork. They were not to follow their comrades until the gun in front of them had safely passed the next cross alley, eighty paces ahead. Cipriano heard the footfalls overhead while they were still some distance from him, and would have moved forward in order to avoid detection had matters been left to his discretion. His orders, however, were plain. He waved his crew to silence and hoped for the best. The approaching defenders were not troubling to conceal their presence. There was a chance that they were merely retracing their path rather than seeking opposition.

Clapping his hand to his side, Cipriano knew he had guessed wrong. An arrow protruded from his side. Softly treading and unseen, Di Gaddo's archers had advanced in parallel with their comrades on the wall. He had time only to utter a hoarse warning before the halberdiers above leapt down among his men.

Blows and shouts echoed all around. Though outnumbered, the eight blackened gunners could barely be seen, while the weapons and perspiring faces of their attackers shone in the dark alley. Their pikes were clumsy at such close quarters. A few landed clumsily and were smashed into insensibility by the short iron billets of their adversaries before they could even regain their footing. Discipline and training were, in these surroundings, no match for crude instinct.

Snapping off the head of the arrow that had passed through his side, Cipriano pulled at the shaft from the other end of the wound. Someone rushed at him with drawn sword. With cold precision, he took the descending blade on his leather-clad upper arm, then drove the barbed arrow point ferociously upward into the pit of his opponent's stomach. Di Gaddo groaned and fell. Cipriano dropped a knee across his throat before wheeling aside, then slid down against the wall. He was grasping the feathered shaft still in his back when his loader collapsed across him, a pike between his shoulders, blood gushing from his mouth. By the time he heaved the dead gunner from him, the fight was nearing its end. Tesoro de Veluti stooped over him.

"The archers?" he asked.

"Good lad," said Cipriano. "They must not escape." He pointed down the alley toward the inner postern gate.

"I see nothing," said Tesoro, "but no matter."

He ran back to the cannon. All around him, men were struggling in the darkness. Swinging back the range screw, he let the muzzle rise and crammed a fistful of small shot down the barrel on top of the single ball already there. He vaulted nimbly back to the breech, tilted the barrel level and wrestled the entire gun about until it was pointing down the alleyway. The slow match, its end burning, was clipped to the side of the carriage. As the last of the swaying combatants cleared from before the cannon, he touched off the fuse, praying that none of his comrades would stumble unwittingly in front of him within the next few seconds.

The gun's fiery explosion seemed to rock the walls at either side of the narrow street, its muzzle flash freezing the figures around him in an unreal tableau which vanished at once in the billowing smoke of its discharge. Ignoring the enraged curses of his fellow gunners, Tesoro sprinted down the alley. Two mutilated corpses were sprawled in a doorway. There seemed to be no more. He was certain, after examining them briefly and by touch, that nobody had survived his ill prepared but lethal shot. He returned to the cannon. The surrounding stones were littered with prostrate soldiers and four upright gunners.

Cipriano called to him from the angle of the wall.

"It was well done, lad," said his crew leader painfully. "The gun is yours. How many are we?"

"Five and you."

"Pray, then," said Cipriano, "that you come across no stairs. Five of you will be enough to roll it on the level."

"Guccio will give us one of his men."

"If the Captain-Gunner agrees. Better not rely on it. Go, boy."

Girolamo Riario stood at a high window overlooking Castelmonte's main square.

"Cecco," he said.

His secretary rose nervously and came to him.

"Yes, my lord?"

"Fetch Stoldo, Buonaccorso and Serpe. Then go to the Count Giovio della Rovere, and tell him to make ready to meet me. He knows where."

"Yes, sir. My lord, what does this . . . what does your lordship think is happening out there?"

Riario turned sharply and struck him full in the face with the back of his hand.

"What I think is no concern of yours," he said. "Begone."

In his room above the massive northwestern portal, Captain Guido Falcone was confronted by Paolo and Ippolito Pazzi, both clearly panic stricken.

"I have spoken with those outside," said Ippolito. "Falcone, they are saying that we . . . that the postern door . . . in short, that we are taken. I do not know what the truth of it may be. But I—"

"Sirs," said Falcone heavily, "calm yourselves, I pray you."

"That is all very well," said Paolo Pazzi. "But this is no time for calm or for delay. We must hold at all costs! What are your dispositions? If we are taken in the rear, how will you answer it? And they are mining us!"

"Be silent," Falcone ordered brusquely. "By God, I find this unseemly. I understand well enough that you are fearful for your skins. But I must tell you plainly, sirs, that I am here to defend a city and not to play wet nurse to a pair of assassins. You have swords, have you not? Use them, if we come to it. Now, get out."

Silencing their protests, he ushered them through the doorway and started in search of his commander. In the passageway outside, however, he was detained by a guard, who held the arm of a filthy and ragged graybeard.

"I cannot understand him properly," said the sentry, "since he is obviously a half-wit. But I think he is saying that he has seen a dead man in the street, blown to pieces by cannon."

Twenty-three

Federigo da Montefeltro was studying the far bank of the river where a company of men and horse was gathering beneath the paling sky.

"At all events," said Guido Falcone, "it seems plain that there is an assault party within our wall, however it may have come there. It follows that their objective must be the gate under our feet."

Montefeltro took his captain's arm and drew him to the embrasure. He pointed.

"And there is the proof of it," he said. "Well, now. Would you care to hazard a guess at the size of this assault party, Guido?"

Captain Falcone rubbed his eyes, grimacing wearily. "Thirty or thereabouts," he said. "They mined the postern, as you said, but they also killed Peruzzi and his detachment. And Di Gaddo has not returned; his party was fifteen strong. They are in force, then, but more than thirty would be unwieldy for a surprise attack."

"And the inner gate?"

"Mined again, I would think."

"Or they are still in the vineyard."

"No," said Falcone.

"No," agreed Montefeltro. "No, they have won the inner gate. Blood of Christ, but we need some knowledge of what has taken place down there!"

"I have sent a reconnaissance party, now that there is light to see by."

"Their information, I fear, will come too late. Well. We have a town to hold, and hold it we shall, Guido, my friend. Where is Rome's Captain-General?"

"I neither know, nor do I care," said Falcone. "What of this cannon, sir?"

"I will believe in it when I see it, and not before," said Montefeltro. The two men looked at each other. "We have seen many things together, you and I. A mine, I am prepared to accept. If I am wrong and they have taken the postern with a cannon, then the rest may be true as well. And if they can fire artillery in the black of night, and that with an accuracy unheard of even by daylight . . . why, then, Guido, you are but an old hound, and I another, and we had best seek our place by the fire to warm ourselves and twitch in our dreams."

The Medici Gunners—thirty-one men strong now, and with their four light artillery-pieces—rolled into the main square and at once crossed it, diagonally, to gain the inner mouth of the covered and sharply angled lane which led from it to the city gates. After Cipriano's skirmish in the alley, they had met with no further opposition; nor, indeed, could they see any sign of life here, though a buzz of turmoil was heard at the lane's farther end, invisible to them because of the defensive bend at its central point.

The square itself lay deserted in the half light. On all sides, the façades of the surrounding buildings rose like the gray walls of a canyon, seeming to press inward upon the space they enclosed. In an upper window, a solitary lantern burned. Everywhere else, the shutters were closed and barred, as though the town had turned her back on civil life and now looked only outward, over tower and parapet, toward the hostile world beyond her guardian river.

Guccio Berotti, in the lead, reached the corner by the lane's entry and swung his gun briskly about to cover the square. Behind him came Tesoro di Veluti, his depleted team restored somewhat by the addition of the remaining target man, presently acting as replacement loader. Pausing only to drop a leather bag of solid shot at Guccio's feet, Tesoro's crew wheeled onward beneath the timbered roof of the lane, to be followed by Agnolo and Scudo, who similarly deposited a bag each with Guccio as they passed him.

Rigo waved at the empty square.

"Keep it as you see it now," he said. "I have no wish to be interrupted by a score or so of pikemen at my back."

"Attend your own business," said Guccio disrespectfully, "and leave me to mine. I am beginning to get the feel of this peagunnery."

Rigo nodded and followed his other three cannon.

"Lay to the left of that corner opposite us," said Guccio promptly to his crew, "and set the range at seventy paces." He sat on his heels behind the gun. "Good," he said. "Fire."

The four-pound shot, its impact velocity barely less than that with which it had left the muzzle a split instant earlier, tore a whole section from the corner pillar of a colonnade as a man might chew out the middle of a carrot. The unsupported upper portion of the column fell from its architrave and toppled into the gutter. Before the smoke had cleared from before the barrel, Guccio's loader was ramming home the wad on top of another measure of powder.

"Now the next," said Guccio, "and stop moving as old women do." He checked the cannon's aim once more. "Fire," he said.

A second column collapsed, spurting dust.

"Again. Fire."

With the decimation of a third column, the entire corner of

the colonnade, together with thirty feet of the face of the building which rested upon it, cracked outward. The gunners reloaded.

"Fire," said Guccio.

A quarter of the building shuddered, split, and fell rumbling across the far corner of the square, blocking two access streets with five hundred tons of masonry and timber.

"Excellent," said Guccio. "Take the corner to our right, and start with the third pillar from the end. It is a very fair little weapon we have here, all things considered. Fire."

Below Riario's feet, the house shook.

He stared, immobile and in fascination, at the drifting powder smoke and the half glimpsed barrel of the gun by the lane.

"Mother of God," said his aide, Buonaccorso, from the doorway behind him. "They will reduce Castelmonte to a heap of rubble!"

"Perhaps," said Riario. "Where is Serpe?"

"Downstairs, my lord."

"Stoldo?"

"By the courtyard gate, sir."

"It is time for us to leave," Riario said. "Find them, and go to the Cappella dei Morti in the Via San Marco, as I told you earlier. Wait there until I arrive, and beware of any treachery on the part of della Rovere and his men."

Tesoro di Veluti, his back against the wall of the lane, checked that his gun could be swiveled quickly and without obstruction so as to point along either arm of the passage.

His task was twofold. Should the defense overcome Guccio in the square, he must prevent them from storming the lane and taking Rigo's rear. And, if need arose, he was to give support to Agnolo and Scudo when they emerged into the piazza behind the main gate itself. Until called upon to perform either of these duties, he would remain where he was.

Like his comrades about him, he stood easily and with his

mouth partly open, a trait which all gunners acquired early and which often gave them the appearance of being half-witted. To stand next to a discharging cannon with jaw set, however, was to invite a ruptured eardrum, especially in the confined space of the tunnel whose center he now occupied.

Fifteen paces away from him, Agnolo and Scudo trained their weapons on the farther mouth of the lane. Rigo stood between his lieutenants. Knowing that they had, perhaps, three or four pulsebeats before their final battle commenced, he pounded each of them on the shoulder in turn as the first of Guccio's shots broke the morning's silence. Dearly though he would have liked to employ these moments, and the sharp edge of surprise they represented, in assessing what lay in the open air ahead, he would be throwing away a badly needed advantage if he did so, and had elected to begin his last assault from where he was.

"After the first volley," he told them, "fire as you will. If there are steps, take them. And, for your lives, recharge your guns quickly."

The dim rectangle of the lane's exit was suddenly filled with oncoming figures. They knew nothing of what they faced, Rigo thought, but they would hardly have been human had they not charged at the sound of Guccio opening fire. The latter's second round thundered from beyond Tesoro di Veluti and was answered without pause by the overpowering twin percussions to the Captain-Gunner's right and left.

Reloading, his crews advanced through swirling fumes and over the fallen bodies of the dead and dying into the piazza which was their ultimate objective.

Some fifty paces directly in front of them were the huge gates—dominating the courtyard—their leaves secured by a bolt half as thick as a man's body and twenty feet from side to side. Above them, the archway supported a narrow and castellated bridge, spanning the gap between a pair of looming turrets. From these, broad stairways led downward and toward the gunners, forming the chief routes of access to the top of the mighty wall that stretched away until it disappeared from sight behind the houses to east and west of the piazza.

In and around this arena, there were, Rigo estimated, a hundred men or more. Down the right hand stairway jostled a party of crossbowmen, closely followed by a ragged stream of halberdiers and men with swords. A group of horsemen was clattering away from him into the alley which followed the base of the western wall. Presumably, he thought, they intended to retake the main square from one of its flanks. In the gateway itself, a somewhat indecisive throng of knights and men-at-arms was milling back and forth, their faces turned in alarm toward the mouth of the lane. He glanced upward and saw more arbalestiers on the rooftops. Bolts sang, and two gunners fell.

His cannon roared again. The crowd in front of him withered like grass before a scythe. Scudo, first to make ready again, shredded the defenders on the stairway, and an instant later Agnolo's gun boomed, filling an arcade with writhing bodies.

Both crews, reloading, dismantled their weapons and fought up the stairways with them, one at each side of the gate, hacking with their boots at those who, wounded, still tried to contest their passage.

Rigo retreated beneath the roof of the lane.

"Tesoro!" he shouted.

"Sir?"

"To me, infant! We have them!"

His third gun rolled to the lane's mouth, thus giving him three sides of the piazza. On the bridge above the gates, he now saw Federigo da Montefeltro, who had emerged from the turret at the right. Rejoicing inwardly, and heedless of the crossbow bolts that still hummed about his ears, he advanced to the middle of the square.

"My lord Duke!" he called.

From the tower opposite, Captain Guido Falcone appeared, to stand beside his commander. Both men took in the scene that confronted them. Montefeltro stepped toward the parapet's rearmost edge, looking down at Rigo.

"Surrender," said the Captain-Gunner. "I hold you in the palm of my hand, as you see. Therefore give up, and save further carnage."

Undecided, Montefeltro turned to the west, where a detachment was rushing toward him along the battlements. Their charge was suicidal. Almost unable to appreciate what was happening, he saw Agnolo Fulvio's crew set down their gun carriage at the stairhead, drop the barrel into position, seat the breech and fire, sweeping the walltop clear of men as a gale scatters chaff. Behind him, he could hear the steady approach of Lorenzo de' Medici at the head of a column of cavalry and foot soldiers. In the doorway of the turret at his right, Paolo and Ippolito Pazzi stood with craven faces. Of his force in the piazza below, more than half were already dead or wounded.

He made up his mind, as a condottiero must. His mercenaries, those left alive, would fight like men if he ordered them to do so, but what he saw about him now was a chicken slaughter rather than a battle. Defeat stared him in the face, but defeat could be survived in the world of the condotta, whereas massacre could not. Fighting to the last drop of blood was the mark not of a soldier, but of a fool.

He raised his hand.

As Leonardo had promised, Lorenzo de' Medici, riding stiffly with the artist at his right and Toscanelli at his left, arrived before the city gates of Castelmonte; he found them—as Leonardo had foretold—open to greet him. So easy did his victory seem, indeed, that he would almost have suspected a trap, had it not been for the sight of his gunners waving from the battlements overhead.

The piazza, when he entered it, was crowded. Immediately opposite him were the guns of Guccio Berotti and Tesoro di Veluti, their crews grime-caked and cheerful. Rigo Leone, his single concession to the formality of the occasion being the discarding of the chain from around his arm, now held Montefeltro's sword and was talking to him, as one professional to another. The dead were already being dragged aside, and the wounded were limping or being carried by their fellows, into the shot scarred buildings.

Toscanelli and Leonardo fell back a little, the latter dismounting and giving his reins to the Florentine mercenary. Lorenzo de' Medici halted a few steps ahead of them, and was approached by Federigo da Montefeltro.

"My lord," said the condottiero simply, "your guns have taken us. Therefore, we surrender this city and all within it, to the mercy and justice of Florence."

Lorenzo gazed coldly past him, his eyes searching. A half minute and more passed in silence before he spoke.

"Give me the Pazzi," he said.

"They are held, sir, at your pleasure."

"It is well for you that they are," said Lorenzo, looking at him for the first time. "Show them to me."

Riario watched this scene with cynical indifference. He was seen by few and recognized by none, since he was wearing the cowl and habit of a friar. He had walked unhurriedly through the covered lane, and now stood some distance past the bend at its center, satisfying himself that the course of action he had chosen was both necessary and correct. Having done so, he turned, and was about to retrace his steps when he was addressed from the ground beside him.

"Bless me, Father," said the mortally wounded soldier who lay against the wall, "for I have sinned."

"As have all men," said Girolamo Riario. "Farewell."

At this, the dying pikeman cried out in rage and desperation. In the lane's mouth, a gunner turned at the sound. Though it was yet dark beneath the roof beams of the tunnel, and despite robes and cowl, Tesoro di Veluti recognized the man he sought as though by instinct.

He would have shouted his hatred and defiance, but restrained himself. The Count of Imola was his meat, and his alone. In the dust, a few paces from him, lay a discarded and bloody rapier. He bent swiftly, snatched it up and ran into the lane like a hare. His sudden departure caused a stir only among those who had been nearest to him. Of these, two men alone instantly perceived the reason for it.

Leonardo gripped Rigo Leone's arm and pointed.

"We are not yet done with Castelmonte," he said.

They detached themselves from the gunners around them, made their way inconspicuously to the lane's entrance and then broke into a run.

By the time they gained its inner end, only Tesoro's back was in sight. He was scrambling over a bank of rubble at the corner to their right, then dropped from view beyond it as they changed their direction to pursue him. Skirting the broken pillars and spills of stucco, which were all that remained of the arcade and housefronts along this side of the main square, Leonardo reached the pile of ruined masonry ahead of the Captain-Gunner, and stretched back to pull him to its summit. Ahead of them, the street lay empty, the first drifts of an early morning mist glistening on its cobbles and gathering at doorsills. They heard the diminishing sound of footsteps in the shadows farther down it, and then nothing more. Rigo, still holding Montefeltro's sword, gestured uncertainly with its tip.

"We cannot leave the boy to his own devices," he said. "Both of us know what he is about."

Tesoro di Veluti took the stairway which led up to the porch of the Cappella dei Morti in three strides and burst open the door with his shoulder, heedless of what he might come upon behind it. For all he cared, he might be entering the very portals of hell itself, so long as he found revenge there for the hideous death of his brother Andrea.

The room in which he found himself was walled in black marble, and filled—or so it seemed to him—with men clad, as his enemy had been, in robes gathered at the waist with knotted cords. At one side of the chapel, for such it clearly was, stood a coffin on a litter. It contained no corpse, but rather a quantity of gold and silver coins, over which two of the seeming friars were in the act of folding a soft cloth.

He understood at once the preparations for flight which he had interrupted. They were not his concern. What enraged him was that he could not distinguish his foe among the fifteen or more similarly dressed figures who now turned menacingly toward him in the gloom. He charged through them, cutting and thrusting with his sword in a white heat of frustration, his eyes flicking about in quest of the murderer he had come to destroy. The sheer fury of his progress carried him to the far end of the nave. At the foot of the chancel steps was a man, his arms grasping the base of a massive stone candlestick as though trying to lift it from its pedestal. His head jerked around, dislodging the cowl from his face. It was the face of the Count Giovio della Rovere, ruler of Castelmonte.

"Dog!" shouted Tesoro di Veluti, and hurled himself forward with thrusting blade. Della Rovere, hampered by the marble cylinder he was trying to support, had no time to draw his sword from beneath his robes. Had he been able to do so, the outcome would have been no different, so violent and uncaring was the young gunner's onslaught. The latter's point ran straight through his body from side to side, tearing open arteries and transfixing his liver. He rolled his eyes, staggered, and collapsed, the mighty candlestick toppling with him.

Across his lifeless body spilled a dazzling tide of emeralds, rubies and diamonds, hidden within the pillar's core and now scattering, as from a cornucopia, over the polished flagstones. Obsessive still in his lust for vengeance, Tesoro ignored them. As he struggled wildly to free his sword, he was barely aware of those who now fell upon him and beat him, senseless, to the floor.

Leonardo and Rigo heard his cry of rage from the street and, crossing it, climbed the stairway to the mortuary chapel.

Most of their opponents were clustered around the fallen gunner, and those nearer to the door were impeded by their monkish costume. Two were already dead, having been slain by Tesoro in his rush toward the altar. They disposed of another pair within moments of their entry, but the odds against them were still heavy.

Rigo Leone seized a lamp from a low cabinet beside him, poised for an instant, and then hurled it at the group by the chancel steps. It burst among them, spreading flame and striking many-colored glints from the gems that lay unheeded all about the marble floor of the nave. Three men, their oil soaked robes aflame, struggled vainly to strip themselves of these. Rigo charged into the remainder, chopping right and left unskillfully but with overpowering strength, and won his way to the choir stalls beyond them, where he overturned the second of the gigantic candlesticks onto those who sought to reach him.

Leonardo, choosing for the moment to stay where he was in order to divide the opposition, found himself assailed by a tall man with a stiletto, upon whose heels followed two more with blades drawn. He picked his spot with care, ran the dagger bearer through the stomach and plucked the weapon from his nerveless fingers as he fell. Left handed and without pause, he flung the dagger with chilling accuracy at the chest of the first man who came behind—sinking it to the hilt—and dropped the other attacker a second later with an upward flick of his rapier that took him in the throat.

There being no more to do at this end of the chapel, he ran the length of the nave to Rigo's assistance. The gunner, standing on a choir bench, had placed the sole of his foot squarely and without ceremony in the face of the nearest and most determined of his attackers, and now straightened his leg with the force of a piston, catapulting his victim backward with a velocity that raised the latter's heels from the ground and spread his arms wildly as though in flight. He was dead even before he landed at the foot of the chancel steps, with the pommel of Leonardo's rapier jammed hard against the small of his back and two feet of its blade jutting forward from his breastbone. His hurtling weight tore the grip from Leonardo's hand. Off-balance, the artist stepped aside, and lost his footing on one of the jewels that littered the ground. He stumbled gracelessly, fighting for poise, and heard Rigo laugh. His hand, seeking a purchase, fell upon the body of Giovio della Rovere. Being now unarmed, he placed his knee against the side of the corpse. He heaved the sword from its rib cage and regained his feet as two of the burned men dashed at him. Their assault lacked both skill and conviction. Leonardo cut one down contemptuously and, whirling aside from the charge of the other, seized him about the neck and ran his skull into the base of the pulpit.

Breathing a little rapidly, he turned once more, his back against the choir screen, only to find that, with the collapse of Rigo's last opponents, there was nobody left to fight.

In a corner beneath the lectern, he saw Tesoro di Veluti begin to stir. Rigo came heavily down the steps into the nave, blood dripping from his sleeve and a grin on his face.

"Riario?" asked Leonardo briefly.

"Nay," said the Captain-Gunner, "you must have killed him yourself. Things have been somewhat hectic these past minutes, but I believe I would have noticed had I done so."

They looked at one another and began to turn over the bodies sprawled all around them. It was Tesoro di Veluti, regaining his senses and perceiving what they were about, who enlightened them.

Clutching his head, the young gunner spoke. "He ran. While I was killing della Rovere."

"He did not come through the door, then," said Rigo, "or he would have passed us."

"No," said Tesoro, pointing. "He went toward the altar, I think."

Leonardo and Rigo climbed the steps to the choir with sinking hearts. Beyond the stalls, a tapestry moved slightly and was still. They wrenched it aside, and revealed a narrow archway and a flight of stairs, from whose foot came a cold and gentle breeze.

The Florentine guards at the postern gate watched the progress of the friar who was making his way across the vineyard, stooping ever and again over the dead as though in blessing. He arrived without haste beneath the outer gate house, and raised a hand in grave salute.

"*Pax vobiscum*," he said.

"*Et tecum, pax*," replied one of the posted men, mechanically. "Here is labor in plenty for you."

"It is ever thus in war," agreed the friar, "and there are more outside that have gone to their Creator. Have I your leave to pass?"

"Of course."

"I thank you for your courtesy," said the Count of Imola. "*Benedicamus Domine*, now and always."

"Amen," said the guard, and stood aside.

Twenty-four

"He held against us last year," said Guido Toscanelli. "It is something, sir, to be considered."

"That was last year," said Lorenzo de' Medici. He was sitting at the head of the table in his library, and turned toward Leonardo, who was at his right. "Things are different now."

"His condotta, nonetheless, is famed," insisted Toscanelli. "The very name of Federigo da Montefeltro—"

"Has been diminished somewhat since yesterday morning," commented Lorenzo drily. "He has paid us a fine of sixty thousand florins. Are you now suggesting that I should give it back to him in hire?"

"By no means," said Toscanelli. "He will come with us for less, since Rome cannot march this way, and he knows it. Offer him his keep and that of his men for nine months, and let him hold Castelmonte for Florence instead of for Rome."

"I will consider it," said Lorenzo. "More to the point is the question of Rome's next move. Sixtus cannot now attack us directly and will seek an alliance with Lucca or Siena; and we cannot afford to stand still while he does so. Captain-Gunner Leone, your task for the present is clear enough, I think. We have all summer before us, and you will want to perfect the use of your new guns. Master Leonardo, how many more should we acquire? Our coffers are full."

"That decision is yours, sir," Leonardo answered.

"Naturally," said Lorenzo, "but I am seeking your advice as their inventor and my engineer."

"With respect, sir, I must point out that I am no longer your engineer. Our bargain is fulfilled."

"So it is. I had not forgotten. What terms do you ask for a further period of engagement in my service?"

"None, sir. I leave Florence at the start of next week."

"I would persuade you otherwise, if I could. What is your destination?"

"I have not yet decided. Perhaps northward, to Milan. Perhaps not. Sir, I owe you my thanks for your forbearance during a time when my intentions cannot have been clear to you. May I ask for it again?"

He rose from the table, bowed and left the room. The others watched him depart.

"An agile mind," said Toscanelli. "But a devious one."

"I am not so certain that it is devious," said Lorenzo de' Medici. "Something else, perhaps. Nonetheless, I would give a great deal to know what his intentions are. Do you have an urge to see Milan, Captain-Gunner Leone?"

"I had not thought about it, sir," said Rigo in some surprise.

"Do so," Lorenzo told him. "The Milanese are excellent gunmakers, and, in any case, it would be no disadvantage to Florence should Sforza decide to join us because of our skill in cannonry, happening, it may be, to hear the tale of the fall of Castelmonte."

Bianca sighed and whispered in the darkness.

"They say that you are a hero. Were we in ancient

Rome, they would have given you a triumphal procession. What does it feel like to be a hero?"

"Very pleasant, for an hour or two," said Leonardo, touching her side. "After that, one begins to wonder whether it is true, and a day later, one concludes that it is not."

"That is what *you* would conclude, of course," she said, slipping away.

"I am not sure what you mean by that."

"I mean that there are a thousand other men who would conclude nothing of the kind. The Prince of Savoy, for instance."

"He is dead," said Leonardo. "And I remain alive, which is all that matters." He came to the window and stood behind her.

"True," said Bianca. "You are right, as ever. Giuliano is dead, too." He put his arms around her and held her close, warming her with his body. "And Constanza weeps. You are here, and if I weep, it is for her grief and my own happiness. What will become of her?"

"I have written on her behalf to Cardinal della Palla."

"So that he may find her a convent?"

"It is what she wishes," said Leonardo.

"I know. I would not choose the life of a nun, were I in her place," Bianca said. "But then, I am not in her place. And she may change her mind when the baby comes . . . No, she will not. I know her too well. She will send it to her aunts. Why Cardinal della Palla?"

Leonardo considered this.

"Because," he said, "he is the nearest I have to a friend, now that Giuliano is gone."

"You have Rigo Leone."

"Not yet," said Leonardo. "Eventually, perhaps, but not yet."

Bianca turned to face him.

"And myself." She put her arms about his neck, and he kissed her. "Friend," she said. "Pupil, always. Lover, for as long as you wish it." She laid a finger against his lips. "And do not start to argue with me, Leonardo, as you always do. You may say yes or no. But I will not listen to your reasons, since love itself is unreasonable."

"Madonna," said Leonardo gently, "in a few days from now, I am leaving Florence."

"I know that too. What has it to do with anything? Giuliano is dead, Constanza will spend her life in a convent and already you are speaking of tomorrow. I will give you anything you ask of me, but tomorrow is not mine to give. If we meet again, we shall rejoice in it; if we do not, how will reason help us?"

Ahead of them, the road led southward into summer. His companion seemed ill at ease, and finally spoke.

"I have a confession to make," he said. "Lorenzo—"

"It is made," said Leonardo cheerfully, "and therefore, let us say no more of it, but, rather, discuss other matters, such as the possible defenses against mobile artillery."

Rigo Leone made no reply to this, and they rode in silence. After another mile had passed:

"This is not the road to Milan," the gunner said.

"I am not going to Milan," said Leonardo, "but to Malta."

"Malta! In God's name, why?"

"For good reasons, or bad. Life is full of surprises, if we but allow them to come to us."

"I had thought . . ." Rigo began. "That is, Lorenzo believes . . ."

Leonardo reached forward and patted his horse's neck. He was laughing.

"I know what you thought," he said, "and Lorenzo. But let us ride together anyway."

About the Authors

MARTIN WOODHOUSE is a pilot, poet, parachutist, machine-tool and computer expert, and a writer. A Royal Air Force veteran, he holds degrees in medicine and experimental psychology and has conducted high altitude research in physiology as well as research on the relationship between human and computer systems. He is the builder of one of the world's first pure logic computers and the designer of a flight instrument that has become standard aeronautical equipment.

As a television writer, Dr. Woodhouse originated the popular series "The Avengers" and is the author of several books—*Tree Frog*, *Bush Baby*, *Phil & Me*, *Mama Doll* and *Blue Bone*. He and his family live on the island of Montserrat in the West Indies.

ROBERT ROSS is a golfer, trout fisherman, poet and chess enthusiast, and has been an advertising writer and creative director for two of the largest advertising agencies in the world. He and his wife, Ranette, also live on the isle of Montserrat.

A lifelong fascination with Leonardo da Vinci has taken Mr. Ross to Leonardo's birthplace in Anchiano, his boyhood town of Vinci, studios in Florence, and the castle of Cloux, near Amboise, where he died. It is the author's firm belief that the lost sections of da Vinci's notebooks will be found one day and will reveal accounts of his adventures and activities while in the service of the great Renaissance houses. *The Medici Guns* is an imaginary re-creation of such a possible exploit, based on fragments taken from these famous notebooks.